A DUEL IN
MERYTON

Renata McMann
&
Summer Hanford

Cover by Summer Hanford

DEDICATION

From Renata and Summer

In loving memory of our favorite editor. Your dedication to and enthusiasm for our work will be sorely missed.

From Summer

To a wonderful woman, who was both mother-in-law and friend. It breaks my heart to write a book you aren't here to read. The world is less without you.

Dear Reader,

By Renata McMann and Summer Hanford

More Than He Seems
After Anne
Their Secret Love
*A Duel in Meryton**
Love, Letters and Lies
The Long Road to Longbourn
*Hypothetically Married**
The Forgiving Season
The Widow Elizabeth
Foiled Elopement
Believing in Darcy
Her Final Wish
Miss Bingley's Christmas
Epiphany with Tea
Courting Elizabeth
The Fire at Netherfield Park
*From Ashes to Heiresses**
Entanglements of Honor
Lady Catherine Regrets
A Death at Rosings
Mary Younge
Poor Mr. Darcy
Mr. Collins' Deception
The Scandalous Stepmother
Caroline and the Footman
Elizabeth's Plight (The Wickham Coin Book II)
Georgiana's Folly (The Wickham Coin Book I)
The Second Mrs. Darcy

*available as an audio book

Collections:

A Dollop of Pride and a Dash of Prejudice:
Includes from above: *Their Secret Love, Miss Bingley's Christmas, Epiphany with Tea* and *From Ashes to Heiresses*.

Pride and Prejudice Villains Revisited – Redeemed – Reimagined
A Collection of Six Short Stories.
Includes from above: *Lady Catherine Regrets, Mary Younge, Mr. Collins' Deception* and *Caroline and the Footman*, along with two the additional flash fiction pieces, *Mrs. Bennet's Triumph* and *Wickham's Journal*.

Georgiana's Folly & Elizabeth's Plight: Wickham Coin Series, Volumes I & II
Includes from above: *Elizabeth's Plight* and *Georgiana's Folly*.

Other Pride and Prejudice variations by Renata McMann
Is Esteem Enough?
Heiress to Longbourn
Pemberley Weddings
The Inconsistency of Caroline Bingley
Three Daughters Married
Anne de Bourgh Manages
The above five works are collected in the book:
Five Pride and Prejudice Variations

A DUEL IN
MERYTON

Chapter One

Every year, just before Easter, Darcy rounded up his favorite cousin, Major Richard Fitzwilliam, and they went to Rosings to visit their widowed aunt, Lady Catherine de Bourgh, and their cousin, Anne de Bourgh. Their visits had become routine and, as such, moderately boring. That would never excuse them, however. Darcy did not consider boredom a valid reason not to dispense his duties, and familial visits were a solemn duty, especially since their uncle, Sir Lewis de Bourgh's, death.

That his cousin felt the same was one of the reasons Darcy got on better with Richard than with either of Richard's brothers, even his twin. Though born some twenty minutes sooner, and therefore older than Richard, Walter Fitzwilliam matured later. Both Walter and the twins' older brother, Arthur, used Lady Catherine's tendency to attempt to manage their lives as a poor excuse not to visit. That excuse would seem more valid if both hadn't gone through times when they were badly in need of such advice. Instead of avoiding Lady Catherine, Richard and Darcy ignored their aunt's well-meaning attempts to run their lives, recognizing she meant well.

"Lady Catherine will expect you to admire Anne's new gown and compliment her Easter bonnet," Richard observed as Darcy's carriage turned up Rosings' tree-lined drive. Richard's voice was perfectly bland, though pitched slightly loud from growing up with boisterous older brothers and his years in the military. His eyes, in contrast, held amusement. Mostly at Darcy's expense.

"Have a care," Darcy warned with mock severity. "Someday I will marry. Aunt Catherine will be forced to put aside her hopes for me and Anne. She will turn her sights on you for our cousin, and you shall be required to notice new bonnets and Easter gowns."

Richard snorted. "You wed, indeed." He shook his head as the carriage rumbled toward Rosings' impressive façade. "For one, you've never shown any such inclination. For another, if you keep gadding about with that new acquaintance of yours, you shall never manage to marry. That one makes calf-eyes at the loveliest woman at each assembly, dances with her, and steals her heart. Now that he's attached himself to you, none of them shall ever notice you, and you aren't the sort to settle for the second most attractive woman in the room."

Darcy frowned. "You mean Charles Bingley? The merchant's son?"

"Aye, that's the fellow."

"He hasn't attached himself to me. He's simply seeking moral and social compass."

"And you are enjoying providing both," Richard observed. "Don't bother to deny it. It pleases you to sculpt him."

Darcy shrugged. "Someone must. He's a decent enough young man, but it takes only a moment or two in his company to realize he could easily be led astray, and he must be doubly careful. Some would quickly use his family's roots in trade to condemn behavior that would be forgiven in someone whose standing is higher."

Richard's gaze narrowed as he studied Darcy. His expression grew more serious. "Darcy, this proclivity of yours to think you know better than others is going to get you into trouble someday."

Darcy shrugged and tugged the curtain wider open. He didn't *think* he knew better than others. He was certain he did. There was no use trying to convince his older cousin of that, though, for Richard possessed the same trait.

"While we're on the subject of your failings," Richard said. "I will add that, since inheriting Pemberley, you've developed a tendency to judge too quickly, and harshly. Walter and Arthur have noted this as well. They nominated me to tell you."

They rounded the curve at the end of the drive. Relief filled Darcy that the journey would soon be over. Normally pleased to travel with his favorite cousin, Darcy didn't like the path of their conversation, though he appreciated that Richard, senior to Darcy by a few years, felt the right to offer his opinions.

"I know you won't heed me, Darcy," Richard said, as they slowed before Rosings. "But at least I've had my say. This way, when your pride brings you trouble someday, I shall win the delight of being able to say I told you as much."

The carriage drew to a halt, saving Darcy from giving an answer, but not keeping his mind from Richard's comment. As they alighted, then mounted the wide front steps, worry weighed on Darcy's broad shoulders. Richard didn't understand. Darcy now had the care of an estate. He had tenants, servants, and property to manage. More importantly, he had the rearing of his young sister, Georgiana. Yes, Richard was her guardian as well, but he had his military duties. Daily, Darcy must make decisions that affected those who looked to him, and those decisions must be stood by.

If he couldn't take a fellow as affable and eager as Charles Bingley and save him from social and financial pitfalls, guide him into being a gentleman rather than some sort of vulgar *nouveau riche*, Darcy was unworthy of filling his father's shoes.

Lady Catherine's butler, Dutton, met them at the door. They traversed the corridors of Rosings in blessed silence, and were shown into the usual parlor, a ghastly red and gold affair, only to find the room fuller than normal. Their aunt was there, of course, and their cousin Anne and her companion, Mrs. Jenkinson, but the chair on Anne's other side was occupied as well. In it sat a jauntily dressed young man, who stood to greet them.

"Darcy. Richard." Lady Catherine held out her hands for them to clasp. "Perfectly punctual, as expected."

"Aunt Catherine," Richard greeted. He placed a kiss on her weathered cheek.

Darcy mimicked the greeting, trying not to stare at the stranger. The young man's visage was comely, his embroidered green coat modish but much too ostentatious for Darcy's tastes. He wore dark hair in a style that was currently fashionable. What piqued a feeling of mistrust, however, was his placement at Anne's side. Much as Darcy loved his cousin, Anne was no beauty, nor an entertaining conversationalist. She was, however, Rosings' sole heir.

Lady Catherine gestured to the unknown gentleman. "Meet your cousin, Mr. Blackmore."

Blackmore bowed, his expression one shade shy of embarrassed. "My mother was merely a second cousin of Sir Lewis de Bourgh," he said. "I am hardly due acknowledgement as a relation."

"Nonsense," Lady Catherine said. "Cousin I say, so cousin you are."

"What brings you to Rosings, Mr. Blackmore?" Richard asked, returning the young man's bow.

"Nostalgia, permitted by your gracious aunt. I visited here once as a child. Your late uncle and this wonderful place made quite the impression, I must admit. I've reminisced over the details nearly daily, longing to return." He made a sweeping gesture and offered Lady

Catherine a smile. "I must say, Rosings and her mistress do not disappoint. If anything, my childhood memories did not do the manor or grounds justice."

Predictably, Lady Catherine bestowed a pleased look on this Mr. Blackmore. Darcy felt his aunt woefully accepting of flattery.

"Yes, Rosings is rather all that, is it not?" Richard said amiably. He turned and bowed to Anne, then Mrs. Jenkinson. "Anne, lovely as ever. Mrs. Jenkinson, it's a pleasure to see you."

"Darcy, greet your new cousin," Lady Catherine ordered. "And Anne. She's been in tumult all day, awaiting your arrival. Haven't you, Anne?"

Anne offered Darcy a grimace, also predictable.

"Anne, Mrs. Jenkinson," Darcy greeted with a bow. He turned to Mr. Blackmore. "Blackmore."

"Cousin Blackmore," Lady Catherine corrected.

Mr. Blackmore offered another apologetic, overly effacing look. "My family wasn't close to Sir Lewis before he married Lady Catherine, and we only kept up a sporadic correspondence after he married. As I said, calling us cousins would be too generous."

"Be generous, Darcy," Lady Catherine snapped. "And do sit down, both of you. Darcy, go sit by Anne. Your *cousin* won't mind moving. Richard, Mr. Blackmore, come sit by me."

They all shuffled about, rearranging themselves to Lady Catherine's satisfaction. Darcy didn't miss Mr. Blackmore's slightly disgruntled look, which he smoothed away before taking his place beside Lady Catherine. Once they were all seated, she looked them over, nodded, and rang for tea.

"Mr. Blackmore saved one of Sir Lewis' letters," Lady Catherine said, aiming the remark at Darcy. "He brought it to me. Your *cousin* has allowed me to keep another memento of my late husband."

Lady Catherine paused, but Darcy, unimpressed, made no comment. Sir Lewis had corresponded with many people. There must be hundreds of letters out there.

"Here, see?" Lady Catherine took out a worn page. She proffered it to Darcy.

Dutifully, he rose to collect the sheet, which looked to have been crumpled at some point, then an effort made to smooth it. Something had been spilled on the address, obscuring it and much of the name, but the letter was largely legible. It was addressed familiarly to George and gave advice about his spending his time at a university. Darcy had received a similar letter. The date put Mr. Blackmore at university at much the same time as Darcy.

Darcy handed the letter back to Lady Catherine and leveled a hard look on Blackmore. "I don't recall seeing you at Cambridge."

"I was at Oxford."

Did Darcy detect a hint of smugness? He retook his seat, realizing he shouldn't have declared what university he'd attended. Not when his uncle's letter hadn't specifically mentioned Cambridge and his words were too general to pinpoint a specific university.

"It's nearly time for dinner," Anne said, speaking for the first time.

Everyone turned to look at her. Anne never spoke. Not unless addressed, or at her mother's command.

"True enough," Richard said.

"Yes, well, off with you all," Lady Catherine said. "Go change. Richard, you're in your usual room. Darcy, I had to give Mr. Blackmore the room beside Anne's. The others we tried all ended up having something wrong with them. We fixed the squeak in the floor of the green bedroom, so you shall take that. The rest, we're still looking into. Mr. Blackmore has overly keen hearing, you see. It interferes with his rest."

Darcy leveled a hard look on the man. "Does it now?"

Mr. Blackmore grimaced. "It's a curse, I'm afraid."

"Suspect that kept you out of regimentals," Richard said. When Mr. Blackmore looked briefly puzzled, Richard explained, "Acute hearing could be a problem for someone who needed to be near firearms."

"That was a consideration, yes," Mr. Blackmore agreed. "Though I should have liked to prove myself and serve my country, as you have, sir."

Richard nodded amiably and stood. "Come, Darcy, I'll help you find the green room. I know you've no notion which it is." He nodded to the assemblage. "Aunt, cousins, Mrs. Jenkinson."

Darcy stood and offered a bow. As he straightened, he aimed another glare at Blackmore, but the other man had turned to bid the ladies adieu. Darcy kept his glower and followed Richard out.

When they reached the upper hall, Richard cast Darcy a look askance. "I don't like this Blackmore fellow."

"Nor do I," Darcy agreed. He offered Richard a nod, then went to the green bedroom, fully aware of its location far down the hall from Anne's room.

At dinner that night, Mr. Blackmore, seated on the other side of Anne from Darcy, spent the first course ignoring him and Richard. Instead, Blackmore focused his conversational efforts on Anne. Darcy couldn't help but note that his cousin proved even more unresponsive than usual. She also leaned away from Mr. Blackmore and thus toward Darcy, whether seeking his presence or simply attempting to put distance between her and Blackmore, Darcy didn't know.

For his part, he endeavored to think of topics on which to engage Anne, to help edge Blackmore out of conversation with her. Unfortunately, idle chatter wasn't one of Darcy's strong suits. He'd never regretted his lack of ability more.

Eventually, a disgruntled look settled over Mr. Blackmore's features. He favored Darcy with an annoyed glance and turned to his other side, to Lady Catherine, who'd so far been content to be entertained by Richard.

"Do you know," Blackmore said into a lull in conversation, "I have such fond memories of Rosings. You'd never guess, but one of them is of the carriage house roof. My brother and I climbed out onto it. Wonderful view from up there."

"Climbed out of where?" Richard asked, frowning. "There's no window leading to the roof."

"The, ah, from the higher bit, onto the lower roof," Mr. Blackmore qualified.

"I don't believe there's a window there," Richard reiterated. He turned to Lady Catherine. "Is there?"

There had been, Darcy remembered. He'd climbed there once with George. No, he wouldn't think of his long-ago companion as George anymore. It was odd that a memory from childhood brought forth Wickham's given name.

Lady Catherine frowned as well. "Once, I think. Long ago? It broke and we had it sealed up. No point in paying tax on it."

"Oh, well, a shame, that," Mr. Blackmore said.

Lady Catherine turned her frown on him.

"Er, not that I can fault your reason," Mr. Blackmore stammered. "Actually, it's certainly better this way. Safer. I daresay it looks better, as well."

"Yes, I daresay it does," Lady Catherine agreed. "What else do you remember?"

Mr. Blackmore went on to describe several more aspects of the home. Lady Catherine seemed to relax, pleased with the steady flow of compliments Mr. Blackmore heaped on Rosings. Darcy only grew more suspicious.

By the time the evening ended, Darcy had reached two conclusions. Mr. Blackmore couldn't be trusted, and Darcy didn't care for the man. All that remained was to convince Lady Catherine to expel Blackmore from Rosings.

Chapter Two

Nearly a week later, Darcy still hadn't found a way to break Blackmore's hold on his aunt, although the man ceased his attempts to engage Anne. Darcy suspected Blackmore's initial interest in his cousin had been an attempt to ingratiate himself to Lady Catherine. Once he realized she didn't approve of such attentions, Blackmore had immediately left off trying to draw out Anne. Even with that respite, however, Anne flagged, overtaken by one of her bouts of ill health. She kept to her rooms more and more, with only brief forays to the library to select books.

Darcy was relieved when Easter morning finally arrived, for Mr. Blackmore was slated to depart the next day. Lady Catherine expressed regrets, but Darcy would be happy to see Blackmore go. He was curious how quickly Anne would recover following the man's departure.

After dressing with extra care out of consideration for Easter service, Darcy descended to the breakfast parlor. Richard joined him almost immediately, followed by Lady Catherine. Dutifully, they both complimented her new gown.

A moment later, Mrs. Jenkinson appeared. "I am afraid Miss de Bourgh isn't feeling well enough for church," she said. "If I may, I should like to remain behind with her."

"Yes, you must," Lady Catherine said, expression worried. "Anne's been unwell for longer than usual. Perhaps I should call in the doctor."

"Call the doctor, for me?" Mr. Blackmore said, appearing in the doorway. He placed the back of a hand against his forehead. "How thoughtful. How did you know I'm under the weather today?"

Lady Catherine turned to him, expression surprised. "You are not well, Mr. Blackmore?"

Darcy took in the other man's appearance. He looked like a man about to attend Easter services, not a man of poor health. "Undoubtedly, we'll meet the doctor at church. You can present your symptoms to him there, Mr. Blackmore."

Mr. Blackmore offered an ingratiating smile, but his eyes held a sly glint. "Please, Mr. Darcy, call me cousin. Or George."

"Darcy, your cousin has asked you numerous times to address him with familiarity, yet you resist and never return the compliment," Lady Catherine observed. "Stop being churlish."

Darcy settled for another glare at Blackmore, unable to make an acceptable reply to his aunt's demand.

Blackmore crossed the room to sink into the nearest chair. "I truly don't believe I can make it to services." He let out a long sigh. "I am trying my best, but I'm in the throes of such terrible malaise." He shot Darcy a look, askance. "In truth, though it reveals how weak I am to admit as much, I believe the source of my malady is my impending departure from Rosings. I can't sleep at night, thinking on it. I might be able to rally for church, if I could know I might remain a few more days. A week, at most."

Darcy eyed his so-called cousin with disdain. "Absolutely not."

"I can speak for myself, Darcy," Lady Catherine snapped. She looked between him and Mr. Blackmore. Her expression softened. "I believe I see what is transpiring, Mr. Blackmore. Anne and Darcy do so look forward to his visit every spring. They rarely get to see one another. You and I, with our chatter and reminiscence, are interrupting their annual reunion, as it were. It's a very important time for them. Darcy is settled in with managing Pemberley now. The moment to take a wife is upon him."

Darcy grimaced. He didn't care one bit for his aunt's interpretation of his dislike of Blackmore. It undermined years of trying to make Lady Catherine see that Anne was not meant to be his wife. He cared for his meek, sickly cousin, but not in the way Lady Catherine wished. Darcy could have looked past his personal feelings, except that, when he did take a wife, he required one able to provide an heir.

Anne seemed to understand all this, and generally sided with Darcy when Lady Catherine pressed for their union. As far as Darcy knew, Anne harbored no amorous feelings for him. If anyone, she fancied Richard. He was the only person whose company she ever sought outside her mother's orders.

Though he disliked deception even in the form of inaction, Darcy held his tongue, and manfully ignored Richard's amused expression. If not refuting Lady Catherine's dreams for him and Anne proved the price of ridding Rosings of Blackmore, Darcy would pay. Silence filled the room. Darcy knew his aunt always took silence for agreement, not realizing that the only thing people agreed upon was they did not want to hear anything more about the issue.

After watching Darcy for a long moment, Lady Catherine turned back to Blackmore. "Sad as it is for me, you must depart as scheduled, Mr. Blackmore. You would imagine Darcy and Anne would be kinder to me, but they are not. We must all bow to the needs of family."

Richard coughed, hiding his expression behind his napkin.

Blackmore slid even lower in his chair, looking like unbaked bread. "Then I truly cannot muster the means by which to attend services. I am too weighed down by sorrow."

Lady Catherine stood from the table. "That is your choice, certainly. I wouldn't wish you to come along, moping the whole way. To have someone who has entertained me so well foist misery on me is unacceptable. Come Darcy, Richard. We shall go enjoy Mr. Grigg's sermon. While we can. I daresay he hasn't many left in him."

Lady Catherine swept from the room. Darcy hastily downed the remainder of his coffee and stood to follow, Richard on his heels. Darcy nodded to Mrs. Jenkinson as he passed, ignoring Blackmore.

Lady Catherine filled the carriage ride with a tirade about Mr. Blackmore's ingratitude. She railed against him becoming disagreeable after not getting his way this one time. Darcy tried to ignore Richard's amusement, aware his cousin felt Lady Catherine mimicked the behavior she decried. For Darcy, the ride passed more amicably than it ought, pleased as he was that Blackmore had finally squandered Lady Catherine's good favor.

When they reached the church and disembarked, Richard held Darcy back as he made to enter the line of people filing in. Darcy turned to his cousin, adopting a quizzical expression.

"I don't believe I trust Blackmore alone at Rosings with Anne," Richard said, voice low.

"She's hardly alone," Darcy countered. Much as he disliked the man, after the first few days of their visit, Blackmore had taken to ignoring Anne. Darcy suspected Blackmore's main goal was to ensure future invitations to Rosings, to soak up Lady Catherine's hospitality. He'd obviously concluded that showing an interest in Anne wouldn't flatter Lady Catherine. It would displease her. "The servants are there, and Mrs. Jenkinson. Besides which, Anne has hardly left her rooms. Surely, she's locked away there even now."

"I'm not certain she is," Richard disagreed. "She was going to the library, but she began encountering Blackmore there. Two nights ago, he cornered her and started talking about love. She tried to discourage him, but he persisted. She ended up running from the room. She told me she doesn't like being confined to her room, but she's only safe in her father's office, because no one can see her if she curls up in her father's chair. I'm worried she may venture out. Mrs. Jenkinson might not even think to tell Anne that Blackmore remained behind."

Darcy stared at Richard. He'd no idea Blackmore had accosted Anne. "I thought Blackmore had decided to leave Anne alone."

"Perhaps in public, or when you're nearby, but no, he doesn't seem to have given up." Richard looked past Darcy, in the direction of Rosings. "I've felt a growing unease the entire ride here. All my instincts tell me something is amiss."

Darcy looked over his shoulder, following Richard's gaze. "Your instincts are rarely wrong." He turned back, taking in the dwindling line of people entering the church. "You'd best take the carriage and go. God will forgive you for missing the Easter service."

Richard nodded. "I'll send the carriage back." He headed toward Lady Catherine's conveyance.

Darcy watched for a moment, then strode toward the church. Within, he found his aunt in her pew and sat down beside her. Mr. Grigg took his position before the assemblage.

"Where is Richard?" Lady Catherine asked.

"He's gone back to Rosings to check on Anne."

"What?" She turned full to Darcy, not bothering to lower her voice. "If anyone should check on Anne, you should, Darcy, but there's no need. She's simply taken with one of her maladies. There's nothing Richard can do for her."

"I believe he's more concerned about the sanctity of her person than her health," Darcy said in a low voice.

"Her person? That's nonsense," Lady Catherine declared. "Call him back."

Darcy looked about. Everyone stared, even Mr. Grigg. They were already making a scene. "It probably is nonsense, but I trust Richard's instincts. I think I'm going to help him."

Darcy stood. Several people gasped. More murmured.

"Fitzwilliam Darcy," Aunt Catherine ordered, "sit back down this moment."

Ignoring his aunt, Darcy offered Mr. Grigg an apologetic nod and headed back up the aisle. Wryly, Darcy reflected that at least following Richard would save him from a repeat of the same sermon Mr. Grigg gave every Easter. Despite Lady Catherine's enthusiasm for the old clergyman, Darcy longed for the day he was replaced. It would be impossible for his aunt to find anyone more boring than Grigg.

Richard and the carriage were already well away as Darcy exited the church. He looked about but saw no ready means of transport. Abandoning decorum in his growing unease, he set off across the lawn toward Rosings at a jog.

He reached Rosings as Lady Catherine's carriage rumbled back down the drive. Ignoring the confused look cast his way by footman and driver, Darcy took the front steps two at a time. As his foot crossed the threshold, a scream rent the air.

Darcy pelted up the staircase toward Anne's room. Another scream sounded. This time, his ears pinpointed it as coming from below. Darcy careened about, nearly falling, and raced back down the steps. A third scream drew him to the north wing of the house, and his uncle's office.

Blackmore had a firm grip on Anne's arm. She was half behind him, struggling against his hold. Blackmore faced Richard, who stood halfway across the room from Blackmore with his hand on the back of a chair. Blackmore pushed Anne to the floor and dove toward Richard.

It took Darcy only a moment to see the sword in Blackmore's hand. Richard pulled the chair between them and stepped farther back. As Blackmore pushed the chair back under the table, Darcy grabbed a forearm-sized vase from a shelf near the door. He aimed for Blackmore's face, but hit his shoulder. As the vase shattered, Darcy realized it was a valuable one from the orient.

Not distracted by the flying shards of porcelain, Richard leapt across the room to pull the mate to Blackmore's weapon from the wall, where the two normally hung, crossed. Richard leapt back toward Blackmore. The swords met with a screech.

As the blades clanked in earnest, Darcy looked about for a means to assist Richard. Anne crouched on the floor behind Blackmore, arms wrapped about her head. Darcy couldn't attack Blackmore from the rear and the space between the table and the wall was too narrow for Darcy to come to Richard's side.

Sobbing, Anne pushed to her feet and stumbled backward, scuttling behind her father's desk. Blackmore sidestepped, keeping his back to

Anne. Darcy grabbed a random book with the intention of throwing it. Before the book could leave Darcy's hand, Blackmore feinted left. Richard, not fooled, drove his blade into his opponent's heart.

Blackmore crumpled to the ground. Darcy went still, book held ready to throw. He tossed the volume aside. It thunked to the floor. Richard whirled, red-coated sword held at the ready. Darcy came to his cousin's side and placed a hand lightly on his shoulder. Blood seeped out from under Blackmore, where he lay on the floor.

Another cry sounded from Anne's direction, this one weak. From where she stood, Darcy suspected she could only see Blackmore's feet. She collapsed slowly, the motion an alarming parody of Blackmore's decent. Richard's sword clattered to the floor as he jumped over Blackmore and raced around the desk. He caught Anne moments before her head collided with the wood planks. Darcy reached them an instant later.

"Is she injured?" he asked.

Richard carefully worked his arms under Anne and lifted her. He carried her around the desk, past Blackmore's still form, and to one of the sofas. Gently, he set her down. He and Darcy both bent low to peer at Anne.

"I don't see any injuries," Richard said after a moment.

Darcy didn't either, but he could see that Anne's sleeve was torn nearly off. Richard pushed the fabric aside to reveal a red welt, likely the beginning of a bruise, on Anne's arm. He and Darcy exchanged a grim look. As one, they turned and stalked over to Blackmore.

Richard poked him with a foot. Blackmore's form moved with the motion, then sank back into place when Richard pulled his foot back. Darcy knelt and checked to see if Blackmore was breathing. He wasn't.

"We'll have to call the magistrate," Richard said.

"You won't be charged."

"No, but we should still send for him."

"What is the meaning of this?" Lady Catherine's voice rang through the manor. "Darcy, Richard, where are you? How dare you walk out on Mr. Grigg's sermon?"

Darcy grimaced. Wry humor sprang up in Richard's eyes. Darcy realized their aunt had left the sermon early as well.

"We're in Sir Lewis' office, Aunt Catherine," Richard called, voice booming.

Anne groaned. Darcy and Richard hurried back to her side. Richard went down on one knee to study her face.

Lady Catherine burst into the room and stilled. "My fifteenth century imperial vase! How dare you…" She whirled toward Darcy, then saw her daughter. "Anne," she gasped.

Anne's eyes flickered open. Her gaze settled on Richard. Her lips pulled up into a rare smile. "You saved me."

"Saved her?" Lady Catherine asked. She turned, slowly, to take in the room. "What happened here? Is that Mr. Blackmore?" Each question came out an octave higher. "Is that blood?"

Anne sat up, Richard supporting her with one arm. "Mr. Blackmore tried to force his attentions on me, Mother. He said I would be made to marry him, and he would have Rosings. Richard saved me."

Lady Catherine swiveled to face Richard. "Is this true?"

"I can't speak to what he said before I found them," Richard said, looking up at her from where he knelt, supporting Anne. "I can say that I returned to find Anne screaming, pinned in the corner by Blackmore."

Anne tried to look around. Darcy realized she couldn't see past Richard. She didn't know there was a body.

"What happened to him?" Anne asked. "Did Mother say there is blood?"

Darcy moved to stand beside Richard, further blocking Anne's view. "Blackmore is dead."

"You slew him for Anne?" Lady Catherine asked, eyes alight.

Darcy shook his head. "I would have been too late. Richard saved Anne. He wielded the blade."

"Thank you," Anne whispered, looking up at Richard.

Lady Catherine sniffed. "Well, you should have been the one to kill him, Darcy. I can't imagine what kept you. Next time, try to be more like Richard."

Darcy kept his expression bland. "Certainly."

"He's really dead?" Anne asked.

Richard glanced at Darcy, who nodded, before turning back to Anne. "He really is," Richard assured her.

She hugged him. "Thank you." She looked over his shoulder at her mother. "I would like to go to my room, please."

"I'll take you." Richard scooped her up. He carried her from the room, angling her in such a way as to conceal the body from her sight.

"Well," Lady Catherine said, looking about. She wrinkled her nose at the body. "I knew I didn't like that man."

Darcy had nothing to say to that.

"You should have been more useful, Darcy," she continued. "You should be the one carrying Anne to her chamber." She let out a sigh and looked about again. "Where is everyone? Where are the servants? Not all of them attended the service."

"A good question. I will find out." He turned to leave the room.

"And send someone to clean this up, Darcy," Aunt Catherine called after him.

Darcy found Rosings oddly silent. Every corridor he walked down proved empty. One of the back parlors held Mrs. Jenkinson asleep on a sofa, but shaking didn't wake her. Hurrying his steps, Darcy continued his search. Finally, he made his way to the kitchen.

Servants, mostly members of the kitchen staff who couldn't be spared to attend church, sprawled in chairs, or even lay on the floor. Several snored loudly. Cups were set out, some with dark liquid still inside. He picked one up and sniffed.

Brandy, and another, odd smell. Most likely drugged. Darcy set the cup back down with a grimace.

He heard a whimper, then another. He followed the sounds to a large cupboard. A wooden spoon was stuck through the handles, jammed in place by a rag. Darcy yanked it free and swung open the door.

A kitchen maid sat inside, squeezed in with several pots, legs pulled tight against her. She saw Darcy and burst into tears. He proffered a hand. She clasped it and he pulled her out.

"What happened?" he asked, gentling his tone.

"That man came in and said they should all drink and I said no, but they all did," she babbled, words spilling out. "And they started falling over and I screamed, and he shut me in the cupboard." Her last word trailed off into another sob, then a hiccup.

"You're safe now," Darcy said. "I need you to go to the church and get the other members of the staff, and the doctor, and the magistrate."

"R-right now?" she asked.

Darcy nodded. "It's important."

"Interrupt the sermon, sir?"

"Yes. Tell them Mr. Darcy told you to. The servants may need a doctor and he should come quickly."

"Y-yes, sir." She twisted her hands.

24

"Go now, out the kitchen door." He didn't want the girl to somehow stumble on Sir Lewis' office. Blackmore's body would further traumatize her.

She nodded and crossed the kitchen to let herself out. Darcy looked about, and grimaced. Blackmore had made quite the mess, and he wasn't even alive to explain himself.

Chapter Three

More than three years later

Darcy sat at Sir Lewis' desk at Rosings, going over the books, though he'd been through them several times already. He sighed and turned back to the household accounts. Aside from one minor arithmetic error, the ledgers were in complete order. Darcy had done everything that he knew how to do. Until Richard came, there was little more to accomplish.

The funerals were over. Darcy hadn't been worried when Richard didn't arrive in time for the first, but concern set in when, almost two weeks later, his cousin still hadn't turned up. Darcy had sent letters to three different places he felt Richard might be, then to four people who might know where he was. Still, nothing.

A wave of dread, inspired by the injuries Richard had suffered in Spain two years ago, lurked at the corners of thought. Darcy shook his head to dislodge the feeling. After what happened in Spain, the earl had seen Richard promoted to Colonel and then ensured he received less precarious assignments. Richard was a third son, true, but his father still valued him. When the earl died, almost a year ago, Darcy had wondered if Richard would push to return to the front lines, but he hadn't.

Darcy pushed back the chair. He detested being idle. Perhaps he would order his horse saddled and go for a ride, under the flimsy excuse that he was looking over the home farm and the tenants' lands. As if he hadn't already done so even more times than he'd gone over the books. He reached for the bell pull but, before he could ring for a servant, footsteps sounded in the hall.

Dutton, Rosings' butler, stepped through the open doorway. "Colonel Fitzwilliam, sir."

Relief surging through him, Darcy nodded to the butler, then turned his attention on his cousin. "Where have you been?"

Richard rocked back slightly. He raised his eyebrows. "Mostly, on my way here. My general said I was required at Rosings with all urgency." His expression clouded. "I heard about Anne."

Darcy gestured to the chair across from him as Dutton disappeared back down the hall.

Richard strode into the room and took the indicated chair. Perhaps because he was in uniform, he held himself stiffly upright. He looked about. "Why are you in Uncle Lewis' office? Is Lady Catherine out?"

"You heard about Anne," Darcy reiterated.

Richard nodded. "It's very sad, but not very surprising. She was always so sickly, and after that incident with Mr. Blackmore, she was even worse." He let out a sigh. "Truth be told, I didn't expect her to last as long as she did. Aunt Catherine must be in quite a state. Is that why you need me?"

"You always were better with our aunt," Darcy conceded. "But, no, that is not why you are required here. Or maybe, in a way, it is."

"You're being convoluted, Darcy," Richard said. "That's not like you. What's wrong? Where is Aunt Catherine?"

Darcy cleared his throat. "Aunt Catherine is dead. We already held the funeral."

Richard stared at him. "Dead?"

Darcy nodded.

"But, Aunt Catherine is…formidable. Indestructible. Practically a force of nature."

Darcy shrugged. "I think losing Anne broke her heart," he said softly.

Richard drummed his fingers on the arm of his chair. "I should have come sooner. The moment I heard Anne died. I wrote, but that wasn't enough. Maybe, with me here, Aunt Catherine—"

"You couldn't have known Lady Catherine would take Anne's loss so hard," Darcy cut in. "And there's no way to guess if you could have done anything for her, if you were here."

Richard nodded, but his expression remained glum. He let out a sigh. "Well, then, let's get on with it. I assume we're coexecutors again? I didn't mean to hold things up, trap you here. I know you have Pemberley to run." He waved a hand at Darcy. "You could have handled this without me, you know. It's not as if I demand you consult me on every little thing with Georgiana, so why would you think I'd balk at you handling Aunt Catherine's affairs? I trust your judgment."

"I appreciate that," Darcy said.

"Although you did hire that disaster of a governess, Mrs. Younge," Richard added with a new frown.

Darcy grimaced. He didn't care to be reminded of Mrs. Younge, which could only serve to bring the incident with Georgiana and Wickham into his thoughts. If Darcy had his way, he would never hear of Mrs. Younge, George Wickham or Ramsgate again. The next time Georgiana wished for a holiday, he would take her to Bath, chaperoning her himself.

"Is that why you called me away from my military duties, because your selection of Mrs. Younge and that near scandal in Ramsgate has you questioning your judgment?" Richard waved off the question, even as he asked. "No, it can't be that. Maybe you need my help tracking people down? Perhaps one of Sir Lewis' relatives inherited Rosings? I believe I've met a few of them, but I can't remember their names and have no idea where they live."

"No." Darcy was beginning to be as frustrated by Richard's presence as he'd been by his absence. Richard, normally amiable but not the least flighty, was particularly garrulous. Darcy was about to suggest his cousin fall silent when Richard looked away and surreptitiously rubbed one eye, then the other.

Anne's and their Aunt Catherine's deaths were harder on Richard, Darcy realized. Richard had always been closer with their cousin and aunt than Darcy had. Lady Catherine had made the right choice.

Richard cleared his throat. "No? Aunt Catherine didn't leave Rosings to Sir Lewis' relatives?" He blinked. "Of course. You need me because I am executor. She left Rosings to you. She always meant for you to marry Anne and have this place. You will take excellent care of Rosings. Aunt Catherine will be happy." He rubbed at his eyes again.

"Richard," Darcy said firmly. "Be silent for a moment, please."

Richard gave him a startled look and nodded.

"First," Darcy enumerated with a finger, "I am sole executor." He saw Richard wanted to interrupt again, so he went on quickly. "Second," another finger went up, "I had no idea of what was in Lady Catherine's will until her lawyer read it to me." He put up a third finger. "Third, several of Sir Lewis' relatives get bequests and I know where those who do are to be found." With his fourth finger up, Darcy concluded, "Fourth, after those bequests, minor bequests to the servants and a few pensions, you are the sole heir."

Richard leaned back in his chair, expression one of utter shock. "Me?"

Darcy returned his hand to the desktop. "You."

Richard blinked several times. He swiveled in his chair to look behind him, as if some other heir might spring up, then turned back to Darcy. "Why not Arthur or Walter? They're both older than I am."

Darcy shrugged. "I can only guess, but I'm certain one factor is that neither of your brothers have visited our aunt in years. More importantly, Lady Catherine appreciated you saving Anne from Blackmore."

The startled look remained on Richard's face. "But still, as a third son, I never expected to inherit anything."

"You are only minutes younger than Walter," Darcy said. Of course, in most ways, it didn't matter if brothers were twenty years apart or twenty minutes, as was the case with the twins, Walter and Richard. The older son was deemed more important.

"Yes, and we were both provided for."

"Walter better than you," Darcy pointed out. The property Walter had inherited brought more money than Richard's military rank.

Richard shrugged. "I care too much for Walter to begrudge him his inheritance." He leaned forward in his chair. "You don't think he'll be upset I'm to have Rosings?"

Darcy certainly hoped not. "I suspect that once the shock wears off, Walter will feel the same way about you inheriting Rosings as you do about his inheritance."

Richard leaned back again. He looked about the office and let out a long breath. "I can't believe Rosings is mine."

"There is one, minor, drawback," Darcy said. He paged through his aunt's will. "Lady Catherine wrote a new will after Anne's death. Essentially, she gave all of Anne's dowry, plus all the funds on hand, to Sir Lewis' relatives and to several of the long-term servants."

Richard frowned. "That seems reasonable to me. I don't need everything."

Darcy shook his head. "It's not a matter of reason. It's a matter of solvency. It takes money to run Rosings."

"Oh, yes, of course," Richard said. "Uh, how much money? Won't more be coming in?"

Darcy nodded. "Yes, but perhaps not quickly enough." He pulled free another page. "I've already found a solution. You can sell the living at Hunsford. Lady Catherine was in the process of finding someone when Anne died. She never took back up the task."

"Mr. Grigg left?" Richard asked. "I didn't know."

"You recall how erratic last Easter's sermon was?" Darcy asked.

"I do. I could have recited it better than he did, I've heard it from him so many times."

"Mr. Grigg's memory is failing him," Darcy said. "Aunt Catherine sent him to live with his youngest daughter shortly after we departed this past Easter. She hadn't found a suitable replacement yet."

"And that would help?" Richard asked.

"It would."

Richard drummed his fingers on the chair arm. "No, I don't want to sell it," he said after a moment.

"I believe Aunt Catherine meant for you to do so," Darcy assured him. "It's my guess, based on her allocation of funds, that she considered the value of the living when she wrote the will. If you sell it for what it is worth, you will have plenty of funds on hand."

"Be that as it may, I don't want to sell it."

Darcy opened his mouth to protest.

Richard held up a finger, a half smile letting Darcy know the gesture for deliberate mimicry. "Remember two years ago, when I was wounded, almost killed?"

"I do." Receiving the news was difficult to forget. Darcy had been considerably alarmed at the prospect of losing his favorite cousin and closest confidant.

"The man who saved my life, the ensign who carried me off the field, he left the service and became a clergyman. I want to offer him the living."

Darcy couldn't deny the rightness of that. "He hasn't found a living yet?"

"Only a curacy," Richard said. "And it's barely enough to scrape by. I owe him, and I like him. And he makes a good clergyman."

"Starting out as an ensign isn't the usual path to become a clergyman," Darcy observed, trying to judge the soundness of Richard's choice.

"It is if you went to university before joining the army."

"He had an education, but signed on regardless?"

Richard shrugged. "He decided his duty lay in the army." He leveled a piercing look on Darcy, a reminder that Darcy had never seen war firsthand. "He wouldn't be the first to change his mind after experiencing a battlefield."

"True." Darcy wondered how much of what Richard said referred to himself.

"He saved my life," Richard reiterated. He looked about the room, their uncle's room. "If I give him the living, will I be able to afford to run Rosings?"

Darcy ran back over the figures in his mind. "Barely. You won't have money for emergencies, but you should make it to quarter day without difficulty. Then you'll have more ready funds."

"And if there is an emergency?" Richard asked.

"I don't recommend it, but you will be able to borrow if you have an emergency."

"What, ah, constitutes an emergency, when it comes to managing an estate?" Richard asked.

It pleased Darcy that Richard was obviously considering the possibility. Running an estate like Rosings took years of practice, and even then, the possibility always existed for something to go wrong. Some factors were beyond control, like the weather, or tenants leaving for various reasons. Death, fire. If Richard truly wished to give the Hunsford living away, he should understand the potential consequences.

"Here," Darcy said, pulling out a clean sheet of paper. "I'll give you some likely obstacles, and how much it should cost to manage them."

He took up a pen, trimmed it, and opened the inkwell. He wrote down likely emergencies and estimates of the amount each would cost. He wanted to give Richard an understanding of what was needed as a reserve fund. Richard had always lived within his income, but Darcy worried that he would feel his wealth allowed him to spend an unlimited amount of money. If there were no emergencies and Richard did not spend more than Lady Catherine had, the reserve fund would build up very soon, and Richard would have more leeway, but until then, there existed a very real danger of being short of funds. Darcy wrote for some time. Finally, he pushed the page across to Richard.

Richard scanned it for a long moment. Finally, he looked up, expression slightly dazed. "I never realized so many things could go wrong with an estate."

"Not could," Darcy corrected. "Will. Eventually, most or even all those things will happen. You can only hope too many don't happen at once, and that you have the funds set aside to deal with them."

Richard dropped his attention to the page again. "Contagious disease?" he said, reading one of the lines, then looked back up, eyebrows raised.

"We had an illness run through Derbyshire during planting season, two years ago," Darcy said. "We needed to bring in extra men to help with the planting or, come autumn, we would have had to buy extra goods, which would have cost much more."

"And in this section under weather, it says too much rain, then too little rain. Not enough sun. Early frost in the autumn. Late frost in the spring. Hail. High winds." He glanced past Darcy, at the office's large window. "I know the weather affects planting, but I never gave it diligent consideration."

"Now, you shall need to."

Twin lines appeared on Richard's brow. "Darcy, I don't know if I'm up to this."

"Of course, you are." Darcy offered a slight smile. "As a man who's seen a battlefield firsthand, you can certainly learn to manage Rosings."

Richard gave a weak chuckle.

Darcy grew serious once more. "And, with your permission, I will remain for a time to assist you." It was not part of Darcy's duty as executor to teach Richard how to be a landowner, but it was an obligation he felt both to Richard as his friend and cousin, as well as to the memory of his aunt and the estate itself.

"That would be greatly appreciated." Richard shifted in his chair. "Several weeks ago, Walter wrote me about some of the difficulties he's suffered. He's having to live very frugally to cover unexpected expenses. I admit, I uncharitably assumed he was at fault. He's always been a bit erratic." Richard tapped the list. "I hadn't realized being a landowner could be so difficult. I hope all the emergencies you spoke of don't happen at once."

As they were cousins, Darcy was somewhat familiar with Walter's estate. Darcy felt it prudent to keep his opinion of Walter's managerial abilities to himself. "I hope so as well, but it's best to be prepared, so you do not need to sink into debt after each unforeseen event. You are lucky Lady Catherine was a good manager. She also has an excellent steward. You should keep him, if he'll stay on."

"Right," Richard said. "I'll ask him." He nodded to the ledgers stacked on the desk. "So, where do we start? I'm sure you already have them memorized."

Instead of refuting that, Darcy pulled one of the volumes from the pile and opened it to a row of figures. He slid it across the table to Richard. "After the bequests, the available funds are enough to run Rosings at a slightly reduced level until quarter day, which will bring in well over two thousand pounds. On top of that, the sale of excess goods from Rosings' farm will bring in a bit more."

Richard looked startled. "It sounds like I will have a great deal of money."

That was the attitude Darcy feared, and must work to stamp out. For Richard's sake, and Lady Catherine's, Darcy would make him a better landholder than his twin brother. "That is two thousand pounds before you pay your expenses and begin the chore of replenishing the reserve fund. In time, you will have some ready cash, of course. Especially if, for now, you are frugal and invest."

Richard nodded, expression suitably serious.

Feeling his cousin was coming to understand the gravity of the task before him, Darcy allowed a slight smile. "You do, however, have a major problem that I cannot solve."

"Do I?" Richard asked, eyebrows raised. "What is this serious problem that you, Fitzwilliam Darcy of Pemberley, cannot solve?"

"One I've been grappling with for years myself. You will be the target of every fortune hunter in England, and all of their relatives."

Chapter Four

Months later

As the dinner hour drew near at Darcy House, his London residence, Darcy looked about the parlor with satisfaction. He hated crowds full of strangers, potentially full of people he would be introduced to who were not worth knowing. He took exception to anyone the least bit vulgar. This, however, was different. Tonight, he'd invited precisely the correct guests, it being his home and his prerogative.

His good friend, Charles Bingley, was staying at Darcy House for a visit after returning from the house he rented in Hertfordshire. That meant the addition of Bingley's always proper and socially adept sisters. One, Miss Caroline Bingley, had not yet wed, making her a particularly good companion to and example for Darcy's sister, Georgiana. The other, a Mrs. Louisa Hurst, had selected an eminently inoffensive gentleman to espouse. Mr. Hurst could be counted on to add little to conversation, politely making Darcy seem less withdrawn, and to admire and consume any and all food offered, which flattered Darcy's cook.

Also present, fortuitously, was Richard. He'd arrived in London only that morning and sent a note informing Darcy of such. Darcy had cheerfully asked his cousin to be a last-minute addition to their dinner. Not only for Richard's conversation, which always proved a good match to Bingley's. Richard would also serve to divert Miss Bingley's attention, at least somewhat, from Darcy. Miss Bingley had the unfortunate habit of over-attending Darcy's words. Since Richard inherited Rosings, however, she'd divided her attention equally between Darcy and Richard, on the one occasion they both were in the room.

Most importantly, Richard would help with Darcy's main goal for the evening, reaccustoming Georgiana to company. Georgiana adored Richard. As Anne had, Darcy's sister often seemed inclined to seek Richard out for conversation. Somehow, he managed to combine the easy-going affability Bingley boasted with Darcy's competence and reliability. Darcy assumed that made Richard a good leader of men. He knew it made their cousin a good confidant for Georgiana. She needed someone with whom to converse, other than her companion, Mrs. Annesley.

Darcy watched his sister as they all assembled in the dining room. She kept her attention on her feet as she walked toward the table. With eight people, all good friends, Darcy hadn't requested place cards or pressed for a formal seating arrangement. He wanted this occasion to be somewhat informal, but he hoped Georgiana would take her place as hostess, especially since she knew he wanted her to do so.

She did and must have realized that Richard would sit on her right, since he was the highest-ranking male guest, because she demurely invited Mr. Hurst to sit on her other side, to Darcy's chagrin. He'd hoped Georgiana would feel comfortable talking to the people on either side of her and had wanted those people to be either Bingley or his sisters, who would socialize with her. Mr. Hurst's primary interest at dinner was, well, dinner. This left her between a man who would be content to say nothing and her cousin. She would not have the experience of talking to Bingley or his sisters. Because he knew them well, Darcy easily read the look Miss Bingley and Mrs. Hurst exchanged. They had wanted Bingley to sit beside Georgiana as well.

Darcy knew they hoped for a match between Bingley and Georgiana, something he would have welcomed. Bingley was a friend and was likely to treat Darcy's sister well. Georgiana, however, showed no inclination toward Bingley. Darcy had broached the subject with her only once. She'd shaken her head no, then become even more withdrawn than ever in Bingley's company. Bingley continued to be friendly toward her and treated her more as a younger sister than as a possible romantic interest. He was sensitive enough not to push his company on her, despite the obvious encouragement his sisters gave.

Darcy would also have welcomed a friendship between Georgiana and either of Bingley's sisters, but she showed no inclination to become friends with them. In truth, aside from Richard, Darcy had no idea with whom his sister conversed. Mrs. Annesley reported to Darcy that Georgiana spoke with her a little but didn't confide in her, and that his sister was no longer even talkative with young women with whom she'd attended school. Darcy wasn't sure if he should describe her as shy or frightened.

Georgiana hadn't always been withdrawn. She hadn't been quiet as a child, or in the years leading up to womanhood. Now, she barely spoke, even to him, and Darcy knew the precise moment of this unwanted change: The incident in Ramsgate with Mr. Wickham.

On the heels of that thought, Darcy clenched his teeth, put Ramsgate and Wickham from his mind, and endeavored to focus on dinner. Georgiana correctly conversed with Richard for the first portion of the meal, although Richard appeared to be doing most of the talking. Earlier than was proper, but with surprising finesse, she switched to talking with Mr. Hurst, thus turning the table and requiring everyone to change those with whom they spoke. Richard took his cue and began conversing with Mrs. Annesley. Darcy removed his attention from Miss Bingley on his left to Mrs. Hurst on his right.

Darcy was glad that Georgiana was handling her position as hostess of a formal dinner, but he had wanted this meal to be informal. That aside, she was doing an admirable job, except for turning the table too early. She spoke little, but Mr. Hurst talked to her throughout the meal. From the tidbits Darcy heard, they spoke about bets Mr. Hurst had made. Darcy was surprised Mr. Hurst chose that topic for a conversation with Georgiana, even though he knew Mr. Hurst enjoyed betting.

Darcy worked to tamp down his disquiet about Mr. Hurst's choice of topic and concentrate on conversing with Mrs. Hurst. Finally, the meal began to wind down. In the same moment he realized dinner was nearing a close, he also realized he'd been neglecting Mrs. Hurst. He turned to her to rectify that, but she was paying him no attention. Instead, she looked across the table at her brother.

"Charles, tell us about the neighbors you've met in Hertfordshire. You told me many of them called on you there," Mrs. Hurst said, surprising Darcy by bringing the informality he'd wished for into the meal by speaking with Bingley, who was not only across the table but one seat over.

"They were very friendly people," Bingley replied cheerfully. "In fact, I thought I might return soon. You are all invited to join me for a couple of months. I've imposed on you long enough, Darcy. I should like to return the hospitality."

"All of us?" Darcy asked.

"Yes. Why not? Unless Miss Darcy is too busy with her studies, that is."

Georgiana raised her gaze to cast Darcy a beseeching look.

"I am certain she can forgo meeting her tutors for a month or two," Darcy said, ignoring his sister's silent plea. It would be good for her to mix more in company, probably better than staying in London and only interacting with her masters and Mrs. Annesley. At his agreement, she dropped her gaze once more, but evidenced no other sign of disappointment, which surprised him. Was she so resigned to staying in the background that she didn't expect him to heed her? He would feel remorse, but he was doing it for her own good.

"Colonel Fitzwilliam," Miss Bingley said. "You are invited also."

"Certainly," Bingley said. "There's always room for you, Colonel."

"That's very kind and, though I've only now arrived in London, I shouldn't mind taking you up on the offer."

Darcy turned a surprised look on his cousin. He'd expected Richard to decline. Since taking over Rosings, Richard had been so social as to be troubling. Tucking himself away in Bingley's somewhat obscure country estate would put an end to that.

Richard cleared his throat. "I should warn you first, however, that I've sold out. I would still be delighted to join you, if you can accept a mere Mr. Fitzwilliam."

Miss Bingley turned to him with bright eyes. "Sold out? Why, Mr. Fitzwilliam, does that mean you're making ready to select a lady for Rosings?"

Darcy knew Richard well enough to see the slight tightening of muscles about his eyes, though his cheerful expression didn't otherwise waver. "If the right woman comes my way," he said. "But it's daunting to select someone to fill Aunt Catherine's role. I certainly never feel that I have."

"Yes, Rosings is quite the responsibility." Mrs. Hurst cast a meaningful look at Miss Bingley. "You need someone firm and well versed in running a household. Caroline, how long did you keep house for our father after our mother died?"

"Oh, several years, as you know," Miss Bingley replied.

"Since it seems everyone else has had their fill, could you pass me the ragout, Darcy?" Mr. Hurst asked.

"What is the estate you're leasing called again, Charles?" Mrs. Hurst asked as Darcy offered the plate of greens to Mr. Hurst. "You mentioned that it is sizeable?"

"Netherfield Park. Lovely place, and large, although it doesn't compare to Pemberley," Bingley supplied.

"Why, that's quite a lot to manage," Mrs. Hurst said. "Don't you think so, Caroline?"

Miss Bingley shook her head. "It doesn't seem so to me, Louisa. I do believe I could manage an estate three times as large, easily. It's as if I've been born to the task, it comes so naturally."

"Yes, you do have a knack," Mrs. Hurst agreed. "Maybe you were born to it, but you've also been very well educated. The perfect combination. Don't you agree Mr. Darcy, Mr. Fitzwilliam?"

Richard met Darcy's gaze, the barest trace of amusement in his eyes. "I cannot help but agree, Mrs. Hurst," Richard said.

"Indeed," Darcy allowed.

"And that aspic, Mrs. Annesley," Mr. Hurst said. "Darcy's cook makes a divine aspic. Best in London. No reason to waste it." He looked up from his plate. "Bingley, you should hire away Darcy's cook."

"Poach Darcy's cook?" Bingley shook his head. "A poor friend I'd be."

"Agreed," Darcy said, though the praise pleased him. One of the staff, waiting unobtrusively about the room, would surely repeat Mr. Hurst's words to Darcy's cook. He might be required to issue a raise, but that was a small price for a happy cook.

"Well, I'll be delighted to see the manor and grounds at your acquisition, Charles, despite the rather remote location," Mrs. Hurst said. "It must be lovely for riding. Caroline, you're such an accomplished rider, so you benefit the most from Charles' choice."

Miss Bingley nodded and turned to Georgiana. "Miss Darcy, have you come any further with your riding? We could explore the park together."

Georgiana shook her head. Riding had never been her strength. Since Ramsgate, Darcy couldn't even get her to attempt it.

A silent moment passed. Darcy's companions always waited, polite and hopeful, for Georgiana to reply. He appreciated their solicitousness of his sister. He wished she would benefit from the kindness.

With a fixed smile, Miss Bingley resumed speaking, turning the conversation to their travel plans. In some way that Darcy didn't quite follow, it was arranged that Georgiana would ride with the Hursts and Bingley, while Mrs. Annesley traveled with Miss Bingley, Darcy and Richard. Normally, Darcy would put an end to such machinations, but Georgiana's continued refusal to speak to those she'd known for years, to emerge from the shell she'd drawn about herself, irked him. When she didn't protest, only leveled a glare on him, Darcy let the matter proceed as Bingley's sisters obviously wished. Perhaps a carriage ride without Darcy, Richard or Mrs. Annesley to speak on her behalf would prove therapeutic to his sister.

Later, after the Hursts departed with Miss Bingley, and Mrs. Annesley and Georgiana retired for the evening, Richard remained, joining Darcy and Bingley in the back parlor. Darcy poured them each a brandy and settled into his favorite chair, fairly content with the evening. Richard and Bingley sat as well, completing a small ring about a low table. This being Darcy's private parlor, there were only armchairs, not sofas.

Darcy turned to Richard. "Joining us in Hertfordshire is a departure from your recent ways." And an odd move for a man Darcy knew didn't wish to encourage Miss Bingley.

"It certainly pleased Caroline that you've agreed to come," Bingley added, the look he leveled on Richard keen. "Is there anything I should know?"

Richard took a sip of his drink. "I'm afraid not, much as you'd make a fine brother, Bingley."

Bingley leaned back deeper into his chair. "I rather thought not. I mean, you're always polite, certainly, but I've never noted you as anything more."

"Why, then?" Darcy asked.

Richard grimaced. "It's my onetime companions. All my military friends assume I will entertain them at Rosings. They also assume I will be happy to send carriage after carriage to London to bring them there and that we will enjoy lavish, out of season fare."

"Is it really that bad?" Bingley asked.

Richard nodded. "Worse than you're imagining, I wager. Take this, and this is only an example, but the wife of my former general wanted me to buy four white horses to carry her around in style. Me. Buy her four white horses."

"To bring her to Rosings?" Bingley asked with a frown.

"No, to bring her everywhere. Four horses, as a gift." Richard's tone betrayed his consternation.

"What did her husband say to that?" Darcy asked. Gifting another man's wife in so extravagant a way, or generally at all, would be quite the scandal.

Richard snorted. "The general said that two horses of any color, as long as they matched, would be a good idea."

"That's ridiculous." Bingley's tone held mild outrage. "Once my fortune became common knowledge, back when I started at university, I faced a similar barrage of demands, although none quite so outrageous. Worse, they were from false friends, for all my friends there were new. Darcy helped me deal with that."

"Yes, Darcy enjoys helping." Richard turned an assessing look on Darcy.

"Do you require my help?" Darcy asked Richard, the words more a challenge than an offer. Richard had required Darcy's help when he first took on Rosings, but that dependence had lasted only a few months.

Richard's expression became equal parts amusement and effrontery. "I do not, but I thank you for the offer." He took another sip of brandy. "No, much as I wanted to please them, I agree with Bingley. They were being ridiculous. Now that I'm no longer in the army, I can be cowardly and run away from them."

"Which is why you resigned your commission," Darcy said.

"Yes, and that was only the first step." Richard nodded to Bingley. "Your offer couldn't have come at a better time. My guests cost me all the funds I had left after administering Aunt Catherine's will and I haven't yet received the money from selling out. I'm living in my rooms off what little I had saved. I was about to humble myself and ask Darcy for board."

Darcy frowned. How much had Richard spent entertaining? It sounded worse even than Darcy had heard. "What about the quarterly income? And the harvest? Rosings usually produces enough that there's some left over to sell."

Richard held up a staying hand. "Don't glower at me, Darcy. Rosings had a bountiful harvest, and the quarterly income is all in, but the parsonage was in dire need of repair. There was dry rot that Mr. Grigg hadn't noticed. I practically had to have the place rebuilt. Given his condition those last few years, I should have thought to check." He narrowed his eyes at Darcy. "That's one possibility you didn't have on that lengthy list of yours."

"I apologize. I didn't consider that."

"List?" Bingley chuckled. "Aback when I was at university, Darcy took me aside and gave me a list of all the reasons people might give as to why I should provide them with funds." His expression became contemplative. "It's a good list. I still have it."

"I should like to see it," Richard said. "This was a good list as well. My brother, Walter, has an estate, as I think you know?"

Bingley nodded.

"I wrote to him about the list," Richard continued. "He said he wished Darcy had given him one, as several of the things on Darcy's list have happened to him and he wasn't prepared. I sent him a copy, and added, parsonage dry rot."

Bingley chuckled.

Richard shook his head, expression contemplative. "Eventually, I suppose, I'll be grateful I inherited Rosings, but now I feel I've less financial security than ever before. It's difficult to be beholden to so many people. I'd like to purchase a new horse, for example. A fine fast animal, for riding, but instead I fixed the parsonage and invested in the maintenance of the farmstead, because a new horse for me wouldn't do the people who look to Rosings any good."

"You could always put up Lady Catherine's house in town to be leased," Darcy said, feeling somewhat responsible for Richard's circumstance, though the dry rot couldn't have been predicted. Who could have guessed, from afar, that Mr. Grigg's condition had deteriorated to the point where he wouldn't think to maintain his home?

"Why not?" Richard agreed. "It's expensive to maintain and I've no intention of taking up residence there. That would necessitate enduring and returning social calls, another expense. I don't need anything fancy."

"It should bring some money," Darcy said, pleased.

Richard nodded, then looked between Darcy and Bingley. "I have a favor to ask."

"What?" Darcy asked.

"Anything," Bingley agreed.

"I know word of me inheriting Rosings is already getting around, but I'd like to stem the tide of gossip as much as possible," Richard said. "Go ahead and tell people that I've sold out because I inherited some property, but don't tell them how much Rosings is worth. I've had husband-hunting women interested in me simply because I was a colonel and the third son of an earl. With Rosings, I won't know a moment's peace."

Darcy shrugged. "I've only discussed your change in circumstance with Bingley and am unlikely to do so with others, but I'm sure word is already out."

"And I've only discussed it with Darcy and my sisters," Bingley said. "But Lady Catherine was known, and her death talked of. Everyone was keen to learn who inherited. I'm sure the whole of London is already aware of your change in circumstance."

"But it's only been a season," Richard protested.

Bingley grinned. "Welcome to London society, Mr. Fitzwilliam."

"I'd draw you up a list of ways to avoid fortune seeking females, but I've yet to find a successful means," Darcy added.

"Oh, you do alright with your high and mighty Mr. Darcy airs," Bingley said, grinning.

"So, the remainder of my life is to be spent running from marriage minded ladies and their determined mamas?" Richard asked.

"No." Bingley shook his head. "Some of your time will be spent in Hertfordshire with Darcy and me hunting, riding, and dancing with country misses who have low expectations of capturing a gentleman like us but a divine eagerness to please."

Darcy shook his head. "But little in the way of wits or beauty with which to do so."

"There are pretty enough girls in Hertfordshire," Bingley said. "You wait and see."

"I doubt there is a single one refined or well-favored enough to tempt me into making an acquaintance that cannot help but be tinged with vulgarity," Darcy countered.

"You see?" Bingley said to Richard. "It's that sort of perfect hauteur that staves off all but the most diligent of fortune hunters." Bingley cast Darcy a look bright with merriment, then turned back to Richard. "And don't worry, I'll be sure to mention to Caroline that Rosings is not yet profitable."

"Meaning no offense, but I'd take that as a kindness," Richard replied.

"Would you like me to tell her the same about Pemberley, Darcy?" Bingley asked.

Darcy shook his head. "I would not have you lie."

Bingley shrugged. "As you wish. I doubt she'd have believed me."

"We should have an interesting time in Hertfordshire," Richard said.

Darcy could only agree.

Chapter Five

Bingley must have told his sisters of Richard's financial hardships, for somehow, despite their earlier plans, Richard ended up riding with the Hursts in Bingley's carriage. In a further show of expert manipulation, Miss Bingley took Darcy aside and sweetly suggested that she could better draw out Georgiana if Mrs. Annesley remained behind. As Georgiana's chaperone's sister was ill and Miss Bingley made a fair point about Georgiana's reticence, Darcy again permitted her machinations to succeed.

Thusly, when the time came to depart London, Darcy's carriage held him, Miss Bingley, Georgiana and Bingley. Darcy didn't expect Richard's reprieve to extend too far beyond riding arrangements, for Rosings was an excellent prize even with some initial hardship, but he could appreciate that Miss Bingley wished to pursue the best option available to her. Her unflaggingly mercenary attitude lent her behavior a soothing predictability. Darcy preferred that to lovestruck, emotional women.

They rumbled through London, the streets filled with wagons bearing goods rather than carriages with the early hour. Georgiana, sharing a seat with Darcy, stared out the window. Across from her, Bingley stifled a yawn.

Seated opposite Darcy, Miss Bingley narrowed her gaze at her brother. "You were eager to get us on the road this morning. I don't see why we had to leave so early. It's only a four-hour trip."

Bingley stifled another yawn. "There's an assembly this evening. It's a good way to meet people."

Miss Bingley sniffed. "I don't think there will be anyone at the assembly who I would like to meet."

Darcy privately agreed.

"According to Sir William, all our neighboring families will be there," Bingley said.

"I've not met Sir William. Is he a baron?" Miss Bingley asked hopefully.

"No. He's a knight." Bingley's expression was bland. "He was in trade, but now owns an estate."

Miss Bingley wrinkled her nose. "I see."

"He's very affable. We should get to know our neighbors."

"You are assuming there is anyone worth knowing." Miss Bingley's tone suggested she didn't believe there would be.

"I rented a manor in the country for the purpose of enjoying myself," Bingley said, a hint of exasperation in his voice. "As much as I appreciate the company journeying with us, I have no intention of spending the next several months in Hertfordshire not mixing with local residents."

"Yes, but an assembly? Anyone could be in attendance. All they need is a sixpence or whatever trifling pittance a countrified region deems acceptable." Miss Bingley sniffed again. "The people there will be nothing to us."

Her harsh tone met with silence. Bingley turned a somewhat vexed look out the window. Darcy agreed with Miss Bingley but saw no reason to pursue the subject.

"I would like to dance at an assembly," Georgiana said into the silence, voice wistful.

Darcy turned to her in surprise. He hadn't even realized she'd been aware of the conversation, she'd been so fixated on the passing buildings as they headed toward the edge of London. "Why?" he asked. "You do not like to be with strangers, and you won't know anyone there. Do you even enjoy dancing?"

Bingley cast him a quick, surprised look. Darcy immediately regretted his harsh words, but Georgiana's declaration confused him. She rarely spoke, not in the months since Ramsgate, but now she wished to enter a hall full of strangers?

"I like dancing," Georgiana said, cheeks turning pink. "But I've only practiced with my dancing master and the girls at school. In Hertfordshire, you could dance with me or Mr. Hurst or Richard or Mr. Bingley. None of you will expect me to talk, so it will be easier."

"But you could dance with any of them in London as well," Miss Bingley pointed out. "I'm sure Charles would always be pleased to partner you."

Georgiana shook her head. "It would matter in London," she said, voice soft. "Before I dance with men where it matters, I would like to try dancing with strangers who don't matter watching me. It may be I could even dance with someone to whom I've just been introduced. Maybe then, when I come out, I'll be more comfortable." She stared at her hands, resting in her lap. "If I make a fool of myself in Hertfordshire, it won't matter."

"Yes, but in going to their assembly, you may be forced to interact with them," Miss Bingley said with another wrinkle of her nose. "And you're rather young to expose to such vulgar personages."

"I would like to go," Georgiana said quietly. She turned questioning eyes on Darcy.

Darcy was more surprised by how much his sister had spoken than by her request. Perhaps she was recovering from the incident at Ramsgate and should be encouraged. He understood Georgiana's point. The people they would meet in Hertfordshire truly didn't matter. Since Ramsgate, his sister lacked confidence. Maybe going to a place where her superior breeding would make her shine would restore some of her poise.

He'd attempted to do so through small gatherings with her equals, to little effect. In Hertfordshire, the absolute lack of consequential people might be exactly what she required. He knew little of girls, but he was aware boys could be cruel to those they thought were weak. Even as a Darcy, his sister would be somewhat subjected to that behavior in London, whereas Georgiana's obvious superiority should make her immune to such treatment at a country assembly.

"If you wish to go to this assembly, you certainly may," he finally said. "You will not have to dance if you are not comfortable doing so. Nor should you feel obligated to speak with your partners. I will take you home the moment you ask."

Miss Bingley made a tisking sound, but Georgiana smiled. That smile only grew as she turned back toward the window, the scene without one of rolling hills now. Sometime during their conversation, they'd passed out of London.

Darcy tried to feel pleased with his decision. Turning from his sister, he listened to Bingley and Miss Bingley discussing how old a child should be to secure employment in a cotton mill, with Miss Bingley arguing for laxer laws so work in the mill might begin at any age. Though he rather vehemently disagreed, Darcy couldn't focus on the conversation, partly because he knew that Miss Bingley would change her opinion to match his as soon as he spoke and partly due to his sister. Anytime he glanced at Georgiana, her face angled slightly toward the passing scenery, his disquiet increased. There was something about her smile, an almost cunning edge, that didn't set well. Such a smile couldn't possibly be because he'd granted her permission to dance with him, Mr. Hurst, Richard or even Mr. Bingley.

The journey to Hertfordshire passed incident-free, which Darcy accounted in large part due to his participation in planning the jaunt. Netherfield Park, as well, proved acceptable. To be certain, the manor and grounds were amiable, even if they lacked the perfect blend of manmade and natural that his family achieved at Pemberley. As well, Pemberley shone with a greater attention to every minute detail. As they made a tour of the Netherfield manor, Darcy reflected that the sort of perfection his home boasted could only be created by years of dedication and would never be found in a property put up for rent.

Still, the satisfactoriness of Bingley's choice in properties did much to ease Darcy's mind. Unfortunately, that state of contentment lasted only until that evening, when their carriages bounced up the drive toward the assembly hall. One look, and all serenity fled.

Not a single carriage in the gaggle they maneuvered toward possessed anywhere near the style or value of theirs. Worse, many people flocked to the event on foot. He saw men without hats. Ladies in desperate need of another strip of lace. One family rolled up the drive in what could only be described as a cart, pulled by a mule.

Georgiana stared out, wide-eyed. Darcy looked from his sister to the scene without and back again, frowning. A glance showed Bingley wore his usual cheerful smile, unfazed.

Miss Bingley leaned forward, peeked around the curtain, and issued a sniff. "How very...rural."

"Are those gentlemen singing and dancing a jig?" Georgiana asked.

Darcy followed the direction of her gaze to see several young men, hopefully not permitted inside, who appeared soused and who were, indeed, dancing. He reached out and tugged the curtain closed. "Let's hope those within are of at least slightly superior quality."

"You may as well ask a horse to speak," Miss Bingley said primly.

"I enjoy a lively gathering," Bingley countered.

Darcy clamped his mouth closed over a rejoinder. He would need to remain close to his sister. Undoubtedly, she would be exposed to a myriad of ill manners that evening.

Inside proved marginally better. It turned out that neither the dancing men nor the family in the cart meant to attend. Apparently, those who weren't even worthy enough to join the hodgepodge assembly routinely gathered without to mingle and observe their betters come and go.

Still, Darcy partnered Georgiana first, to gain time to observe the room and form a plan to protect her. He made no attempt at conversation, intent on studying the other occupants of the hall. Nor did his sister speak. She did, however, dance well. Her skill proved a surprise, and noticeable enough to penetrate his distraction.

He relinquished Georgiana into Richard's care, then stood up with Miss Bingley, followed by a set with Mrs. Hurst. During that set, Georgiana danced with Bingley. The few glimpses Darcy got of her showed she spoke little to Richard, and even less to Bingley. She then danced a set with Mr. Hurst, while Darcy watched on, relieved he wouldn't be called on to dance again that evening. He'd done his duty to his party. Now, he could concentrate on chaperoning Georgiana.

Oddly, his sister spoke more with Mr. Hurst than any of her previous partners. As they danced, he even smiled several times. After her set with him ended, Darcy expected she would decline whichever man next approached her. By tradition, that refusal would end her participation in dancing for the evening. He might take her home soon, as there was nothing to occupy them save being accosted by country gentry. Her set with Mr. Hurst drew to a close, and Darcy gestured to catch their attention, waving Georgiana over.

She saw him but turned away as a young man approached her and Mr. Hurst. The man chatted with Mr. Hurst, who introduced him to Georgiana. Before Darcy fully grasped his sister's intention, Mr. Hurst strode toward him and Georgiana began the next set with the unknown young man.

Darcy didn't hide his frown as Hurst joined him along the wall. "With whom is my sister dancing?"

"A young Mr. Lucas," Hurst said. "Seemed an amiable chap. Eldest son of Sir William Lucas. If you remember, Bingley introduced us when we entered."

Darcy couldn't find any actual fault with that. He turned his attention back to watching his sister. Oddly, she seemed to be carrying on an animated conversation with the young man. She looked rather…happy. When the set ended, the two were approached by another young man, and Georgiana danced again.

Darcy's frown deepened. Perhaps he'd been mad to let her attend. She wasn't out. Not really. She would come out with a grand party in London, or at Pemberley. Eventually. In a year. Maybe two. After the incident in Ramsgate with Wickham, Darcy wanted Georgiana kept away from all men until she was old enough to make intelligent decisions.

An excess of giggling caught his attention. He sought the source with his gaze to find an older woman, several younger ones beside her, chortling in an unacceptable manner. Darcy watched for a moment as the older woman leaned over and whispered to the youngest of her companions, the one he'd spotted without who required more lace. They both laughed in an over-loud way. Looking at the eldest of the bunch, it occurred to him that he may have to keep Georgiana away from men for longer than he'd thought. It appeared some women never attained the ability to make intelligent decisions.

"That's Mrs. Bennet," Hurst informed him. "Those are three of her daughters. She has five, and no sons, poor woman. I'm going to inspect the card room. You should dance, Darcy. There isn't a woman here who wouldn't be happy to stand up with you."

Darcy shook his head and returned to glaring at Georgiana and her partner. As he watched, both Richard and Bingley sailed by, each with an unknown young woman as their dance partner. Darcy tried to calculate for how long he'd be made to remain. He began to wish he'd brought Mrs. Annesley after all, for she could have escorted Georgiana back to Netherfield Park.

As the evening wore on, Darcy couldn't avoid certain introductions. Each proved less acceptable than the last, yet he'd no opportunity to depart. Georgiana danced on. Richard and Bingley were enjoying themselves. Both danced indiscriminately with anyone who happened to be available. They weren't even exclusively partnering the attractive women. Early on, they both danced with Miss Lucas, sister to Georgiana's first partner outside their group, who was very plain.

After what felt like hours, Richard left off dancing and headed Darcy's way. Darcy dared to hope his cousin had come to his senses. It was high time they headed back to Netherfield Park.

50

"Georgiana isn't going to come to any harm," Richard said. "You should dance."

Darcy grimaced. "Why? You know how I detest it unless I am particularly acquainted with my partner. I danced once already with Georgiana and both of Bingley's sisters. All are engaged now."

"You shouldn't need me to point it out to you, but there are other women here," Richard said. "Many of whom are in want of a partner each set, there being a shortage of gentlemen."

Darcy shook his head. "Bingley is monopolizing the only beautiful woman in the room. There is no one else here who is pretty enough to dance with."

Richard looked over to where Bingley spoke with a young woman Darcy had come to understand was Miss Bennet, eldest of the five Bennet sisters, whom Mr. Hurst had mentioned.

"She is beautiful, and very pleasant as well," Richard said. He turned back to Darcy, grinned, and held up a finger. "First, it is your duty as a gentleman to dance." He added a finger. "Second, as I warned you long ago, Bingley is wont to monopolize the most beautiful woman in every room." A third finger, and a pleasant expression aimed over Darcy's shoulder. "Third, Miss Bennet's sister, Miss Elizabeth Bennet, is very pretty, and she is behind you. I could introduce you to her."

"Which do you mean?" Darcy turned around and caught the eyes of a young woman who stood a few paces away, beside Miss Lucas. Her interested expression revealed she eavesdropped on their conversation. Her impudence caused him to frown. "She is tolerable, but not beautiful enough to tempt me; I am in no humor at present to give consequence to young ladies who are slighted by other men."

The young woman's eyes, which were far more tolerable than he'd acknowledged to Richard, widened slightly. Beside her, Miss Lucas issued a small gasp.

Darcy hid a wince. Perhaps, in his ire, he'd gone too far, but he wouldn't apologize. He was a Darcy, after all, and these people were beneath him. There was little anyone, even Richard, could say to convince him otherwise.

Chapter Six

Richard stepped around him, obscuring the two women and filling Darcy's vision. "Darcy, come with me," he said in a tone he had probably used for ordering troops.

Puzzled, Darcy took in his cousin's hard expression. Richard gestured for Darcy to follow, then led the way toward an empty corner of the room, far from the dancing. Since the musicians were taking a break, conversations were increasingly filling the room, with everyone speaking louder to be heard over the din.

Richard reached the wall and turned. His censorious expression hadn't slackened. "Darcy, you did me a great favor by helping me with Rosings and I'm going to do you one now."

"I beg your pardon?" Darcy said, for Richard didn't appear in the mood to grant a favor, but rather like he wished to lecture.

Richard's mouth quirked in a wry smile. "The difference is, I appreciated your intervention. You will resent mine."

Darcy held up a hand. "Can it not wait, then? This evening is already intolerable."

Richard's face became once more devoid of humor. "No, I do not believe it can wait," he said, tone serious. "You behaved insufferably just now. You insulted a lady. Not only that, she overheard you. I don't care how wealthy you are or how distinguished your ancestors were. I've heard from others that you are resented by many. I didn't understand it before. Now I realize that is because I've only seen your behavior among people you respect."

"Come now, it can hardly matter what I do here," Darcy cut in defensively, chagrin surging through him.

"It always matters," Richard said, implacable. "Good manners aren't only about behaving properly when you want to. For no reason at all, you insulted a woman. If she'd any brothers, they'd be tempted to challenge you." Richard shook his head. "I thought you were taught better than that. Your father would never have behaved that way."

Annoyance and humiliation did war in Darcy's gut. "My father knew how to insult people," he muttered. "I've heard him do it."

"Yes. So, have I, but he did so deliberately and when he had a reason. That woman did nothing to deserve your insult."

"She didn't have a partner," Darcy said, that paltry excuse ringing hollow.

"What if it had been me?"

Darcy whirled to find Georgiana behind him. He stared at her in surprise.

"I said, what if it had been me?" she repeated, steely eyed.

Darcy had never seen his sister so angry. "You shouldn't listen in on a private conversation," he said stiffly.

That, after all, was how this Miss Elizabeth Bennet had become insulted. The fault for her mortification resided with her, for eavesdropping, not with him, for speaking the plain truth. Looking between his sister and cousin, he decided not to voice that thought aloud.

"I heard very little of what you and Richard are discussing, but I can guess," Georgiana said. "I overheard Mr. Lucas tell his brother about your insult." She maintained her glare. "Must I repeat my question a third time?"

Was any conversation private here? "It couldn't have been you," Darcy said to stave off that repetition. "You wouldn't be without a partner." He could all but feel the disapproval radiating off his sister and Richard. Within Darcy, annoyance began to win out over mortification.

"Only because of my wealth," Georgiana stated. "There are more women here than men. If that happened in London, I could easily be without a partner. Would that make me worthy of insult?"

Darcy clamped his mouth closed, having no good reply. Why did Georgiana have to choose this moment to find her voice?

Georgiana moved closer to glare up at him. "Besides which, Miss Elizabeth Bennet is prettier than I am. She dances better, too. Are you saying that, without my connections and dowry, I wouldn't be worthy of a dance? I, myself, have no merit beyond what you and our father chose to provide me?"

Darcy looked from his sister to his cousin. There was no give in either's expression. He did not think he'd done anything so terribly wrong. Certainly not wrong enough to warrant so much disapproval, but he was willing to placate them, people he did respect, even if they were being trying. "If I dance with her, will that make you both happy?"

"Yes," Richard said slowly. "But I bet she won't dance with you."

"You bet? What do you bet?" Darcy wasn't one to wager, but he was sufficiently irritated to pounce on Richard's turn of phrase. What right did they have to lecture him about his behavior before such a countrified gathering? Why, Georgiana had postulated only that morning, in the carriage, that what they did in Hertfordshire didn't matter.

"What do I bet?" Richard drawled. "How about, if you lose, you have to ask the least attractive woman in the room to dance with you. If you win, I will dance with the woman you decide is the ugliest."

Georgiana looked between them with wide eyes. "But I've already danced with both of you."

"Don't be absurd, Georgiana," Darcy protested.

"You are lovely as ever, cousin," Richard said.

Georgiana's mouth quirked in a smile. "Pick," she commanded to Darcy.

"Miss Lucas," Darcy said. He eyed Richard. "And you'd best hope I lose, because you've already danced with the lady once this evening. I shouldn't want you to create a misunderstanding. That would be very ill mannered of you."

Richard snorted. "Don't worry about *my* manners, Darcy."

Darcy scowled at him.

"You do realize that you're both behaving badly now?" Georgiana's balled hands found her hips as she spoke.

Richard grimaced and offered a slight nod. "She's right, Darcy. Although Miss Lucas and Miss Elizabeth cannot hear us, we ought not speak as we are."

"Trying to get out of our wager already?" Darcy asked stiffly. Let Richard feel guilt. Darcy only felt annoyance. His sister and cousin had stung his pride. They must suffer the consequence.

"Only because entering the wager was wrong."

Darcy locked gazes with his cousin.

Georgiana let out an exaggerated sigh and muttered something under her breath. She turned to Darcy and took his arm. "Come. I shall introduce you to Miss Elizabeth so we can lay this to rest."

Turning from Richard, Georgiana set them off across the room. Many people watched their progress. Some wore looks of disapproval. Darcy reminded himself that their opinions didn't have any consequence. The back of Miss Elizabeth's head, long neck a graceful sweep below her curls, came into view. Miss Lucas stood before her. She said something, and Miss Elizabeth turned.

"I'm not sure I wish to do this to Miss Elizabeth," Georgiana said from the side of her mouth.

"Make me dance with her?" Darcy asked, further piqued. "I am not so bad as that."

"No, make her sit out the rest of the night. She's sure to refuse you, you know."

"If she refuses me, which a woman of her station never would, and doesn't dance for the remainder of the evening, again questionable given her likely lack of honor, I will somehow make it up to her."

Georgiana gave him a quick look, which included rolling her eyes heavenward. Fortunately, they'd drawn too near their goal for further reprimand. They stopped before the two. Darcy bowed.

"Miss Lucas, Miss Elizabeth, this is my brother, Mr. Darcy," Georgiana said. "If you'll excuse me." She released his arm and walked away.

Darcy looked after her for a moment, taken aback by her abrupt departure. He turned back to Miss Elizabeth and offered another bow. "Miss Elizabeth, may I have the honor of the next set?"

She looked surprised, then speculative. A spark lit deep in her eyes, amplifying their already pretty cast. "I am sorry, sir, but I have decided not to dance anymore this evening. Thank you for your offer." She curtsied and walked away.

Darcy stared after her, flabbergasted.

Miss Lucas offered a flat smile. "Please excuse Elizabeth, Mr. Darcy. She's not one to prevaricate."

Richard appeared beside Darcy, a malicious gleam in his eye. "Turned you down. I told you."

Darcy frowned, still following Miss Elizabeth's progress across the room. She seemed determined to put as much distance between them as the space allowed. "I wonder if she will keep her word and not dance anymore tonight." Darcy wanted her to dance. He wanted to find a flaw in her.

"Certainly, she will keep her word," Miss Lucas said stiffly.

"I'll advise her not to," Richard said. "She should enjoy herself, despite certain…" He offered Darcy a disapproving frown. "…circumstances. Miss Lucas, Darcy, if you'll excuse me." With a bow, Richard headed after Miss Elizabeth.

Darcy resignedly turned to Miss Lucas. "Miss Lucas, as we both seem to have been abandoned, would you offer me the pleasure of a dance?"

Miss Lucas hesitated for long enough to stir mortification. Finally, she nodded. Darcy offered his hand. He led her toward the dancing.

As they danced, Miss Lucas did not press him for conversation, though she made enough of an attempt that he could have conversed had he wished to. On top of that, she danced well. Partnering her wasn't as taxing a payment of the debt as he'd anticipated, but it annoyed Darcy that Richard was right, and he was wrong. Worse, while Darcy and Miss Lucas danced, he spotted Miss Elizabeth in cheerful conversation with Richard, those lovely eyes sparkling with humor and intelligence. She spoke and Richard laughed, casting a glance Darcy's way. He ground his teeth, certain they spoke of him. Yet, Richard wouldn't have brought him up. Miss Elizabeth must have.

After his set with Miss Lucas, Darcy retreated to a dark corner of the room, obscured by a collection of potted plants. Secure he was unobserved, indeed could hardly be seen, he permitted himself to glower at the dancers. The night progressed even worse than he'd feared, now that it included his sister and cousin both angry with him, and a nobody country miss too haughty to accept a dance. Well, if he must, he would remain off to the side until his party chose to leave. He'd enough mortification for one night. He checked his pocket watch then leaned against the wall to watch several sets before checking, then stowing, his timepiece again.

"I suspect Mr. Darcy only danced with me because of a bet," a low voice said, nearby.

Darcy blinked. Though they'd spoken little, and the words were quiet, the speaker must be Miss Lucas. After all, he'd only danced with four women and would recognize the voice of any of the other three immediately. He peeked around the largest plant to see two forms on that dark edge of the room, rendered somewhat indistinct by the light behind them.

Then the meaning of Miss Lucas' words registered. She had guessed. Darcy felt an unfamiliar emotion…shame.

"Why do you think that?" Miss Elizabeth's voice asked.

The revelation that she was the second form amplified his mortification.

"For several reasons," Miss Lucas replied. "Mr. Darcy didn't say more than a few words while we danced. I spoke to him twice and he hardly responded. When the set ended, he did his duty and escorted me to a chair. A single chair with none vacant nearby."

"Absolving him of any additional attempts at conversation," Miss Elizabeth observed.

"Yes. Then Mr. Fitzwilliam danced with me a second time. The first time we danced, we spoke of the usual trivial things one talks of with strangers. The second time, we had a real conversation. He tried to get to know me, which is suspicious."

"Not so," Miss Elizabeth protested. "You undersell yourself, Charlotte. You are a wonderful dancer and a pleasure to speak with."

Miss Elizabeth may not prevaricate, according to Miss Lucas, but Darcy measured her a staunch friend.

"I may be an adept dancer and able to carry on conversation, Lizzy, but I am no man's first choice for a partner. Mr. Fitzwilliam was being deliberately kind. I suspect he felt a touch guilty."

Darcy added intelligence to his list of Miss Lucas' qualities, and an even temperament. Many women would sound angry, but she did not. If anything, wry humor touched her voice.

"Still, you couldn't have minded dancing with Mr. Fitzwilliam twice," Miss Elizabeth said. "He is a very pleasant conversationalist. I was sorry I had to refuse to dance with him a second time."

Miss Lucas let out a small sigh. "Yes, he does both dance and speak well. I'm sorry I can't count his second dance as hinting at any attraction. What did you two talk about while I had to bear Mr. Darcy company?"

Bear him company? Darcy bristled. His company was sought. Especially by unwed ladies.

"We talked of new books and of music." Miss Elizabeth's voice had a warm tone that further evoked Darcy's ire. Everyone always found Richard amiable. "And of traveling and staying home. It was very entertaining."

"That sounds lovely," Miss Lucas said, a hint of sorrow in her tone. "He's a kind gentleman."

"You can't know for certain his dancing with you a second time had to do with a wager," Miss Elizabeth said.

"I'm sure it did," Miss Lucas said. "Furthermore, Mr. Darcy dancing with me wasn't a reward. It was a punishment. Whatever the bet was, he lost."

"How can you say that?" Miss Elizabeth protested. "We already established that you dance very well."

Darcy repressed the urge to add his assurance to that praise. Miss Lucas did dance well. His guilt over employing her as part of a wager might be salvaged by saying as much.

But he could not permit them to know he listened. More guilt layered atop the first, for he was doing exactly that for which he'd condemned both Miss Elizabeth and Georgiana. Eavesdropping. But what else could he do? To move would reveal him.

"I've never been pretty," Miss Lucas said, voice quiet. "And as the years pass, I am only less so. I'm twenty-seven and look it."

"You have so many other qualities," Miss Elizabeth said firmly.

Darcy noted that she did not, indeed, lie. She offered no outright attempt to deny Miss Lucas' assessment of herself yet provided what support and solace she could.

"You are kind, Lizzy," Miss Lucas said. "And perhaps I do have laudable qualities, but they are not readily visible on a dance floor."

"They could be, if you dance often enough with the same gentleman for him to come to know you," Miss Elizabeth said. "Which will never happen if we linger in this corner gossiping. Come. I may not be able to dance again this evening, but you certainly shall."

Darcy peeked out to see the slenderer of the two forms take the other by the arm. They headed back toward the better lit, more crowded area of the hall. Once he felt sure they were away, he stepped out from behind the planting, before he could be trapped into eavesdropping again. A glance back showed how flimsy his hiding place had been. He could only thank heaven that neither of them had looked his way.

Chapter Seven

A few weeks later found Darcy on the way back from dining with the officers. As he enjoyed Colonel Forster's company, the evening had been convivial. Mr. Hurst was already snoring, slumped against the corner of the carriage next to Darcy. Experience taught them all that he would sleep soundly until they arrived at Netherfield Park, but then be ready for cards. Richard, who shared the seat across the carriage with Bingley, also appeared to have had a pleasant time. Darcy supposed his cousin somewhat missed his regimental days, though not enough to return to them now that he was a landowner.

Bingley, in contrast, was rather distracted that evening. Not his usual talkative self. Even now, he drummed his fingers on his leg, peering out the carriage window at their progress.

"Do you suppose Miss Bennet is still at Netherfield?" he asked.

"Doubtful," Darcy replied. "It is late."

"Because you suddenly became loquacious," Bingley muttered, gaze still out the window.

Richard cast an amused look between them. Darcy wondered if his cousin guessed why they'd remained with the officers for so long. Darcy had no desire for his friend to meet Miss Jane Bennet any more often than required, and Bingley's sisters had invited the lady to dine with them that evening.

Darcy had no qualms with Miss Bennet as an individual. In truth, it pleased him for her to dine at Netherfield. He hoped she would be a positive influence on Georgiana, who rarely spoke to Bingley's sisters.

No, his qualms, such as they were, stemmed from Bingley's infatuation with the woman. Darcy hadn't spent years molding and guiding his friend for Bingley to become entangled with a country miss who had an abhorrent family, no connections and no dowry. Worse, Miss Bennet wasn't the sort with which Bingley usually became enamored, the more worldly and jaded young ladies of London. Miss Bennet would assume his interest to have true meaning. When Bingley's ardor cooled, as it always did, she would be left shamed and distraught. Therefore, Darcy had kept them out late enough that Miss Bennet was sure to be gone by the time they returned to Netherfield Park.

"I don't see what you found so interesting about Colonel Forster and his men," Bingley said, attention trained out at the passing night and the bobbing rings of lanternlight surrounding the carriage. "Mr. Fitzwilliam has common ground with them, to be certain, but you've always been a landowner, Darcy. When I brought up the possibility of buying an estate, there was hardly any discussion about it."

Bingley's complaint wasn't reasonable. In London, they often addressed several of the evening's topics, with Bingley a willing participant. Silence, uncomfortable after Bingley's sullen tone of accusation, filled the carriage, only punctuated by Hurst's snores.

Richard shifted in his seat. "On the subject of landowning, and knowing I can count on your discretion, Bingley."

More silence followed.

"Bingley?" Richard prompted.

"What?" Bingley swiveled toward Richard, expression questioning.

"May I count on your discretion?" Richard prompted.

"Oh, yes, certainly." Bingley turned back to the window.

Richard cast him an amused look before refocusing on Darcy. "Walter is still having trouble with his estate," Richard said. "At first, I thought he was hinting for a loan, but now I think he just wanted someone to talk to. He knows I'm short of funds myself."

Darcy grimaced. "I don't feel it is—"

Richard held up a staying hand. "I'm not asking you to give him a loan. I'm asking, and I'll write his permission first, if I may confide his troubles to you for your advice."

"Certainly," Darcy said, relieved. He didn't begrudge the money, but loaning money to family tended to create resentments. "Write to him first thing in the morning. I have some letters going out. My man will post yours for you."

"Thank you, but one more day won't do any harm. I'll write him tomorrow afternoon."

Darcy frowned. Richard's daily habits weren't his concern, but he couldn't help asking, "Why? You always breakfast early. There will be time in the morning."

"I'm riding in the morning."

"You rode yesterday morning," Darcy countered.

"I prefer to ride every morning, directly following breakfast," Richard said, tone firm. "It's good for my constitution."

"Is this a new occupation?" Darcy didn't recall such a routine during their many stays at Rosings. "Perhaps I will join you."

"I need to keep fit now that I'm no longer in regimentals, and I prefer to head out alone."

Darcy eyed his cousin with suspicion.

"Did you order your driver to set this interminable pace, Darcy?" Bingley groused. Darcy hadn't, sure his delaying tactics at dinner had already bought him enough time.

"In fact, I believe we're about to turn up the drive," Richard said.

Richard's assessment proved correct. The carriage turned a moment later, to rumble up the drive. Bingley alighted as soon as they arrived, hopping out to splash unceremoniously into a puddle. He let out a curse for his shoes, while Darcy shook Hurst awake and followed with more decorum, Richard and Hurst behind him. They entered the well-lit entrance hall to find Miss Bingley before her brother, in midsentence.

"...oaked through when she arrived." Miss Bingley's tone betrayed annoyance. "Can you imagine, riding over in this weather? Hoydens, the lot of them."

"You lent her a dress, I assume?" Bingley asked. He shot an anxious look up the staircase.

Darcy hid a grimace. "Am I to understand Miss Bennet remains?"

Miss Bingley offered him a nod before returning her attention to her brother. "Of course, we lent her a gown. Georgiana did, as they're of a height. We also sat Miss Bennet by the fire. None of it proved any avail. She was ill before dinner finished."

"It was good of you to offer her a room, Caroline," Bingley said. "You did well."

"Certainly, I offered her a room. It would have been cruel to send her home in her condition, riding back through the rain."

"You could have lent her the use of Bingley's carriage," Darcy argued as he began stripping off his gloves. Servants waited to the side, ready to receive their outerwear.

Miss Bingley shook her head, expression sour. "My brother's coachman believed this evening the best time to address some minor wear, with us remaining in and you four employing your conveyance, Mr. Darcy. He had the carriage in a state of disorder."

"Fortuitously," Bingley said hotly. "To send her out into the cold when she's ill would be the height of irresponsibility." He looked up the staircase again, as if he might rush to Miss Bennet's side.

Darcy rather thought riding over in clearly inclement weather was the height of irresponsibility. Had no one in the Bennet household any sense?

"You sent word to her family, I assume," Richard asked, coming to stand beside Darcy.

"I did." Miss Bingley sounded a touch annoyed by the question.

"Her poor mother must be so worried," Bingley said.

"Her poor mother likely put her up to it," Miss Bingley replied with a sniff. "I'd blame Miss Bennet herself, but she hasn't a conniving bone in her body."

Darcy agreed with both parts of that sentiment.

"I'm sure Mrs. Bennet wouldn't deliberately put her daughter at risk," Bingley declared. "More likely, they misjudged the weather."

To Darcy's mind, the silence that met Bingley's declaration was a clear sign no one agreed with him.

"Yes, well, it's only a sniffle," Miss Bingley said. "We can hope she'll be gone tomorrow."

Darcy offered silent agreement as he passed his outerwear to a waiting footman.

"A hand of whist, anyone?" Richard suggested in a light voice.

Miss Bingley's expression morphed into one of amiability. "Only if you will partner me, Mr. Fitzwilliam. That way, I shall count this evening not as a loss, but as one of the most pleasant so far in Hertfordshire."

"I believe I have partnered you in whist five times already, Miss Bingley," Richard said in an amiable tone as he moved forward to offer his arm.

"And each time we have won, sir, marking us as a formidable coupling," Miss Bingley said as they moved off together down the hall.

Darcy watched in bemusement. He didn't mind a cessation of Miss Bingley's pursuit of him. He only hoped Richard knew what he was about. The woman could be tenacious. Or did Richard seek the match? Richard had denied as much to Bingley, but that was some weeks ago. Miss Bingley had social grace and a large dowry. Darcy glanced to Bingley to gauge his reaction to the flirtation, only to find him still gazing up the staircase.

"Bingley, Darcy, one of you must join me in whist," Mr. Hurst said. "If I play with my wife as a partner again, I will lose all patience with her. It is up to one of you to ensure harmony in our marriage."

"Come, Bingley, you are her brother," Darcy said, worried his friend might actually seek Miss Bennet. "It is your duty to promote marital accord."

"Hm? What?" Bingley asked, turning toward Darcy.

"Whist. Come." Darcy gestured Bingley to precede him, with little hope his friend would be able to concentrate well enough on the game to have a chance against Miss Bingley and Richard.

Bingley nodded and headed down the hall, casting one final look toward the staircase. Darcy followed, intending to read the newspaper he had missed earlier. He offered a second wish for Miss Bennet, and her hold over Bingley, to depart come morning.

As he followed, Darcy reviewed his discussion with Richard in the carriage. Odd, that Richard should make such a point of swearing Bingley to secrecy. First, because Richard grew up on such an estate and he'd had neighbors. He knew most losses to an estate were not secret. Walter's problems were probably well known by people who lived near him, and thus, by anyone with whom they cared to gossip. Second, swearing Bingley to secrecy called attention to the conversation and made it more significant. After a good meal with a bit of wine, Bingley might easily pay little attention and even less heed.

Darcy's gaze narrowed. His cousin might decry Darcy for managing other peoples' lives, but Richard was at least as bad, though more subtle. With Bingley considering the purchase of an estate, Darcy suspected Richard wished Bingley to understand that buying such an estate, complete with tenant farms, was a great and unpredictable responsibility. It was the only explanation for Richard's behavior. A private conversation with Darcy at some other time would hardly be difficult to come by, in a location without Bingley or Mr. Hurst, who could have woken at any moment.

A new, more horrifying notion hit Darcy. Bingley's considering buying an estate might mean he was planning to put down roots, and roots might be a prelude to him getting married. To Miss Bennet.

Darcy entered the parlor with a scowl on his face to find Richard, Bingley, Hurst and Miss Bingley assembling for cards. Mrs. Hurst read in a chair near the fire, Georgiana similarly occupied across from her.

She looked up, took in Darcy's scowl, rolled her eyes and returned to her book.

Darcy spent an interminable evening reading the paper, waiting for an acceptable time to retire. This he followed with a restless sleep, visions of Mrs. Bennet marauding about Bingley's home with her relatives filling his mind. Darcy would never be able to visit again. When morning finally came, he descended to break his fast with the hope of seeing Miss Bennet up, well, and back in her own gown. In short, ready to depart.

He entered the breakfast parlor to find it empty of all but Richard, who greeted him with a nod. Darcy nodded back and selected a seat. A footman hurried over to offer coffee.

"Any news on Miss Bennet?" Darcy asked.

"Only rumor, but that says she is, sadly, not improved."

Darcy wondered if that were true or Miss Bennet simply wished to remain at Netherfield in hopes of capturing Bingley. Were it in any way appropriate, Darcy would personally assess her condition. Instead, he frowned and said, "We should send for a doctor."

"I believe Bingley already has."

"Bingley is about already?" Darcy asked, surprised. Bingley generally slept well into the morning.

"He rose early out of concern for Miss Bennet," Richard said, tone neutral. "It seems she's a good influence on him."

Darcy cast his cousin a sharp look. Richard obviously suspected Darcy didn't wish Bingley's prospects squandered on Miss Bennet. Did Richard disapprove?

"Why, what a pleasant way to break my fast," Miss Bingley said, entering the room. "Mr. Fitzwilliam and Mr. Darcy, all to myself. Good morning, gentlemen."

Darcy stood, Richard mimicking the movement across the table from him. Miss Bingley took the seat at the head, between them. She nodded to a footman who brought her tea.

"You've seen Miss Bennet this morning?" Darcy asked, for he could count on Miss Bingley for an honest opinion of the lady's state.

Miss Bingley grimaced. "I have. Charles insisted. Practically dragged me from my bed and shoved me into her room, with no care that I might be exposed to a contagion. The poor thing is quite ill, I'm afraid. Charles went dashing off after a doctor. He means to pass by the Bennet residence on his way back, to advise them." A line marred her brow. "What do they call the place? Longthorn?"

"Longbourn, I believe," Richard said, slathering butter on a bun.

Miss Bingley shrugged. "Well, whatever they call it, do you know what I heard? They shan't even keep it. It's entailed away, to some cousin somewhere. That's part of the reason Mrs. Bennet is so desperate to get all those daughters into wealthy hands. She'll need to live with any man foolish enough to wed one."

At least that somewhat explained the woman's willingness to let Miss Bennet ride out in inclement weather. Darcy didn't envy anyone five daughters and no sons. Even someone as silly and crass as Mrs. Bennet didn't deserve such a fate.

"That's a shame," Richard said. "The world would be better served if the Bennet sisters were able to marry for affection, rather than fortune. They're a biddable, attractive lot."

Miss Bingley turned to him with wide eyes. "Perhaps we speak of a different Bennet family, Mr. Fitzwilliam. I count only Miss Bennet as attractive or biddable."

"If that is what you see, then we must indeed be speaking of different Bennet sisters," Richard replied. "I'll grant that the middle sister holds a touch less charm than the other four, but that is as far as I shall bend."

"Less charm?" Miss Bingley's voice sparked with mirth. "Miss Mary is as plain and drab as week old bread. She speaks with no intelligence, plays poorly and squawks like a dying mallard when she sings."

"That seems a touch harsh," Richard murmured.

Darcy recognized Richard's mild tone as disapproval. He'd been on the receiving end of that tone often enough.

"And as for the youngest two," Miss Bingley continued, undaunted, "they're such hoydens as to render any initial impression of beauty moot. Attractiveness is not, after all, simply a matter of skin tone. It's an assemblage of accomplishments, wit and manners."

"Then you must allow Miss Elizabeth to be attractive, at least," Richard said. "I've been told she plays and sings well, though I've yet to have the privilege. She's well read, lovely to converse with, a fine dancer, elegant of manner and keen of wit."

Darcy hadn't heard of Miss Elizabeth's playing and singing or had the opportunity to assess how well read she was. She'd avoided his company since their first meeting at the assembly. It galled him that, although both Miss Elizabeth and Miss Lucas had guessed a wager underway, only he seemed to suffer censure. Richard, they accepted with all amiability.

Miss Bingley shook her head. "I can only assume you were subjected to women of such poor quality on the Continent that your sense of measure is askew, Mr. Fitzwilliam. Pray, do not make any hasty choices until you've reacclimated. You'll soon find your infatuation with Miss Elizabeth very ill-placed."

"Infatuation?" Richard shook his head. "I simply listed the lady's qualities as any man would see them."

"Any infatuated man," Miss Bingley countered. She turned to Darcy, obviously seeking an ally. "Mr. Darcy, you be the judge. Is Miss Elizabeth as lovely as Miss Bennet, or even passable by any true measure?"

Darcy frowned, annoyed to be included in such a frivolous, gossip-laden conversation.

"Yes, Darcy, do give us your opinion of Miss Elizabeth," Richard said, tone one of challenge.

"I cannot speak to the young lady's accomplishments, but her eyes are quite fine," Darcy admitted. "They lend a moderate attraction to her countenance."

"What is this?" Miss Bingley asked in feigned shock. "Moderate attraction? High praise indeed. I stand corrected, Mr. Fitzwilliam. One of Miss Bennet's sisters has a single, moderately attractive feature. Therefore, any man should be happy to wed her and enjoy her lack of consequence and her overbearing dam."

"On the topic of things anyone should be pleased to endure," Richard said, turning slightly to Darcy, "the day dawns fine. It's high time for my morning ride."

"But with the rain, the ground shall be mud," Miss Bingley protested.

"I believe, from time to time, I've endured worse than mud," Richard said, and stood. "Miss Bingley. Darcy." With a nod to each of them, he quit the room.

"Well, even more fortuitous. I am able to dine alone with you, Mr. Darcy," Miss Bingley said, and launched into a one-sided conversation about ideal walking weather.

Darcy responded as little as possible, all the while wondering that Miss Bingley couldn't see how her belittlement of the Bennet sisters put off Richard. Then, she never seemed to notice Darcy's attempts to hint at his lack of interest in her advances. Miss Bingley quite obviously lived in a world highly colored by delusion.

Soon, they were joined by the Hursts, then Georgiana. Bingley didn't return until they'd all finished their morning meals and Richard had come back, notably cheerful, from his ride. Bingley let them know he'd broken his return from seeking the doctor, who was to arrive later by gig, with a stop at Longbourn.

With that information, they settled into one of the larger parlors. Darcy perused a book to avoid further conversation, while his sister sat near a window, embroidering. Bingley, Miss Bingley, Mrs. Hurst and Richard elected cards once more, while Mr. Hurst dozed on a sofa with the paper.

The time for luncheon was still far from upon them when Andrews, Netherfield's butler, appeared. "A Miss Elizabeth Bennet to see you, sir."

Bingley's expression showed surprise, but he nodded. "Show her in, please."

Andrews' retreat was soon followed by his reappearance. Miss Elizabeth arrived in his wake, then glided past him into the room. Along with the other gentlemen, Darcy stood, unable to avoid studying the subject of their morning conversation.

Her eyes were as fine as he recalled, alight with interest. Her skin glowed with health. Though in appearance free of dyes or powders, her lips were a pink bow. Dark curls framed a face that more correctly matched Richard's description than Darcy's, for Miss Elizabeth was, indeed, a rather beguiling creature.

"Miss Elizabeth, welcome," Bingley said, striding forward.

"Mr. Bingley." She dropped a slight curtsy. "I do not mean to be presumptuous, but this morning, when you said I might come tend to Jane, I felt I must take you at your word."

"Yes, of course. Certainly. I hoped you would," Bingley said. "She'll be all the better for your attentions. The doctor will be by this afternoon. I'm afraid he was setting a leg when I called on him."

"Miss Elizabeth," Mrs. Hurst said. "Whatever has befallen your dress?"

"My dress?" Miss Elizabeth looked down.

Darcy followed her gaze to take in a hem dampened several inches and kissed with mud.

"I daresay it's still rather wet without," Miss Elizabeth said. "I came across the fields."

"On foot?" Miss Bingley asked, tone shocked.

"Alone?" Mrs. Hurst added, expression aghast.

"It's not a long walk," Miss Elizabeth assured her. "Miss Lucas and I regularly walk the long way to Oakham Mount and back, which is nearly twice as far."

"Mayhap it's not far for a country miss," Mrs. Hurst said, her tone implying censure.

"I walk a great deal at Pemberley," Georgiana said. Though quiet, her words were clear. Miss Bingley and Mrs. Hurst clamped their mouths closed.

"Do you require anything, Miss Elizabeth?" Richard asked.

A slight snore sounded from Mr. Hurst's sofa, where he dozed with the paper open, draped across his chest.

"No, thank you, Mr. Fitzwilliam," Elizabeth replied, expression warming as she turned to him. "I should like to see Jane, if I may?"

"I'll ring for a maid," Miss Bingley said.

"I'll show Miss Elizabeth the way," Georgiana said, standing.

Darcy turned to his sister, surprised.

"I require my shawl," Georgiana continued.

"A maid can get it," Miss Bingley said with a frown, but Georgiana was already crossing the room.

Darcy watched, bemused, as his sister gestured for Miss Elizabeth to join her. Miss Elizabeth offered a second curtsy, gaze glossing over Darcy as she scanned the room, and led the way back into the hall. Even with a damp, muddy hem, she walked straight backed and with a slight, smooth sway of her hips.

Darcy retook his seat, a touch put out at her lack of any acknowledgement toward him. He didn't know what he expected, as their longest interaction thus far was his insult and subsequent offer to dance, but she acted as if he bore no more consequence than the sofa on which he sat. When she returned, perhaps he would engage her in conversation. In the few weeks they'd spent in Hertfordshire thus far, he'd watched her speak with Richard often enough to know conversing with Miss Elizabeth would offer a certain amount of diversion.

He need only wait a quarter hour. Miss Elizabeth would reappear momentarily, a declaration of Miss Bennet's continued repose on her lips. With a house full of eligible men, Miss Elizabeth couldn't mean to spend much time with her sister. As was always the case with the fairer sex, her real goal must be matrimony.

Time ticked by on the mantle clock. Georgiana, not wearing a shawl, reappeared and took back up her needle and thread. Darcy made to focus on his book but, somehow, his gaze kept drifting to the doorway. Every moment, he expected Miss Elizabeth to reappear. The more he thought on her, the more convinced he became that her frank conversation would be a welcome change from Georgiana's silence and Miss Bingley's and Mrs. Hurst's not-so-subtle guile.

The time for luncheon arrived, still with no sign of their guest. When sent an invitation to join them, Miss Elizabeth refused. Finally, nearly an hour after they'd dined, she reappeared in the parlor doorway. Along with the other gentlemen, Darcy stood, but her focus was on Miss Bingley, who composed a letter at the writing desk.

Miss Elizabeth crossed the parlor to her side. "Miss Bingley, I apologize for interrupting."

"Your sister is ready to return to Longbourn?" Miss Bingley asked, looking up from her page.

"Quite the opposite," Miss Elizabeth replied. "I'm very concerned for her. I shouldn't like to move her. Is there any word on when the doctor will arrive?"

"He should be here," Bingley said with a frown. "I'll discover what's delayed him." He nodded to Miss Elizabeth and hurried from the room.

Miss Bingley glanced about, taking in the eyes on her and Miss Elizabeth. "So, you wish to depart? I'm sure Charles would loan you the use of his carriage to take you home."

Miss Elizabeth shook her head. "Jane is very ill. I should like to remain to tend her. It is for that I've come to you. Would my addition be too much of an imposition?"

Miss Bingley looked about again. She met her sister's eyes. Mrs. Hurst offered a slight shake of her head. Miss Bingley opened her mouth to speak. Oddly, it perturbed Darcy to realize she would decline Miss Elizabeth's request.

"I'm certain Bingley would wish you to remain to tend Miss Bennet," Richard said. "Who better to nurse her back to health than her dear sister?"

"Well, yes," Miss Bingley said flatly. "We can ask him, to be sure."

"Bingley is all amiability," Richard said. "He's certain to agree."

"Agree to what?" Bingley said, striding back into the room. "I've sent several footmen after the doctor. He'll come this time or have a very fine reason for not."

"Miss Elizabeth wishes to remain to tend her sister," Richard said.

"Yes, you must. I insist on it," came Bingley's predictable reply. "I'll send someone to advise your father and request a case be packed for you."

"Thank you, Mr. Bingley." Elizabeth dipped her head to him. "And you, Miss Bingley, for your hospitality." To this, she added a conspiratorial smile, aimed at Richard.

Richard returned the look, much to Darcy's irritation. Why must Richard flirt with every woman he met? He didn't even seem to care if they were comely, which Miss Elizabeth was. He must win over them all. With Bingley always snatching up the prettiest, and Richard the most enjoyable, was it any wonder Darcy held himself aloof?

"If you'll excuse me, I must return to Jane," Miss Elizabeth said. With another beguiling retreat, she disappeared.

Chapter Eight

The remainder of the afternoon found Darcy out of sorts. Not that any would notice, he suspected, for he made a show of reading. Georgiana continued her needlework. Miss Bingley endeavored to keep Richard by her side. Mrs. Hurst complained continuously of losing at cards, for she partnered a very distracted Bingley. Mr. Hurst rose from the sofa at some point and wandered from the room.

The doctor arrived and Bingley ushered him upstairs, where he remained for what Darcy felt to be an overly long time. When he came down, Bingley jumped to his feet.

"How is she?" he asked, hurrying across the room. "How is Miss Bennet?"

The doctor nodded in greeting. "She is very ill, Mr. Bingley. You were right not to move her. I've given Miss Elizabeth a tonic, and instructions. If Miss Bennet doesn't show improvement over the next two days, you must send for me again, sir."

"Certainly, I will."

"When will the poor dear be able to return to the comfort of her family?" Mrs. Hurst asked.

"If she improves from this point, she must still remain for several days," the doctor replied.

"Several days?" Miss Bingley repeated sharply. "How shall we know when we might move her?"

"You may send for me, if you like, or you may trust Miss Elizabeth's judgment."

"Miss Elizabeth's?" Miss Bingley sniffed. "She will wish to remain for so long as possible."

"Doctor Flynn said she will know, Caroline," Bingley admonished.

The doctor nodded. "I know the Bennet's well, having called on Mrs. Bennet on many occasions. Touch of the nerves, you see." He blinked a few times, peering through thick spectacles. "Miss Elizabeth is keen minded and steady. Her judgment on when it is safe to remove Miss Bennet may be trusted."

"Thank you, Doctor," Bingley said, leveling a quelling look at Miss Bingley. He offered a bow, which Doctor Flynn returned.

"It's a shame Miss Bennet is of such a sickly nature," Mrs. Hurst said in an overloud voice. "And even with country living. I daresay it's a blessing the poor thing isn't made to endure London."

"Sickly?" the doctor repeated, pausing in turning away. "Nay, the Bennet girls are a hearty lot. Rarely have I been required for any reasons other than Mrs. Bennet's nerves. Even Miss Kitty, with her cough, is otherwise of fine health. Mr. Bennet is lucky in that. Sir William has a house full of lads. They require frequent setting and stitching. So much so, that Miss Lucas has become quite adept at both. Both Miss Lucas and Miss Elizabeth possess singular intelligence for women."

"Yes, well, thank you, Doctor," Bingley repeated, casting a grimace toward his sisters. "Let me walk you out."

With a gesture, Bingley gestured the doctor from the room, leaving the others to return to their amusements, though those at the table had to await his return for cards. Darcy took back up his pretense of reading.

Finally, the dinner hour arrived. Miss Elizabeth joined them, her gown simple and modest. Miss Bingley had set out place cards, saying they must impress their guest. In truth, Darcy suspected she wished to keep Miss Elizabeth as far from any eligible gentleman as possible, while at the same time monopolizing them and putting Georgiana near Bingley. This theory was born of Darcy's and Richard's placements on either side of Miss Bingley, with Miss Elizabeth and Georgiana flanking Bingley at the other end. The Hursts were opposite each other in the center of the table, but since talking across the table was gauche at a formal dinner, that was acceptable enough.

As dinner wore on, Darcy was amused to note that the few sentences his sister uttered were when Miss Elizabeth joined the conversation with Bingley. Georgiana spoke in monosyllables when Mrs. Hurst tried to talk to her. Richard acted like the dinner was informal and spoke to Darcy. They didn't exclude Miss Bingley, but she rarely had a private conversation with either man. Bingley and Georgiana were largely silent when Miss Elizabeth talked to Mr. Hurst. Darcy wondered how she knew to talk to him about betting. He'd no opportunity to find out for, when dinner ended, Miss Elizabeth departed with immediacy. She took with her much of the brightness in the room.

Once the gentlemen rejoined the ladies, Miss Bingley suggested another game of cards. Darcy, along with his cousin, Bingley and the Hursts, agreed. Darcy didn't wish to pretend to read any longer. It annoyed him that his attention had kept wandering from his book to the doorway, every sense alert for Miss Elizabeth's return. The strange hold she had over him was unsettling. Cards would prove a distraction.

Only Georgiana declined to join the game, moving instead to the pianoforte. Soon, music filled the room. Though his sister was quite skilled, Darcy couldn't help but wonder if he should have the opportunity to hear Miss Elizabeth play.

Cards served Darcy little better than the book had. He struggled to keep track of whose play they waited on, or what cards had been put down. His attention wandered repeatedly to the parlor doorway. He wished often for the interminable evening to end, yet couldn't bear to retire, sure Miss Elizabeth would come down the moment he did.

When, late in the evening, she finally appeared in the doorway, Darcy felt a lightness in his chest. It was as if a weight had pressed down, but now lifted, enabling him to better breath. The other gentlemen stood. Darcy belatedly followed suit.

"Miss Elizabeth, how is Miss Bennet?" Bingley asked.

"She finally sleeps peacefully," Miss Elizabeth said.

Darcy noticed a slight weariness in her. Did it come from worry for her sister, or the strain of tending her these many hours? He hoped the latter. For so much as he didn't condone Bingley's interest in the lady, Darcy wished Miss Bennet no ill.

"Would you care to join us at cards, Miss Bennet?" Richard asked.

Darcy wished he'd thought to voice the question.

"No, thank you, Mr. Fitzwilliam. I believe I should like to read."

"Our loss," Richard replied with a smile.

Miss Elizabeth returned the expression then, as they all retook their seats, headed toward the sofa on which Darcy had spent much of the day. Several books rested on the table nearby, for that particular sofa provided the best light for reading, day or night. Out of the corner of his eye, Darcy watched Miss Elizabeth peruse the table's offerings. She took up the very book he'd been attempting to read. She sat and, soon, regularly turned pages.

"I say, Darcy," Bingley's voice broke into his musings. "It's your turn to deal."

Darcy accepted the cards Bingley proffered and set to attending the game. On the other side of the room, the song Georgiana played came to an end. Instead of beginning another, his sister rose and went to sit beside Miss Elizabeth, who set aside the book and turned to Georgiana attentively.

The two began to speak in low voices. Play about the table recommenced. Darcy set down a card, ears straining to hear what his sister and Miss Elizabeth said. His inattention to the game caused him to lose when he should have won. He then realized his eavesdropping was not only insulting to his fellow card players but wrong. Grimly, he forced himself to play well. He had resisted the arguments Richard and Georgiana gave at the assembly because the people there didn't matter. The people at the card table did matter.

No. The people in the room mattered. When had Elizabeth changed from someone who didn't matter to someone who did?

Elizabeth stood. "I'm rather tired. I believe I shall retire. I bid you all a good evening."

Darcy rose, sorry to see her go, but relieved as well. Maintaining attention to the card game had been difficult. Elizabeth offered a nod to the room at large. Darcy's gaze followed her departure.

Before anyone could retake their seats, Georgiana stood as well. She turned to him. "I am tired, too," she said, and left the room.

Miss Bingley sniffed. "Miss Darcy is young and spent much of the day on her needlework, always tiring, but I've no idea what excuse Miss Elizabeth can give for being such a poor guest."

"I daresay one of breeding," Mrs. Hurst offered.

"Or being spent after spending the day tending her ill sister," Richard said in a mild voice. "It's your play, Mrs. Hurst."

As they all returned to the game, Darcy couldn't help but wonder if his sister and Elizabeth intended to continue their conversation in the privacy of one of their rooms but could think of nothing to do to prevent them. He only hoped his impression and the doctor's recommendation were correct, that Elizabeth was of a responsible nature. In truth, it pleased Darcy to see Georgiana converse with someone. He simply wished he could oversee their conversations. Since eavesdropping was wrong, in the future he would have to monitor their exchanges by joining them.

He attempted his planned insinuation multiple times over the following days, but it turned out to be difficult. Georgiana stopped talking whenever he joined them. Then, one or the other would cry off, followed by the next. Darcy suspected they rendezvoused and carried on without him.

He would have thought that notion paranoid, but he had ample opportunity to test their behavior. With Miss Bennet ill and in their care, Bingley seemed to feel they must remain in during the evenings. Staying at Netherfield Park troubled Darcy not at all. Little company existed in Hertfordshire to tempt him. Being uncertain what his sister and Elizabeth found to speak on, however, left him routinely cross.

Over those days of voluntary exile from Hertfordshire society, Georgiana spent a surprising amount of time not only with Elizabeth, but with Miss Bennet as well, visiting her multiple times each day. With amusement, Darcy noted that even though Bingley's sisters spoke often about entertaining Miss Bennet, their brief visits to the sick room occurred only when the gentlemen were unavailable. It was rare, if not unheard of, for Darcy and Richard to be about the manor without Miss Bingley's attention.

Elizabeth, on the other hand, came down only for dinner each evening, taking her other meals with Miss Bennet in her room. Elizabeth then always returned to her sister until quite late. Generally, she spoke with Georgiana, though one evening she engaged in a lengthy conversation with Richard, keeping him from his usual place as Miss Bingley's partner at cards, before excusing herself for the night.

"You must be careful, Mr. Fitzwilliam," Miss Bingley said as Richard returned to the card table on that occasion.

"Oh? Have Darcy and Bingley suddenly become more skillful opponents?" Richard quipped, nodding toward them.

"They shall never outplay us, sir," Miss Bingley declared. "I speak, rather, of your conversation with Miss Elizabeth."

"I find it difficult to see any danger in speaking with Miss Elizabeth," Richard said, tone overly light.

"That is because you are new to your fortune, sir," Miss Bingley said as she lay down a card. "A woman like Miss Elizabeth is always seeking to attach a man of circumstance. Be wary she doesn't snare you."

"Snare me? By arguing against my assessment of the East India Company Act?"

They all waited for Bingley to play. Craning his neck, he peered in the direction of the staircase, as if Miss Bennet might spring from her sickbed and grace them with her company.

Miss Bingley nodded. "She is devious, sir. Be on your guard against her moneygrubbing."

"If it's a fortune she wishes, she'd rather address her efforts toward Darcy," Richard observed. "I may have inherited Rosings, but he's still far wealthier than I."

Darcy wished Elizabeth were a fortune hunter. Then, he might have more opportunity to speak with her. She never sought his company. They only conversed if he addressed her. Otherwise, she avoided him, which he attributed to his initial insult several weeks ago at their first assembly. Words he much regretted now, for her conversation delighted far beyond any other available to him, with the possible exception of Richard.

"I'm sure she realizes Mr. Darcy is too far above her to even attempt, which is why she's set her sights on you, and speaks to you with such animation. She wishes to take advantage of your lack of familiarity in dealing with fortune hunters." Miss Bingley aimed a frown at her brother. "Charles, stop woolgathering and take your turn."

"What?" Bingley turned back toward the table. "Oh, right, yes," he said, and placed down a completely useless card.

"Speaks to me with animation?" Amusement colored Richard's tone. "Apparently, she's going after Georgiana as well, then. I happened to be out for an early morning walk and found them strolling arm in arm. I heard my cousin tell Miss Elizabeth about some incident at school. I haven't been able to get much more than monosyllables from Georgiana for several months." He set down a card.

Darcy played an uninspired card, for Bingley had given him nothing with which to work.

Miss Bingley's eyes narrowed. "Perhaps that is her angle for attracting you, then, Mr. Darcy. We all know how you treasure your sister."

"If it's an angle, I daresay it's working," Richard said before Darcy could formulate a reply. "I know I find Miss Elizabeth's success in drawing out Georgiana attractive, and I am merely her doting cousin." As he played a card, Richard turned an exceedingly bland look on Darcy. "How say you, Darcy? Is Miss Elizabeth's ability to engage Georgiana alluring?"

"I find it shameful," Miss Bingley said. She slapped a card down on the table. "It's unkind to manipulate Miss Darcy so, pretending to be her friend and find interest in her."

"Darcy?" Richard pressed.

"It pleases me to know Georgiana is conversing with Miss Elizabeth," Darcy allowed. "She was once talkative." He felt a familiar surge of anger toward Mr. Wickham, since Georgiana's reticence was his fault.

Miss Bingley offered a sweet smile. "It's the way of young ladies her age to change. I'll speak to her about her reticence. I'm sure she would be better served confiding in me than in the likes of Miss Elizabeth."

Darcy shrugged. He hoped his sister wouldn't confide in anyone. No one should know her shameful secret.

"Charles," Miss Bingley snapped. "Play a card. Really, if you aren't going to attend the game, you shouldn't play."

As Bingley turned back to the table and fumbled with his hand, Darcy suppressed a sigh. Even if she chose to speak with Richard and not him, Darcy wished Elizabeth would return to brighten his evening.

Chapter Nine

Their hosts gathered in the entrance hall as Elizabeth assisted Jane down Netherfield Park's grand staircase. Still pale and weak, Jane nonetheless wore a smile, her focus on Mr. Bingley. He gazed up at her as if words of devotion might burst from his mouth at any moment. Elizabeth heartily wished they would, certain Jane returned the sentiment.

Mrs. Hurst and Miss Bingley flanked their brother, each a half step ahead of him, as if to bar his way should he move toward Jane. Elizabeth attempted to hide her amusement at their obvious horror over the prospect of their brother wedding her sister. They should have visited Jane more often in her sickroom. Anyone who knew Jane would be delighted to have her for a sister, no matter what size her dowry.

Mr. Hurst wasn't in evidence and Elizabeth suspected he enjoyed his post breakfast nap. Mr. Fitzwilliam stood below, however, looking up from beside Miss Bingley. As always, he wore a convivial expression. Elizabeth quite enjoyed his company and felt a deep gratitude toward him. Without Mr. Fitzwilliam and Miss Darcy, her time at Netherfield should have been truly excruciating.

Beside Mr. Fitzwilliam stood, to Elizabeth's surprise, Mr. Darcy. As usual, a severe expression marred his handsome countenance. As far as Elizabeth could ascertain, Mr. Darcy lived in a rather dismal world, where something always existed with which to be displeased. This seemed especially true when she was about, for she often found him watching her with a frown. She could not be in the same room with him without his eyes upon her, a dour twist to his mouth.

As Elizabeth and Jane reached the bottom step, Miss Darcy rushed forward, almost unnoticed in her brother's shadow. She extended her hands to them. "Miss Bennet, Miss Elizabeth, you shall be missed," she said, voice low.

Jane offered a smile. "We will miss you, too, Miss Darcy."

"We shall not be so very far away," Elizabeth said. "We would be happy for you to call."

"It brings joy to my heart to see you improved, Miss Bennet," Mr. Bingley said, stepping past his sisters. "I only wish your stay with us could have been under easier circumstances."

"Thank you for permitting me to remain, Mr. Bingley," Jane murmured.

"And for the use of your carriage," Elizabeth added.

"It is not my carriage," Mr. Bingley said. "Mr. Darcy has provided his."

Elizabeth turned to him, eyebrows raised in question. "Has he?"

"We deemed it the most comfortable," Mr. Fitzwilliam said into the following pause.

Elizabeth had noticed the care of Mr. Darcy's cousin and Mr. Bingley. They often paused to give Mr. Darcy the opportunity to speak. He rarely availed himself. Still, she schooled the amusement with which she met Mr. Fitzwilliam's eyes and turned to Mr. Darcy. "Then we thank you, sir, for the kind use of your carriage. We shall send it back with all haste."

"There is no need for haste," he said in a rare act of addressing her directly.

"Oh, but there is. Surely our sisters will attempt to appropriate it." She knew it was mean to tease so rigid a man but could hardly help herself. A wince on his part rewarded her words, then Jane's elbow dug into Elizabeth's side.

"Thank you, sir," Jane said.

Mr. Darcy offered a bow.

"Miss Bennet, allow me to assist you to the carriage," Mr. Bingley said, presenting Jane his arm.

She accepted and he led her out, freeing Elizabeth to turn back to face Mr. Bingley's sisters. "Thank you for your hospitality."

"Yes," Miss Bingley said in that nasally, supercilious way she had.

"Please know you are always welcome at Longbourn," Elizabeth added, to emphasize Miss Bingley's lack of warmth.

Miss Bingley grimaced. Mrs. Hurst coughed. Miss Darcy offered a smile, which Mr. Darcy observed with a frown. Elizabeth worked to check her mirth. Such a stodgy lot. It was no wonder Miss Darcy sought out Elizabeth and Jane.

"I am sure we shall all meet again soon," Mr. Fitzwilliam temporized.

Elizabeth offered him another amused look, dipped her head, and turned to follow Jane and Mr. Bingley.

Mr. Darcy's carriage did prove amazingly comfortable and offered a ride so smooth, Elizabeth couldn't imagine Jane suffered in any way. Though she hid her worry, Jane's paleness troubled Elizabeth. She'd never known her elder sister to be this ill. She truly was grateful she'd been permitted to remain to tend Jane. Elizabeth wouldn't have entrusted her sister's care to anyone else.

"It's a lovely carriage, but I should have preferred Mr. Bingley's," Jane said softly, turning from the window, where she'd watched until Netherfield, and Mr. Bingley, dwindled from sight.

"Oh?" Elizabeth had yet to wring a confession from Jane but felt very sure her sister was in love.

"I should like to ride once in Mr. Bingley's carriage, for the memory."

Elizabeth frowned. "Surely, you aspire to more with Mr. Bingley than simply a memory of his carriage?"

Jane shook her head. "How can I? He is far above me, Lizzy."

"I do not believe Mr. Bingley cares. He's clearly taken with you. My guess is that only his sisters stand between him offering for you."

"His sisters?" Jane frowned. "They are very kind. I'm sure it's simply a practical consideration. We are not of their circle."

"Only you would find Mrs. Hurst and Miss Bingley kind," Elizabeth observed, but without censure.

"You are too quick to judge people," Jane replied. "Have they said one unkind thing to you?"

Elizabeth smiled. She loved Jane's idealism. "No, they have not." They had implied many.

Jane answered with a smile, which turned into a slight frown. "Unlike Mr. Darcy, who was terribly hurtful at the assembly. I'm sorry my illness forced you to endure him."

Elizabeth shrugged. "There was nothing to endure. He's hardly spoken to me these many days."

"Which is rather rude of him."

"I suppose it is." Elizabeth didn't add that Mrs. Hurst and Miss Bingley also avoided speaking with her whenever possible. Mr. Hurst seemed indifferent, though it was difficult to tell. Mr. Fitzwilliam, Miss

Darcy and, of course, Mr. Bingley had all been convivial. Plus, to balance out her worry for Jane, Elizabeth had been spared the silliness of their mother and younger sisters. Overall, she rated her stay at Netherfield Park pleasant enough.

After a short carriage ride, they arrived home to find Longbourn blessedly quiet. As they hadn't sent ahead, their mother and sisters were out, much to Elizabeth's relief.

"Jane, it is good to have you back," Mr. Bennet said, appearing in the entrance hall.

"Thank you, Papa," Jane replied, smile weak. Even their brief, comfortable ride had tired her.

"And you as well, Lizzy."

"Thank you, Papa." Elizabeth's words were addressed partially to her father's back, as he already turned back toward his library. Elizabeth offered his retreating form an amused look, then proffered her arm to Jane. Taking advantage of the calm, she settled Jane in bed.

Returning downstairs, Elizabeth found their father seated at his desk, though he'd left the library door open. She hesitated on the threshold until he looked up.

"Lizzy, come in."

She entered to take the chair across from him, her worry for Jane allayed by the familiar room. She loved being surrounded by rows upon rows of books as well as the quiet that generally permeated the space. As he intended, her father's library was a sanctuary in their often-chaotic home. Today, more than usual, he appeared as though he required one, looking abnormally tired. Elizabeth imagined her mother and sisters were more difficult for him to endure without her and Jane to mitigate them.

"How is Jane?" Mr. Bennet asked, marking his place in the large volume before him.

"She is improved, but still quite ill," Elizabeth said, some of her ease stealing away. "She's been very unwell, Papa."

He nodded. "Doctor Flynn was by several times to give us updates. He said you did wonderfully. He also said Mr. Bingley paid his fees. Is there something I should know?"

Elizabeth shook her head. "Nothing certain. By my estimation, Mr. Bingley is enamored of Jane, but his sisters do not approve of the connection."

"And Jane?"

"She will not admit as much, but she is taken with him, as well." Elizabeth grimaced. "She feels she is too far beneath him to hold any hope of a proposal."

Mr. Bennet steepled his fingers, expression thoughtful. "It seems your mother's machinations have failed, then, unless her only goal was to make Jane quite ill."

Elizabeth shrugged. "Time will tell. I hold hope both families will be reasonable."

Mr. Bennet cocked an eyebrow. "Do you? That is because you are young."

"Papa," she chided.

Mr. Bennet dropped his hands to his book. "If Jane does not care for him enough to aspire to him, and he does not care for her enough to ignore the protestations of his sisters, it is not meant to be," he declared, and opened his book.

Elizabeth knew that as a dismissal. She stood and crossed to the shelves to select a volume. As she turned to leave, she asked, "When do you expect Mother and my sisters home?"

"We can pray not until evening. They've gone to torment Lady Lucas into holding a party, since I told Mrs. Bennet we cannot have one here until Jane is fully recovered."

Elizabeth nodded. Lady Lucas did not realize it, but if she refused, her torment would only grow. With Jane no longer in his care, Mr. Bingley and his company would be out and about once more. The neighborhood would clamor for a party. Every young woman in ten miles wished for a chance to dance with Mr. Bingley and Mr. Fitzwilliam. Mr. Darcy, though they'd all thought him handsome and fine at first, had been branded too proud and aloof to pursue, undoubtedly his intention.

By the dinner hour, Elizabeth's mother and sisters returned, plunging Longbourn into a more usual level of chaos. This state prevailed through the evening and spilled into breakfast the following morning. Ignoring the conversation around her, Elizabeth watched Jane carefully as they drank their morning tea, but her sister seemed stronger than she had in days. Perhaps coming home truly was what Jane required to fully recover.

"If you could all break from the ever-important discussion of ribbons," Mr. Bennet said loudly from his place at one end of the breakfast table. "I have an announcement."

"An announcement?" Mrs. Bennet repeated, tone already filled with accusation.

"Yes, Mrs. Bennet. News."

"You have news you've kept from us?" Mrs. Bennet cried. "You are too thoughtless, Mr. Bennet."

"Is this like when Mr. Bingley came to town, Papa?" Lydia asked eagerly. "Is there another new gentleman?"

A look of amusement so keen as to put Elizabeth on guard crossed her father's features. "Why yes, Lydia, there is."

"Who is he?" Lydia asked, at the same time as Mrs. Bennet let out a wail, lamenting her husband's heartless behavior and Kitty cried, "Another gentleman, Papa?" while Mary launched into a sermon about propriety.

A vision of the frown Mr. Darcy would unleash on them all popped into Elizabeth's head. She used her napkin to cover a giggle, not wanting to add to the silliness. Only Jane sat calmly, waiting for their father to elaborate. Finally, the din died down.

"Do not keep us in suspense any longer, Mr. Bennet," Mrs. Bennet cried.

"I should have told you long ere now if I'd any hope of being heard," Mr. Bennet observed. He paused, but silence prevailed, although Lydia fidgeted, tearing little pieces from a bun. "Yes, another gentleman is coming to Hertfordshire. To Longbourn itself, in actuality. Your cousin, Mr. Collins."

"Mr. Collins?" Mrs. Bennet gasped.

"The man Longbourn is entailed to?" Elizabeth asked.

"Yes. The man who will turn you out of your home when I die," Mr. Bennet replied.

All around the table, shocked looks met his declaration, the feeling mirrored in Elizabeth. Mr. Bennet was not usually so dramatic. He seemed in the mood to stir trouble.

"Why is he coming here?" Mrs. Bennet asked, recovering first. "I don't want to see him. He is probably coming to see what he'll inherit. I won't have that man in my house."

"I think it is proper for him to come," Mary said. "He is, after all, our cousin. Family is important. We are all richer for our connections."

"He isn't an officer, is he?" Lydia asked, still delighted the militia had come to their community. Her only interest lately was officers.

"Wouldn't that be grand, to have an officer staying here?" Kitty said. She shared Lydia's interest in redcoats, though Elizabeth felt Kitty to be less consumed by it.

"Undoubtedly it would," Mr. Bennet said in a dry tone. "But one will not. Your cousin is a clergyman."

"He is?" Mary said, expression pleased.

Lydia turned to Kitty and pulled a face.

Kitty giggled.

"Why is he coming?" Mrs. Bennet asked, tone querulous.

"Why don't we ask him when he arrives this afternoon," Mr. Bennet replied.

"This afternoon?" Mrs. Bennet cried. "Oh, Mr. Bennet, how could you." She jumped from her chair and hurried from the room. "Jane, Lizzy," she cried, her voice carrying back from the direction of the kitchen.

Elizabeth set down her napkin. "Mary and I will go," she said, standing. "You rest, Jane."

Jane nodded her agreement, a sure sign she still didn't feel well. Elizabeth gestured to Mary. Together, they went off in pursuit of their mother. In their wake, Elizabeth could hear Kitty and Lydia take up a conversation about the superiority of officers to men of the cloth.

Elizabeth and Mary spent the rest of the day diligently assisting their mother. Mary with great enthusiasm, for she was eager to meet their cousin and enamored with the notion of a clergyman in the family. Elizabeth completed her tasks cheerfully as well, happy for occupation and to let Jane rest. Kitty and Lydia, in contrast, did their best to hide from Mrs. Bennet, while primping and preening as if an officer, indeed, came to dine.

Chapter Ten

"To find a wife," Mr. Collins said at dinner when Lydia bluntly asked why he'd come.

Elizabeth eyed their cousin with burgeoning dislike. A large, heavy-looking man, his florid complexion and tendency to ramble did not appear to be helped by his third or fourth glass of wine, which he even now sipped. He had an overbearing sanctimoniousness about him that seemed little borne out by personal merit and much applied to the judgment of others.

"I would like to heal the breach that existed between my father and yours," he continued, still addressing Lydia. "I believe taking one of you to wife should suffice."

About the table, Elizabeth's sisters exchanged horrified looks. Mrs. Bennet regarded Mr. Collins through narrowed, calculating eyes. Only their father seemed indifferent, picking at the food on his plate.

"If you want a wife, why is this the first we've seen of you?" Lydia pressed, tone unconvinced. "You are old enough to have married already."

Mr. Collins flushed and gulped the remainder of his wine. Elizabeth felt a stab of guilt for not curtailing her sister. They all bore blame for Lydia's brashness. They let her get away with such impunity because she asked what they wanted to know.

"I could not afford to come earlier," Mr. Collins said stiffly. "I was unable to persuade anyone to give me a living. I used most of my remaining capital to buy one. The tithes bring in only three hundred pounds. I thought I could increase my income by farming the glebe, but I cannot farm, manage a parish and run a household. Therefore, I require a wife."

"You want a housekeeper, not a wife," Lydia accused.

"Every wife must be a housekeeper," Mr. Collins said in haughty tones. "In the highest households, it is her duty to see that the person with the title of housekeeper does a proper job. In the lowest household, it is the woman's job to see to it that her family lives comfortably. It is a noble role."

Lydia made a sound of disgust.

"And you have, sight unseen, settled on one of my daughters for this noble role?" Mr. Bennet said softly.

Mr. Collins nodded. He poured another glass of wine. Three hundred pounds a year wasn't much. Perhaps Mr. Collins drank so much because he couldn't afford wine, or perhaps to make him brave enough to speak of taking a wife. Her father, Elizabeth noted, hadn't even finished his one glass.

"I wanted to compensate my fair cousins for what, in the normal course of events, will be the loss of their home," Mr. Collins said, expression filling with condescension. "I do this out of the kindness of my heart and a sense of what is right."

"What is right?" Mrs. Bennet gasped. "Right would be not to evict us, sir."

Mr. Collins turned to her with that same patronizing expression. "When Mr. Bennet is gone, madam, I do not see myself as being required to support a widow or orphaned children. That would go against the purpose of the entail. Still, taking care of one of your daughters would diminish the burden on you and the others, and would ease my conscience over requiring you to leave."

Elizabeth's mother sputtered, fortuitously unable to find words, unusual for her.

"That is very noble of you," Jane said.

Elizabeth raised an eyebrow. Only Jane could say that without sarcasm. Mr. Collins' desire to fulfill his sense of right obviously stemmed from complete selfishness.

"My kindness toward you all is not entirely nobility," Mr. Collins said, a wide smile cutting across his face. He looked about the table. "Seeing the fair countenances of my charming cousins, I am eager to see which of you will make me the happiest of men."

"You think we're all beautiful?" Mary said, voice a bit breathless.

Elizabeth cast her middle sister a horrified look.

Mr. Collin nodded, but trained his attention on their father. "I think you all fair, as I said, but as none of you are married, it is obvious that your beauty has not the means to attract suitors."

Mary's expression soured.

"How dare you," Mrs. Bennet began. "My daugh—"

"Mrs. Bennet." Mr. Bennet held up a staying hand.

To Elizabeth's surprise, her mother fell silent.

"What are you saying, Mr. Collins?" Mr. Bennet continued.

"That I am willing to overlook your daughters' lack of appeal to other men, and their lack of dowry. I only require you to supply fifty pounds a year and guarantee one fifth of what money is settled on Mrs. Bennet after both of your deaths."

A chill went through Elizabeth. Mr. Collins had now mentioned their father's passing more than once, and added their mother's as well? How could he be so callous as to speak of her parents in such a way? At their table, no less.

"You not only want a housekeeper, you want an income," Mr. Bennet observed.

"I want my due," Mr. Collins stated. "I am here to provide for one of your daughters. I won't be taken advantage of."

"I'm surprised you haven't yet found a wife," Mrs. Bennet said, voice saturated with disdain. "Surely, there are women who would marry you and give you a dowry, considering you are planning to throw us out of our house."

"When Mr. Bennet dies, it will be my house," Mr. Collins said.

He reached again for the wine. Mary's eyes narrowed. Her lips pressed thin with disapproval.

"It must have been expensive to come here, all for the sake of one of us," Kitty said, tone oddly devoid of rancor.

Mr. Collins turned a pleased expression on her. "It was, but I did this for you. One of you, at least, I can spare the loss of your home."

"Yet, you took a risk, sir," Elizabeth couldn't resist saying. "You can hardly be assured your money and time are well spent. You are guaranteed no success in finding a wife."

"I thought..." Mr. Collins looked about the table, taking in their expressions. His curdled. He set down the wine.

"I think he couldn't find anyone anywhere else who would marry him," Lydia declared.

Again, no one bothered to reprimand her. Not even their father, who eyed Collins wearily. Mr. Bennet set down his fork, though he'd hardly touched his food.

"There are farmers' daughters aplenty who would be happy to marry me," Mr. Collins declared, anger touching his voice.

"So, go marry them," Lydia suggested with a toss of her curls.

"Lydia," Jane murmured.

"Let not the wise man boast in his wisdom, le—" Mary began, her words aimed at Mr. Collins.

"Ug," Lydia cut in. "Not one of your sermons."

"You read the Bible, Cousin Mary?" Mr. Collins said, tone a bit desperate.

Elizabeth imagined the evening wasn't progressing as he'd planned. His cheeks were red from wine. His gaze a bit dull. Maybe another reason he drank so much was in celebration, but he now found himself with nothing to celebrate.

"Daily," Mary replied primly. "As is my Christian duty."

Mr. Collins regarded her with an expression of hope.

"Why didn't you marry them?" Kitty cut in, voice over loud. "The farmers' daughters?"

Everyone turned to her, varying degrees of surprise on their faces.

"Was it because..." Kitty flushed. "Do they cough?"

Mr. Collins' brow furrowed. "No. I don't believe so. Not that it matters." He shook his head. "No, the trouble is, the ones I've met can't even read. Most of the neighborhood where my living is consists of people who are too poor or too wealthy. I need more from a wife than an illiterate milkmaid, yet none of my wealthier parish members believe I will inherit an income of two thousand pounds. They don't believe I'm really a gentleman. I don't understand why not," he continued, tone querulous. "I'm telling the truth."

"So, you came here, where we are well aware of all you shall inherit," Elizabeth said.

Mr. Collins looked about the table again, expression baffled. "I assumed at least one of you would realize how advantageous a marriage to me would be. Your father will not live forever. In fact, he looks ill to me. He hardly ate anything."

"You are right," Mr. Bennet said, standing. "I do feel ill." He walked from the room.

Elizabeth stared after him in shock, then looked about the room to find her sisters and mother all wore similar expressions. One by one, these morphed into varying degrees of hostility. Soon, a table full of women glared at Mr. Collins.

"I, um, don't feel well myself," Mr. Collins said, rising. "If you'll excuse me?" When no answer proved forthcoming, he offered a jerky bow and hurried from the room.

***

In a state of mild trepidation, Elizabeth trailed Jane down to breakfast the following morning. Their first evening with their cousin had not gone well. After his abrupt departure from dinner, they had seen no more of Mr. Collins, or Mr. Bennet.

Elizabeth entered to find she and Jane were first to arrive, which did nothing to quell her nerves. Their father usually rose before any of them. Trying to ignore her worry for him, Elizabeth put on a good face, for Jane still appeared paler than normal. Elizabeth didn't wish to fret her.

They were joined shortly by Mary, then Kitty and Lydia. By that time, Elizabeth had eaten her fill, but Jane hadn't consumed much. Elizabeth remained, trying to encourage Jane to eat.

Heavy steps sounded in the hall. They all stilled to watch Mr. Collins enter. He paused in the doorway and gaped at them. He raised a hand to rub his forehead and Elizabeth took in his pallor.

"Join us, Mr. Collins?" Kitty said.

He nodded and tromped into the room.

"Not feeling yourself this morning, Mr. Collins?" Mary asked, tone over-sweet.

"I... I am not accustomed to wine with dinner," he mumbled. He made his way to the sideboard.

"Don't most real gentlemen have wine with dinner?" Lydia asked.

Mr. Collins made no reply as he selected his fare. Elizabeth cast her youngest sister an amused look, but Jane and Kitty frowned. Mary appeared smug.

Mr. Collins came to the table and sat. "I thought, after breakfast, I might read Fordyce's sermons to you all."

"Ug," Lydia replied.

"Oh?" Mary asked. "Why not something from Ephesians? Perhaps around 5:18."

"No reading," Lydia said. "I'm going into town to see Aunt Phillips."

"You have tasks here," Mary said. "Idle hands, Lydia."

"We must introduce our cousin around," Lydia countered. "He's spent all his funds to come here and find a wife."

"Who is Aunt Phillips?" Mr. Collins asked. He took a long sip of coffee.

"She is our mother's sister," Kitty said. "That makes her a connection, especially if you marry one of us."

Mary wrinkled her nose, mirroring Elizabeth's feelings on that subject.

"I'm sure you'd like to meet Aunt Phillips," Lydia declared.

"Does she have any daughters?" Mr. Collins asked hopefully.

"No, but she knows all the unmarried women in town, and she entertains frequently," said Jane.

Mr. Collins' expression brightened. He took another swallow of coffee. "I should like to meet your aunt. I have much of Fordyce memorized. I can recite to you along the way."

"Wonderful," Lydia said flatly. She turned to Kitty. "Do we still wish to go?"

Kitty nodded.

"I should like to walk, if you don't plan a rapid pace," Jane said. "I've been indoors a very long while."

"Why is that, Cousin Jane?" Mr. Collins asked.

"Jane has been very ill," Kitty said.

"I am sorry to learn that," Mr. Collins said, but Elizabeth could practically see him adding 'sickly' to his list of her sister's qualities.

"I will remain here and practice," Mary declared. "I've nearly perfected that new sheet music I bought last month."

Lydia opened her mouth, but Elizabeth cast her a glare and spoke first, "And I shall remain to see to some tasks I've neglected."

"Neglected?" Mr. Collins echoed.

"Indeed. For at least a week." Elizabeth didn't elaborate that she'd been at Netherfield tending Jane. She watched Mr. Collins add a lack of industry to his mental list regarding her. "I'll tell my mother where you've gone."

Elizabeth saw the others off, and Mary into the parlor and at the pianoforte, before hurrying above stairs to check on her parents. She knocked on her mother's door first and was bade enter. Elizabeth pushed open the door of her mother's small sitting room to find Mrs. Bennet seated before a lavish spread.

"Jane, Kitty and Lydia have taken Mr. Collins to town to meet Aunt Phillips," Elizabeth said.

"Thank heavens," Mrs. Bennet said. "I cannot endure that man's presence in my home. Look at me, forced to hide in my room while I breakfast."

Elizabeth forwent pointing out that Mrs. Bennet routinely used any excuse to have food brought to her. "Have you seen Father yet this morning?"

"Mr. Bennet?" Mrs. Bennet frowned. "Why would I?"

"He said he felt unwell last evening," Elizabeth reminded her mother.

"Posh. He's simply avoiding that odious Mr. Collins."

Elizabeth nodded. "I'll go make certain." She closed her mother's door and went down the hall to the next, even though her mother's sitting room adjoined her father's bedchamber. If Mr. Bennet wished to see his wife, he would have opened the door. A knock on her father's door brought his valet.

"Mr. Simmons, is my father awake?" Elizabeth asked. "He didn't come to breakfast."

"Your father is not feeling himself, miss," Mr. Simmons said.

"Is that Lizzy?" her father's voice called. "Let her in."

Mr. Simmons backed into the room with a bow.

Elizabeth followed to find her father propped up in bed. He hadn't shaved, his countenance pale. She hurried to his side.

"Papa?" she cried, the word a question. She scooped his hand from atop the coverlet to hold in both her own. "Whatever is the matter?"

"Nothing. I simply do not feel well."

"I'd hoped you'd only tired of Mr. Collins."

Her father offered a slight smile. "That, too."

"I shall send for Doctor Flynn."

"Why?" her father asked. "He can't make Collins any more bearable."

Elizabeth tried to smile at her father's joke, but his sudden illness robbed the expression of amusement. Or was it sudden? She recalled how tired he'd appeared when she and Jane returned the previous morning. She hadn't seen her father in over a week, having been at Netherfield. "How long have you been feeling unwell? Has the doctor been yet?"

Mr. Bennet looked past her with a grimace. "Mr. Simmons insisted we call him several days ago."

Elizabeth swiveled to see her father's valet still waited by the door. "What did Doctor Flynn say, Mr. Simmons?"

"He said I am perfectly well," Mr. Bennet said

Elizabeth didn't turn back to her father, her gaze leveled on his valet.

"Doctor Flynn said your father must rest and not tax himself," Mr. Simmons said.

"Thank you." Elizabeth turned back to her father, hiding a frown. "In that case, I shall not reprimand you, but instead shall offer to read to you," she said with as much cheer as she could muster.

Her father let out a relieved sigh. "That would be kind of you, Lizzy."

"I'll return shortly. May I assume you wish to continue with the book on your desk?"

He settled lower in his pile of pillows. "You may, though I warn you'll find it dry. I'm making a study of history."

"Which part?"

"All of it."

Elizabeth nodded and rose from his side. She maintained her pleasant expression until her father's door closed behind her, then gave in to a frown. Her father was never unwell. Then, neither was Jane. Could it be the same illness? Jane was younger, and strong, and she'd grown quite sick. Elizabeth schooled her features, unsure whom she might encounter as she traversed the halls and fetched her father's book.

She was glad she hadn't joined the others on their walk. Her father needed her, no matter that he wouldn't have asked. Besides which, she reflected with a wry smile, whatever her father was reading was likely to be more interesting than Fordyce's Sermons. Gibbon may have said that history was 'little more than the register of the crimes, follies, and misfortunes of mankind,' but any part of it must be more interesting than listening to Mr. Collins recite Fordyce's version of how women should behave.

Elizabeth read to her father for two hours, detailing various Roman exploits. He complained that she skipped some, and she reread a bit. She then switched to *Aesop's Fables*, which she found by his bed, since, unlike history, these did not have to be read in order, so she could skip to her favorites. Eventually, his eyes drifted closed and his breathing evened out. When he started snoring, she decided he was deeply asleep. She marked their place and closed the book.

As she stepped into the hall, Jane topped the staircase. She hurried forward with a smile, looking better than she had since before falling ill.

Not wishing to disturb their father, Elizabeth gestured Jane to silence and then into their room.

"Would you like to do some mending?" Jane asked. "I thought I might. Mama chided us all for our lack of industry. She was waiting for us in the parlor when we returned."

"Did you have a pleasant walk?" Elizabeth took in the bright sparkle in Jane's eyes. "Did you meet anyone in particular?"

A flush colored Jane's cheeks, but her smile only grew. "We met several people. At Aunt Philips, we met a Mr. Wickham. He's an officer. He recently joined the regiment here."

"Oh?" Elizabeth pressed, sure a new officer couldn't be the source of Jane's smile.

"He's rather handsome, and friendly. You will like him, Lizzy. He'll be at Aunt Phillips tomorrow evening. Oh, Lydia accomplished her goal. Aunt Phillips invited us all to dine there tomorrow evening, along with several officers."

"That's good news," Elizabeth said. She eyed her older sister. "But I'm certain it is not all of your news. Come now, who else did you meet, Jane?"

The pink in Jane's cheeks brightened. "We also happened to meet Mr. Darcy and Mr. Bingley. They were riding in the lane. They were on their way here to ask after me."

"How considerate of them," Elizabeth said. Having drawn the truth from Jane, she saw no reason to tease her sister further. "Was Mr. Fitzwilliam with them?" Elizabeth felt mild curiosity as to whether the gentleman had asked after her. He'd been a pleasant companion at Netherfield.

Jane shook her head. "He was calling on the Lucases."

"Indeed? I wonder why."

Jane shrugged. "Who can say? They did ask after you, though, the gentlemen."

Elizabeth issued a wry smile. "Both of them?"

"Well, Mr. Bingley did," Jane amended. "Mr. Darcy appeared interested in the reply, however."

Mr. Darcy probably hoped Elizabeth had fallen ill, given the way he'd constantly glowered at her at Netherfield. "That was very kind of Mr. Bingley."

"And of Mr. Darcy," Jane said.

Elizabeth shook her head but didn't press her sister. Jane would never admit ill of anyone, even someone as quarrelsome as Mr. Darcy. "Did you say you intend to do mending?"

Jane nodded.

"Would you mind very much mending in Father's room?" Elizabeth asked, for she'd tasks in the garden she might see to, if someone else would stay with their father. Elizabeth didn't wish to make too fine a point of it, but she'd been indoors the entire day, and much of those previous.

"In Father's room?" Jane echoed, brow creasing.

"He's not feeling well," Elizabeth said. "I've been reading to him, but he's asleep now. I should like someone to be there when he wakes."

"He's unwell?" Jane's tone held worry. "I thought he simply didn't wish to dine with Mr. Collins any longer."

"I thought so, too," Elizabeth said. "Apparently, he's been increasingly unwell while we were away. So far, he's kept his condition from all but Simmons."

"Have you called Doctor Flynn?" Jane asked, expression anxious.

"He's already been. He advocates rest and quiet."

"Certainly, I will go sit with Father," Jane said. "It's the least I can do, and you've only recently spent more than a week nursing me."

"I would never begrudge either of you even a moment of my care."

"I know." Jane smiled. She went around the bed to retrieve her mending. "Should we tell Mama?"

Elizabeth shook her head. "We'll let Father decide when to do that. Who knows? He may be much improved tomorrow and we shan't need to."

"Yes, of course." Jane smiled. "I'm sure he'll be well tomorrow."

Chapter Eleven

The following morning, Elizabeth headed out for a walk while Jane read to their father. She went first toward the Lucases, thinking she might invite Charlotte along and regale her with tales of Mr. Collins. When she neared, however, she spotted Mr. Fitzwilliam's horse tied out front. Much as Elizabeth had enjoyed his company at Netherfield, she veered away. She didn't wish to interrupt whatever business Mr. Fitzwilliam had with Sir William Lucas. Nor did she wish to be caught indoors socializing, or to endure possible questions about the wellness of her family.

Instead, she indulged in a long, brisk walk with only her thoughts as companions. This proved an error, as those thoughts kept returning to Mr. Darcy and how aggravating he was. Why she must constantly think on the man she couldn't fathom. They'd only his insult at the assembly and a few brief words at Netherfield between them. Yet, whenever she found no ready means of distraction, his image rose in her consciousness.

She disapproved but felt it quite possible her preoccupation sprang from stung pride. No gentleman had ever insulted her so directly before, or so harshly. What a contrast Mr. Darcy was to his sister, who'd been a lovely companion, a bright spot in Elizabeth's time at Netherfield. Miss Darcy seemed to genuinely care about Jane, and to enjoy her and Elizabeth's company. Elizabeth would be eternally glad that Miss Darcy and Mr. Fitzwilliam had been there.

Mr. Bennet was asleep when Elizabeth returned from her walk and remained so for most of the day, but woke shortly before they were due at the Phillips for dinner. Elizabeth readily volunteered to stay home with him. Jane had spent the morning reading to their father, and she'd even less opportunity to enjoy society recently than Elizabeth had. Mary offered to remain as well, but Elizabeth knew how hard her younger sister had been working on her new sheet music and how much she longed to entertain with it and refused her.

Predictably, neither Kitty nor Lydia offered to stay. Not that Elizabeth would have accepted. She wouldn't torment her father thusly. What she did do, was read to him until he fell asleep. She then watched him for a time, trying to believe he breathed easier than the day before. When the hour grew late and the others still hadn't returned from the Phillips, Elizabeth tiptoed from her father's room and sought her bed.

Unsurprisingly, given how late it seemed when Jane joined her in their room, Elizabeth arrived downstairs for breakfast before any of the others. Her sisters and cousin trickled in, all conversing amiably about their dinner at the Phillips. Elizabeth marveled at the difference of a day. The morning before, her sisters could hardly stomach Mr. Collins. Now, they conversed as friends. Occupied with her thoughts and not blessed with her sisters' more favorable attitude toward the man, Elizabeth didn't attend to their conversation. As she poured her second cup of tea, Mrs. Bennet came in. She leveled a frown at Mr. Collins but said nothing as she took her seat.

"…was raised alongside Mr. Darcy like they were brothers," Lydia said, Mr. Darcy's name catching Elizabeth's attention.

"Who is like Mr. Darcy's brother?" Elizabeth asked.

"Mr. Wickham," Kitty said.

"The officer I mentioned." Jane dabbed her mouth with her napkin. "The new one we met at dinner last night."

Mary frowned. "He was too handsome."

"Nonsense," Mrs. Bennet said. "An officer can't be too handsome. Jane, pass me the preserves."

"What does the too-handsome Mr. Wickham have to do with Mr. Darcy?" Elizabeth asked as Jane proffered the preserves to their mother.

"Mr. Wickham was the son of old Mr. Darcy's steward and they were raised together," Lydia said.

Mrs. Bennet smeared a spoonful of preserves on a roll as she said, "Mr. Wickham said that Mr. Darcy was supposed to give him a living, but when the incumbent died, that horrible Mr. Darcy gave it to someone else."

"And do we believe this Mr. Wickham?" Elizabeth asked. For all Mr. Darcy seemed overly dour, he didn't strike her as dishonest.

"He's an officer," Lydia said. "And he's too handsome to lie."

Elizabeth exchanged an amused glance with Jane. "I don't believe it works that way," Elizabeth murmured. Aesop said that people are known by the company they keep. Mr. Darcy kept company with Mr.

Fitzwilliam and Mr. Bingley. More importantly, they kept company with him.

"I find his story unlikely," Mr. Collins said. "If Mr. Darcy did deny Mr. Wickham what was owed to him, he should be able to seek legal recourse."

"We asked about that," Kitty said. "Mr. Wickham said there was a minor technicality in the wording of old Mr. Darcy's will that made it so he couldn't seek legal recourse."

Lydia popped a piece of bread into her mouth, then spoke around it. "Besides, Mr. Wickham said he respected Mr. Darcy's father so much that he didn't want to bring shame on the man's son."

"Don't talk with your mouth full, dear," Mrs. Bennet said.

Lydia swallowed. "I think Mr. Darcy deserves shame."

"Oh, Mr. Wickham also said that Miss Darcy is terribly stuck up, like her brother," Kitty added.

Elizabeth frowned at that.

Jane shook her head. "I didn't find Miss Darcy stuck up."

"You don't find Mr. Bingley's sisters stuck up, either," Lydia said, as if that proved Jane's judgment was unreliable.

Mary eyed Jane speculatively. "I didn't have the chance to speak with Miss Darcy at the assembly, but she danced with everyone who asked, regardless of station."

"I hear Sir Williams' eldest is quite taken with her," Mrs. Bennet said.

"Well, Mr. Wickham said she's awful," Lydia said. She turned toward where Elizabeth and Jane sat side by side. "I bet you had a dreadful time at Netherfield Park. Between Miss Darcy, Miss Bingley, and Mrs. Hurst, you had to deal with three women whose noses are so high in the air, you would think something important was written on the ceiling."

Kitty giggled.

"It's not wrong for people of standing to act as befits their station," Mr. Collins said.

Kitty's mirth vanished as she flushed.

"I'm sure Miss Darcy is horrible," Lydia declared.

"When she was not with her brother, she seeme—" A knock on the door interrupted Elizabeth's defense of Miss Darcy.

"Who is calling at this hour?" Mrs. Bennet asked. "It must be Lady Lucas with gossip about the Phillips' party."

With great interest, they all turned toward the door. Miss Darcy was ushered into the breakfast parlor. Elizabeth stared at her, surprised. She wondered which Miss Darcy had come to call; the cheerful one who walked with Elizabeth and spent time with her and Jane, or the sullen one who haunted the parlors of Netherfield. Elizabeth hadn't yet dared ask for the reason behind Miss Darcy's dual personality, worried the answer would only further prejudice her against Mr. Darcy, whose presence they must all endure for the duration of his time in Hertfordshire.

Miss Darcy met their curious gazes with a smile. "Good, you're still eating," she said, moving toward a vacant chair. "May I have a roll? I skipped breakfast to come here. I left a note. I wanted so much to visit you again, but no one has been willing to come with me. So, this morning, I gave up asking and walked over."

"Yes, certainly," Elizabeth said when no one else replied, her question answered. This was the talkative Miss Darcy.

If Miss Darcy noticed the others were too stunned by her appearance to speak, she gave no indication. She yanked out the chair before a footman could come forward to help her and perched on the edge of the seat. "May I have more than a roll? It was a longer walk than I supposed. I'm famished."

"You may have whatever you like," Elizabeth said. "It's pleasant to see you again so soon, Miss Darcy. Have you met my mother and younger sisters?"

A footman set a plate before Miss Darcy. She reached for a roll from the basket on the table. "I saw you all at that assembly, when we first arrived, but I do not believe we were introduced."

Elizabeth nodded. "Miss Darcy, my mother, Mrs. Bennet. My sisters, Mary, Kitty and Lydia, and this is our cousin, Mr. Collins."

"He's a clergyman," Kitty added.

"Mother, Mr. Collins, Mary, Kitty, Lydia, this is Miss Darcy," Elizabeth finished.

"It's very nice to meet you all," Miss Darcy said. "Thank you for letting me intrude on your breakfast. I didn't mean to interrupt."

"You aren't interrupting," Jane said.

"We were talking about the officers stationed in Meryton," Lydia added.

"I've seen them about," Miss Darcy said. "They're so handsome in their uniforms." She rolled her eyes. "My brother tries to keep me from socializing with them, even though my cousin, Mr. Fitzwilliam, was an officer."

"He was?" Lydia asked.

"Oh yes. A colonel."

"Why ever did he give it up?" Mrs. Bennet asked. "He's not yet wed. Women love an officer."

Miss Darcy shrugged. "I'm not sure. Maybe to better run the estate my aunt left to him."

Mrs. Bennet's eyes brightened. "I'd heard something about an estate. Is that true? Mr. Fitzwilliam has an estate?"

Miss Darcy nodded. "It's in some sort of straits, though. I've heard him and my brother speaking of it."

"Oh." Mrs. Bennet grimaced. "Well, he best not be looking here for a dowry to help set things right. My girls are not to be squandered on a man with pockets to let."

Elizabeth turned her laugh into a cough. She or her sisters would be fortunate to attract Mr. Fitzwilliam. A kind, affable, intelligent man with any sort of estate would be a catch for any of them. Most any gentleman would be, for they'd a dearth of prospects in Hertfordshire.

"I don't think it can be all that bad," Miss Darcy said. "My aunt's estate is quite grand. I don't believe my cousin is in the market for a wife, though. But if he were, I should love him to choose one of you. If you're all like Miss Bennet and Miss Elizabeth, I should be overjoyed to have any one of you as a cousin."

"Of course, you would," Mrs. Bennet said, preening.

Elizabeth realized Miss Darcy had no notion how small their dowries were. If Mr. Fitzwilliam were in need of funds, he should look to the likes of Miss Bingley, who'd hung on his every word when Elizabeth was at Netherfield, not to Elizabeth and her sisters, who possessed little in the way of dowries or connections.

Miss Darcy waved a footman over and requested tea and a plate of food from the sideboard, then looked about the table with bright eyes. "It's so much nicer here. Miss Bingley makes it so stuffy at Netherfield."

Elizabeth raised her eyebrows, finding Miss Darcy's statement a touch rude, even if it happened to be true.

"Miss Bingley makes everywhere she goes stuffy," Lydia said.

"I have not yet had the pleasure of meeting the lady," Mr. Collins said, tone one of mild censure.

"If you had, you wouldn't refer to it as a pleasure," Miss Darcy replied on a laugh.

Lydia giggled. Kitty glanced at Mr. Collins' disapproving expression and crushed her napkin to her lips. Her eyes danced.

Bemusement stole through Elizabeth. When she and Jane had interacted with Miss Darcy at Netherfield Park, she'd been ladylike. At Longbourn, she seemed more relaxed, and bubbled with a silliness that approached Kitty and Lydia's. For the first time, it occurred to Elizabeth that Miss Darcy must be about Lydia's age. She'd seemed much more grown up at Netherfield, under the shadow of Mr. Darcy.

"You said I interrupted a conversation about redcoats?" Miss Darcy prompted.

Lydia regarded Miss Darcy, eyes bright with curiosity. "You know one of them. Mr. Wickham. He said he was raised with your brother."

Miss Darcy nodded. "He was. They were like brothers, only the same age. Not twins. They were very different."

"You mean, Mr. Wickham is charming, and your brother is not," Lydia said.

That was too unkind even for Lydia, Elizabeth thought. She opened her mouth to protest Lydia's statement.

Miss Darcy burst out laughing. "Mr. Wickham is very charming, but he lies, he loses at cards, and he doesn't pay his debts. His mother, his father, my father and my brother each, at least once that I know of, paid Mr. Wickham's debts."

"All of them?" Jane asked, sounding surprised.

"If he's that unrepentant, why would they keep paying for him?" Mary asked, frowning.

Miss Darcy shrugged. "I don't think any of them knew he'd gone to any of the others. They each thought it was the only time he needed help."

"Then how do you come to know?" Mrs. Bennet asked.

"I pieced things together after he left." Miss Darcy's smile held smugness. "I knew about my father and my brother paying Mr. Wickham's debts. My brother thought he was sparing our father from discovering his favorite's flaws. I can only assume my father thought Wickham had learned his lesson and saw no reason to involve my brother." She grimaced. "My brother can be rather unforgiving."

"Did your father and brother tell you that?" Kitty asked, eyes wide.

Miss Darcy offered another shrug. "No, but I see and hear a lot more than they give me credit for."

"Eavesdropping is a sin," Mary said primly.

"Not directly so," Mr. Collins said.

"Also take no heed unto all words that are spoken; lest thou hear thy servant curse thee," Mary countered.

"That's right," Miss Darcy said to Mary, then shrugged. "They knew I was there but didn't think I could hear them when I played the pianoforte."

Mr. Collins looked back and forth between then, then opened his mouth to speak.

Lydia screwed up her face. "How do you know Mr. Wickham's parents paid his debts?" she asked, loudly, cutting off Mr. Collins.

"A girl who worked in the Wickham household became my maid," Miss Darcy said. "She knew all about his parents bailing him out."

Kitty looked from a frowning Mr. Collins to Miss Darcy. "So, it's true?"

"But he is so charming," Lydia protested. "And so gentlemanly, and so handsome."

"Oh, he is," Miss Darcy said. "I once spent weeks with him turning his charm on me."

"When was that?" Lydia asked. "And why did he stop?"

Elizabeth tried to catch Miss Darcy's gaze. She willed Miss Darcy not to answer. Elizabeth knew not where the tale headed but felt it couldn't be anywhere appropriate. All about the table, Elizabeth's mother and sisters watched Miss Darcy with wide eyes.

Chapter Twelve

"Not that long ago, and he wouldn't have stopped," Miss Darcy replied. "He was after my dowry, and rather determined."

"Really?" Lydia asked, eyes alight with interest.

"Yes," Miss Darcy said.

Elizabeth redoubled her prayers that their guest might revert into her more silent self.

"How did that happen?" Mrs. Bennet asked at the same time as Kitty blurted, "How did you know?"

Miss Darcy looked about the table, expression thoughtful. "It started when I left school. My brother decided I needed a governess. He hired a woman named Mrs. Younge to chaperone me and oversee the continuation of my education. She took me to all the masters he hired, but she wasn't very strict. I think she wanted me to like her."

"Did you?" Jane asked.

Miss Darcy shook her head. "Not really."

"What has she to do with Mr. Wickham?" Mrs. Bennet asked eagerly.

Elizabeth's leeriness grew. Miss Darcy shouldn't be so open. She knew Elizabeth and Jane. Undoubtedly, she judged the remainder of their family based on her interactions with the two of them. Miss Darcy couldn't know it didn't do to tell their mother and sisters anything. Especially not anything private. As for Mr. Collins, who still frowned, Elizabeth had no idea if he could keep a secret. Not that it would matter. Her mother and youngest two sisters could not.

"I'm getting to Mr. Wickham," Miss Darcy said. "You see, Mrs. Younge told my brother I needed a holiday, because I was studying too hard. Only, I wasn't. I was doing much less than I had in school."

"And you got a holiday?" Lydia asked.

"Yes. In a way." Miss Darcy's expression clouded. "We went to Ramsgate. Suddenly, Mrs. Younge became very strict. I wasn't permitted to see anyone but her and the servants. We would take walks and speak only in French or Italian. I had to describe the ocean or the houses or the people in whichever language we were using that day. Then we met Mr. Wickham, supposedly by chance. Mrs. Younge permitted me to spend as much time with him as I wanted. She didn't chaperone us, even when we went on walks that lasted for hours. I'm certain Mr. Wickham orchestrated the entire thing."

"What was he trying to do?" Mr. Collins asked, frown deepening.

"Marry me, of course."

The frank way she said it took Elizabeth aback, for the situation sounded horrifying. Looking at how young Miss Darcy was, she couldn't have been more than fifteen, if that, when her tale took place. Far from charming, Mr. Wickham sounded like a monster.

"But he couldn't marry you without the permission of your guardian," Mr. Collins said.

"Guardians," Miss Darcy corrected. "Mr. Fitzwilliam is also my guardian, along with my brother. That wouldn't have stopped Wickham, though. He wanted me to elope with him to Scotland."

"Oh dear," Jane breathed.

Lydia listened with avid interest. "Did you want to run away with him?"

"Not one bit." Miss Darcy grimaced.

"But it would be so romantic," Lydia protested.

"I think Mrs. Younge hoped I would believe so," Miss Darcy said. "She kept having me translate French and Italian works. Ones that idealized true love. I believe she thought she was being subtle."

"Did you fall in love with Mr. Wickham?" Kitty asked Miss Darcy. "It wouldn't be so bad to marry him if you loved him."

"Until the money ran out," Miss Darcy said, with a wryness that belied her youth.

"Why do you think the money would run out?" Mary asked.

"I've seen how quickly Mr. Wickham can squander three thousand pounds. I doubt it would take him much longer to spend ten."

"How did he get three thousand pounds?" Elizabeth asked, despite her desire for Miss Darcy to halt her tale. Three thousand pounds was a considerable sum, to have or to spend.

Miss Darcy turned to Elizabeth. "Mr. Wickham asked my brother to give him three thousand pounds to compensate him for a living he was supposed to receive. It was in my father's will. A dying wish, but Mr.

Wickham said he would rather have the money than be a clergyman. Then he spent most of it."

"How would you come to know that?" Mrs. Bennet asked.

"He admitted it to me." Miss Darcy took a bite of toast and chewed. They all sat silent, waiting for her to continue. "He claimed to still have a thousand pounds left, invested to give him fifty pounds a year, but I'm not sure he told the truth. He wasn't happy that I knew about his selling his right to the living."

"Still, if you loved him, you would have been happy," Kitty said.

"It would still be wrong to elope," Mr. Collins said.

"And how would you have lived?" Mary added.

"Mr. Darcy gave Mr. Wickham money before," Lydia said. "With them married, he'd surely have given you more." She turned to Miss Darcy. "Wouldn't he?"

Miss Darcy nodded. "My brother would see we didn't starve, but he wouldn't send us money, because Mr. Wickham would spend it on himself, not me or any children we had. Mr. Wickham is very selfish. That's why I knew I couldn't love him."

Mrs. Bennet nodded her approval. "No woman should settle for a selfish man. It brings only sorrow."

"But what happened then?" Kitty asked. "You were with him, and he wanted you to go to Scotland, and it doesn't sound as if your governess would prevent that."

Miss Darcy took a sip of tea. "I wrote my brother to tell him that Mr. Wickham was with us, because I knew he wouldn't approve, but I am pretty certain the letter wasn't sent."

Jane and Mary gasped. Mrs. Bennet looked confused.

"Do you mean, your governess took the letter?" Mr. Collins asked, tone affronted.

Miss Darcy nodded again. "I'm certain she did, because my brother never replied."

"That's villainous," Jane said.

"I suppose it is," Miss Darcy agreed.

"If you couldn't write, and you couldn't see anyone, what did you do?" Kitty asked.

Miss Darcy's eyes sparkled. Elizabeth realized she was enjoying telling her tale. To how many others had she confessed the story? Her brother and Mr. Fitzwilliam knew, surely.

"Normally, I wrote weekly," Miss Darcy said. "So, the following week, I made sure Mr. Wickham's name was mentioned on every sheet of my letter. I thought Mrs. Young would have to send at least one page. If my brother didn't hear from me for too long, he would worry."

"Did she send it?" Mary asked, finally appearing caught up in the tale.

Miss Darcy shook her head. "She told me that I had given enough information about Mr. Wickham in my previous letter and should rewrite that one without mentioning him."

"So, she had read the first one," Elizabeth observed.

"For shame," Mrs. Bennet said.

"It was her duty, as governess," Mary observed, but without her usual censure.

"She had no right to come between you and your guardian," Mr. Collins said.

"Did you rewrite it?" Lydia asked.

"I did not," Miss Darcy said. "And Mrs. Younge sent me to bed without supper when I refused. After thinking about it, and feeling quite hungry, I stayed up very late and wrote a long letter using all the descriptions she made me give her in Italian and French. My brother doesn't know Italian, but he speaks passable French. I wrote the French ones in French, using the excuse that Mrs. Younge wanted me to practice my French. I believe I made many mistakes, but I didn't care."

"If you wrote the Italian ones in Italian, I'll bet Mr. Darcy would guess something was wrong," Elizabeth said, trying to guess Miss Darcy's plan.

"He would have," Miss Darcy agreed. "But Mrs. Younge knew he doesn't speak Italian."

"So, you wrote them in English?" Jane asked, frowning.

"The idea was to write so much, it would take a very long time to read it all," Miss Darcy said. "In the middle of a long paragraph describing the ocean, I wrote, 'I am happy here.' I deliberately left a space between 'am' and 'happy.' Not a large space. Only enough so that I could write 'un' connected to happy. I also made sure the letter had other places where the spacing was erratic."

Lydia yawned and looked about the table. Elizabeth could see her youngest sister was becoming bored with the story, now that talk of elopement and dowries had been replaced by French, Italian and letter writing. A glance confirmed Mrs. Bennet had returned to eating her meal, vacant expression angled toward the wall. Lydia reached for another roll.

Elizabeth, in contrast, was increasingly intrigued. "How did you get the 'un' into the letter?"

Miss Darcy offered a smug smile. "I bribed a maid with a bracelet. I arranged that when I coughed three times in a row and then once, the maid would head into the adjoining room and knock something over." Miss Darcy's smugness grew. "As soon as Mrs. Younge finished reading the letter, I coughed. Before she could seal it, something smashed in the next room. She went to investigate. She even lectured the girl for several minutes. I had more than enough time to add a couple letters."

"She didn't look at the letter when she returned?" Elizabeth asked.

"She looked at it, but not carefully enough," Miss Darcy said. "After that, there was no more mention of letters. Mrs. Younge pretended I hadn't received any from my brother."

"Why?" Jane asked.

"My brother must have said something," Miss Darcy said. "Not only didn't Mrs. Young give me any more letters or insist I write any, Mr. Wickham increased his insistence that we elope."

Lydia perked up, turning back their way. "But you must not have eloped."

Sympathy welled in Elizabeth. "How did you put him off?" She hadn't yet met this odious Mr. Wickham, but it must have been difficult for a young woman, a girl really, to fend off the advances of a grown man.

"At first, I pretended I had no idea what Mr. Wickham wanted."

Jane nodded, obviously approving of the strategy. Kitty watched with a worried look, which increased Elizabeth's respect for her younger sister. Usually, Kitty and Lydia couldn't be bothered to have empathy.

"Later, when Mr. Wickham persisted, I said I would wait for him," Miss Darcy continued. "That if he still loved me when I was twenty-one, I wouldn't need my brother's consent." She grimaced. "That didn't suit him at all. He went on and on about how wonderful it would be if we eloped."

"And you still didn't?" Lydia breathed, eyes dreamy.

Elizabeth wondered exactly how handsome Mr. Wickham was. She glanced at Jane. Even her older sister had labeled him of fine mien. Normally, Jane spoke only of a person's nature, not their countenance.

Miss Darcy's expression firmed. "Even if I desperately loved him, I wouldn't have eloped. I would never hurt my brother and cousin that way."

"I should think they deserve to be hurt after hiring such a despicable governess," Mrs. Bennet said, alerting them to her renewed interest in the conversation.

"My brother hired her," Miss Darcy said. "My cousin was on the Continent."

"At war," Lydia said, tone even more enamored.

"I haven't had the pleasure of meeting your cousin," Mr. Collins said. "Or your brother."

"My brother? He is perfect. Just ask Miss Bingley," Miss Darcy said.

"Mr. Darcy is a singularly upright individual," Elizabeth cut in. She didn't object to Miss Darcy mocking Miss Bingley and could appreciate that Miss Darcy felt the right to make light at her brother's expense, but she worried their guest didn't realize how fully her mother and younger sisters would repeat her every word. With Miss Darcy's tale of Mr. Wickham and her time spent unchaperoned in his company, enough damage had been done without Mr. Darcy hearing he'd been mocked behind his back by his sister, although Elizabeth privately reserved the right to mock him to his face.

Miss Darcy cast Elizabeth a measuring look. She turned back to Mr. Collins. "My brother is always pleased to meet a member of the clergy, as is Mr. Fitzwilliam."

"If Mr. Fitzwilliam was so far away, it's possible Mr. Wickham felt you would be easier to suborn, since you had only one guardian nearby," Mary said.

"Maybe," Miss Darcy allowed. "Mr. Wickham dislikes my brother, but he's afraid of my cousin."

"Afraid of Mr. Fitzwilliam?" Elizabeth was startled into asking. "He's the most convivial of men." Mr. Darcy appeared much more formidable, with his endless glowers. Then again, Elizabeth knew no intimidation when it came to him. What more could he do? Insult her publicly again?

Miss Darcy set down her third piece of toast and leaned forward. "My cousin," she said, voice lowered, "is rumored to have killed a man in a duel."

Gasps sounded around the table, Elizabeth's among them.

Of course, Lydia and Kitty wanted to know about that. Miss Darcy firmly held everyone's attention once more. As Elizabeth watched her speak, she realized two things. One was that Miss Darcy didn't really know much about the purported duel. The other was that their unexpected breakfast guest enjoyed being the center of attention.

After nearly two hours, Miss Darcy seemed to run out of stories to tell. Breakfast finally broke up. Mr. Bennet sent Simmons to ask if any of his daughters felt enough gratitude to him for giving them sustenance and shelter to read to him, a duty for which Jane promptly volunteered. Kitty, to Elizabeth's surprise, cajoled Lydia and Mary into listening to Mr. Collins read while they did mending. As much for Miss Darcy's company as to avoid that, Elizabeth offered to walk their guest home. She led Miss Darcy outside, proffered her arm, and angled them toward Netherfield.

"This isn't the way I came," Miss Darcy said as they walked across a meadow arm in arm. "I followed the road."

"No wonder you arrived famished." Elizabeth smiled. "That way is nearly three miles. This will be quicker."

"But, were it early morning or right after a rain, our hems would become much damper," Miss Darcy noted with a smirk.

Elizabeth chuckled. "Aye, they certainly would, to our enduring shame, I'm sure." She sobered, casting Miss Darcy a sidelong look. "I could think of no way to warn you at breakfast, but you should be aware, my mother and youngest two sisters are terrible gossips. They will repeat your tale."

Miss Darcy nodded. "I suspected as much."

"Yet, you spoke regardless." Elizabeth couldn't fathom why.

"Mr. Wickham is a liar and a cheat, and not to be trusted. Everyone should know."

"Even if it impugns your reputation?" Elizabeth asked.

Miss Darcy threw back her shoulders, chin high. "I did nothing wrong. Besides, stories are bound to get out, eventually. I've lived my whole life as a Darcy. I know how the ton works. You cannot hide these things."

Elizabeth nodded. Stories did always come out. If not Miss Darcy's version, then another. Mr. Wickham, from what Elizabeth had already gleaned, enjoyed spreading tales. He'd been very free with his accusations that Mr. Darcy had cheated him, and that Miss Darcy was a snob. He would likely be free with other stories as well.

Miss Darcy's reply satisfied Elizabeth as to the source of her unexpected frankness at breakfast, but Elizabeth was still troubled by one aspect of the tale. "Your brother came simply because you said you were unhappy?" Elizabeth tried to reconcile such behavior with a man who had openly insulted her, likely lost a wager concerning her and Charlotte, and had hardly spoken to her at Netherfield.

"Yes." Miss Darcy nodded. "I knew the moment my brother read that I was unhappy, he would set out for Ramsgate."

Elizabeth frowned, still filled with mild disbelief. "What happened when he arrived?"

Miss Darcy let out a sigh. Their skirts brushed through the tall grass, seeming to echo the sound. "He was very angry."

"With you?"

"With me. With Wickham. With Mrs. Younge and the rest of the staff. It's difficult to say, and I didn't want lengthy discussion or an argument with him." She angled her face toward the bright blue of the sky. "He can become very unreasonable and dig in his heels and I wanted to get out of there. I speak lightly of it now, but it was terrible, the weeks of Mr. Wickham pressing me, every hour of every day. It wore on me."

Elizabeth squeezed Miss Darcy's arm. She could imagine how awful it must have been.

"I told my brother that I had agreed to elope with Mr. Wickham and had changed my mind, so he would take me away immediately," Miss Darcy continued. "I thought that if I tried to explain everything, my brother would spend days endeavoring to assign the exact amount of proper blame to everyone. He tends to be very meticulous."

"You mean, Mr. Darcy believes you meant to elope?" Elizabeth cut in. "I thought you didn't wish to hurt him."

"His sensibilities aren't that tender," Miss Darcy protested. "Thinking of eloping and actually eloping aren't the same at all."

Elizabeth wondered if Mr. Darcy saw it that way. "Did he remove you quickly, as you hoped?"

Miss Darcy nodded, expression glum. "He did. I was right that my lie got me out of there, but you wouldn't believe how many lectures I received from my brother, as well as from my cousin when he returned. They've also talked about delaying my coming out until I'm eighteen, or possibly longer."

"Why don't you admit you lied?" Elizabeth asked.

Miss Darcy shook her head vigorously. "My brother hates liars."

"You must do something to mend things," Elizabeth said.

"I am. I am acting contrite."

That explained the difference in Miss Darcy's loquaciousness when around her brother and Mr. Fitzwilliam. "Is it working, do you think?"

"I don't know, and it's been very difficult." Miss Darcy glanced Elizabeth's way with a tentative smile. "I'm not certain of the difference between being silently contrite and being silently sullen." Her expression grew contemplative. "Maybe you can help me."

"I can certainly try," Elizabeth said, wondering how.

Chapter Thirteen

Darcy, dressed for the midday meal, strode through Netherfield manor in increasing agitation. It was after noon and he could not locate his sister. Nor had he seen her since the evening before. He turned into the parlor the ladies frequented during the day, and found Mrs. Hurst and Miss Bingley, both reading. A glance showed the room did not hold his sister.

"Do you know where Georgiana is?" he asked.

Mrs. Hurst looked up from her book. "I haven't seen her yet this morning. Caroline?"

"Isn't she in her room?" Miss Bingley asked.

Darcy shook his head, worry mounting. "I knocked and there was no response. She went to bed quite early. She should be up by now."

Perhaps he should open her door. Could she be ill? She could have contracted what Miss Bennet had. Wouldn't her maid have thought to inform him?

Miss Bingley frowned, face adopting the expression with practiced ease. "She went to bed early, yes, but she said she planned to stay up until she finished translating something from Italian. She is so conscientious about her studies that I assumed she stayed up late and was still asleep."

Darcy mimicked Miss Bingley's expression. It wasn't unusual for Georgiana to study into the night, or even to miss breakfast, but it was late, even for her. She should have appeared by now. His worry mounted, but he forced his frown to ease.

"That's likely it," he said, not wishing to promote agitation. "Or she's gone for one of her walks and I missed her."

Miss Bingley tipped her head with a thoughtful look. "I believe she keeps her cloak in her room. I will gladly check for you." She set aside her book.

"I will check," Darcy said.

Miss Bingley stood. "I'm already up. Besides, if the door is locked, you will need my key."

Darcy pressed his mouth into a thin line, having no civilized way to deter Miss Bingley. Together, they left the parlor and returned to the hall where Miss Bingley had given Darcy, Richard and Georgiana rooms. Miss Bingley knocked on Georgiana's. No response came.

"If she were within, her maid would be as well," Miss Bingley reasoned. She tried the knob. It turned under her hand. Miss Bingley swung the door open and entered.

Darcy followed to find the room in perfect order and the bed made. A folded paper lay on the coverlet, unsealed, but with his name readily apparent on the outside. Miss Bingley plucked it up. Darcy could read her indecision. He held out his hand. She passed it to him, still folded, eyes bright with curiosity.

Darcy flipped the note open. *I wanted more congenial company. I'll be back early in the afternoon.*

"What does she say?" Miss Bingley leaned around him, trying to read the page.

Darcy folded it shut, then in half, and shoved it in his pocket. He would speak to Georgiana about leaving an unsealed insult to their hostess in plain sight. "She said she has gone out and will be back by early afternoon."

"Without one of us?" Miss Bingley asked. "Did she take her maid?"

"It doesn't say." How could Georgiana behave so irresponsibly as to leave Netherfield without informing him? Where had she gone? He schooled his features, so as not to alert Miss Bingley to his level of agitation.

"I will ask the servants if they know her whereabouts or if anyone accompanied her," Miss Bingley declared.

"Thank you, but that won't be necessary." The last thing he wished was to involve the staff. That would only stir gossip. "I will speak with Richard. Likely, Georgiana told him where she went."

"He went out for his morning ride," Miss Bingley said, "but he usually arrives back about now and changes for lunch."

"He'll know where Georgiana is," Darcy reiterated.

Hoping Miss Bingley believed his unworried demeanor, Darcy stepped aside and gestured for her to precede him from the room. As she set off down the hall, he crossed to knock on Richard's door.

The door opened to reveal Richard's valet, his former batman. "Good afternoon, Mr. Darcy."

"Good afternoon, Disher. Is Richard in?"

"Let him in, Disher," Richard's voice called. "Darcy's seen me in a state of undress before."

Darcy entered to find Richard in trousers, in the act of donning his shirt. While Darcy had certainly seen his cousin in many states during a youth spent charging about the countryside together, he hadn't seen Richard shirtless since before Spain. Though the white cloth dropped quickly into place, Darcy caught a glimpse of scars. He swallowed at that too-real reminder of how close those bullets had come to taking Richard from his life.

"What can I do for you, Darcy?" Richard asked, tucking in his shirt.

"I'm looking for Georgiana." Darcy strove for a natural tone, rattled by both his sister's defection and his older cousin's mortality. "She hasn't been seen since last night, and I found this note on her bed." He retrieved and proffered the page.

Richard finished with his shirt and took the paper. He unfolded it, snorted in amusement, and handed it back. "It sounds as if she'll be home any moment."

"Yes, but where did she go? Why not inform me?"

Richard turned to put his arms through the waistcoat Disher held out, but not quickly enough to hide the look of worry that crossed his face. "Likely for a longer than usual walk."

"You know something," Darcy accused, shoving the note back into his pocket.

"Nothing about Georgiana, per se." Richard set to buttoning his waistcoat.

"You will make me drag it from you?"

Richard looked up, meeting Darcy's gaze. "I visited the Lucases this morning. A new officer has joined the regiment stationed in Meryton. Everyone is abuzz about him." Richard grimaced. "It's Wickham."

Something quite akin to fear ricocheted through Darcy. "You think Georgiana has gone to meet him?"

Richard returned to his buttons. "How would she know he's arrived? I only learned this morning."

Darcy frowned. He didn't know how Georgiana might have found out, but he feared she had. "Maybe I should permit Miss Bingley to quiz the servants. She offered."

Expression neutral, Disher stepped forward with Richard's cravat.

Richard shook his head at Darcy, accepting the length of cloth from his valet. "If we make a general inquiry about when Georgiana left, it will cause concerns that would not reflect well on her. You already dissuaded Miss Bingley from investigating?"

"I did."

"How? She's generally quite tenacious, I've noticed."

Darcy shrugged. "I asked her not to."

Richard flashed a grin as he used the mirror to tie his cravat. "I sometimes forget that your word is law to her. Should I be jealous that she's still chasing you?"

That brought a slight smile, as Richard undoubtedly intended. "You should be relieved, as I am, that her attention is divided. She's more bearable." Darcy briefly wondered how Miss Bingley would react if he and Richard disagreed about something, but his levity fled. "If Georgiana is lying in a ditch somewhere, I don't care what concerns are raised."

"She'll likely be back any moment, Darcy. She's not a child."

"Nor is she a woman grown," he countered.

"Um, sirs, if I may?" Disher asked.

Startled by the interruption, Darcy turned to Disher. Richard's valet had his gaze trained out the window. He stepped to one side and held the curtain back to give them a better view. Georgiana, arm in arm with Elizabeth, strode across the lawn toward the manor. Relief washed through Darcy.

"Well, that answers our questions," Richard said lightly.

As quickly as his relief had come, Darcy's anger flared. "I'll go speak to her."

"Darcy," Richard called as Darcy strode across the room.

Darcy whirled back.

"She isn't a child," Richard reiterated, tone mild.

Darcy deepened his scowl and lengthened his stride. He'd prefer to meet the two in the garden, where they would have less of an audience. He had a few choice words for his sister for running off alone, and for Elizabeth for encouraging such behavior. Unfortunately, as he descended toward the entrance hall, Miss Bingley's voice, gaining in clarity, alerted him that he'd failed to meet his sister and Elizabeth outdoors.

"...uppose you think now you'll get to spend the night, since you walked Miss Darcy home?" Miss Bingley's voice held rancor.

"No, thank you," Elizabeth said pleasantly. She glanced up, expression touched with amusement, as Darcy neared the bottom step.

Wrenching his gaze from Elizabeth and her bright eyes, Darcy reached the entrance hall and turned to his sister. "Where have you been?" he asked, unable to keep a note of anger from his voice.

"At Longbourn," Georgiana said cheerfully. "Miss Elizabeth insisted on walking me home." She turned to Elizabeth. "You ought to stay a while. You must rest a bit and, if my brother's coat is any indication, it's time for luncheon." Georgiana cast a look toward Miss Bingley.

Silence filled the entrance hall. Miss Bingley frowned. She glanced about, as if seeking aid. "Yes, you must stay," she finally said, tone flat. "You walked Miss Darcy home. A half hour would be appropriate."

Elizabeth shook her head. "Thank you, but no. I should get back. I've been away from home too much of late and there are matters to which I must attend."

"At least let us send for a carriage," Georgiana said. "To save you time."

"I will walk Miss Elizabeth back," Darcy snapped. He leveled a look on his sister meant to inform her that he would speak with her later. First, he would deal with Elizabeth.

"How gracious of you," Elizabeth said. Far from appearing daunted by his obvious displeasure, she still looked amused.

"I'm sure Charles will lend his carriage if yours is unavailable," Miss Bingley said, gaze going from him to Elizabeth and back again. "You needn't miss luncheon, Mr. Darcy."

"I will walk Miss Elizabeth back," Darcy repeated. With a glare that dared Elizabeth to refuse, he proffered his arm.

She raised her eyebrows but nodded. "Thank you for a lovely visit, Miss Darcy, and a convivial walk."

"You are welcome, Miss Elizabeth," Georgiana said, tone equally light.

Darcy had no notion what his sister and Elizabeth found so humorous. Nor did he care. He proffered his arm again.

Elizabeth placed a long-fingered hand atop his sleeve. "Miss Bingley, please give my regards to your family."

Miss Bingley offered a stiff nod.

Darcy paused to give Miss Bingley time to return the courtesy, but her mouth remained clamped closed. He turned Elizabeth back toward the door. The butler, Andrews, stepped forward from where he'd stood unobtrusively against the wall and swung the door open to reveal a day that would have been lovely were Darcy in a less foul mood.

He marched Elizabeth down the steps and out into the drive. "Why did you not send a note telling me where Georgiana was?" he asked as gravel crunched beneath their feet. Belatedly, he realized the door behind them had not yet closed. Likely, Miss Bingley, Georgiana and any nearby staff had heard him.

Elizabeth cast him one of her mirthful looks. She said nothing. A moment later, they could hear Netherfield's front door shut.

"If you were to knock on our door, unlikely as that is, should we send a note to Mr. Bingley informing him of your whereabouts?" Elizabeth asked.

"I am a grown man," Darcy snapped, then winced. He sounded a bit like a sullen boy. "Georgiana is not yet of age," he added in a more reasonable tone.

"If Miss Bingley calls, shall we send a note to her brother? She is not yet of age." Elizabeth affected a startled expression. "Oh dear, I am not of age either. Do you wish to return to Netherfield and compose a note to my father? You could have someone ride over with it while we walk."

Darcy fixed his gaze on the end of the drive, still some ways off, and struggled to stave off additional petulant comments. Elizabeth made a fair point. Still, she and Miss Bingley were nearly of age. Georgiana was but fifteen.

"Our duty was to see to her safety while she was at Longbourn," Elizabeth said gently.

"A duty you exceeded when you walked her home."

She cast him a startled look, glimpsed from the corner of his eye.

Darcy drew in a long breath. "I apologize. I overreacted. I was worried."

"It was reasonable for you to worry," she said. "I had no notion you didn't know where she was, or I truly would have sent word."

"She left a note saying when she would return but not where she had gone," he said, struggling to keep his anger from rekindling. "As she left it on her bed and sent no word she was going out, I didn't find it until I discovered she was missing and started to search."

Elizabeth shook her head, sending dark curls swishing. "She said she left a note. It didn't occur to me she would place it out of the way and not include where she was headed." She cast him a sidelong look. "It's not my place to say, but would Miss Darcy benefit from another governess?"

"She has one. Mrs. Annesley."

"And is not Mrs. Annesley meant to look after her?" Miss Elizabeth asked as they turned into the lane.

"Miss Bingley suggested that Georgiana might benefit from some time without Mrs. Annesley to do her speaking for her."

Elizabeth chuckled. "You mean, Miss Bingley maneuvered to deprive your sister of any female companionship, thus forcing Miss Darcy to spend time with her and Mrs. Hurst."

"That was likely her goal, yes," he admitted. "As Mrs. Annesley has been Georgiana's only companion, and it is my wish for Georgiana to recover some of her former talkative behavior, I agreed to Miss Bingley's unsubtle machinations. Mrs. Annesley also had a family matter to attend to, so leaving her in London seemed the best course for all." Darcy suppressed a sigh. All he'd accomplished was even greater silence from his sister, who bore Bingley's sisters a dislike. He also realized he'd revealed Georgiana had a problem, by his use of the word former. He glanced at Elizabeth askance again, wondering if she'd noticed his slip, and how he came to be so unguarded with her.

Not that Elizabeth's perception of Georgiana mattered, for they should likely leave Hertfordshire. Now that Mr. Wickham was in town, Georgiana would be isolated further. Darcy couldn't risk an encounter between the two. "Perhaps we should return to London. Or Pemberley."

"Pemberley? Your home? Are there young ladies Miss Darcy's age with whom she may socialize?"

As the answer was no, Darcy ignored the question.

Elizabeth stopped, forcing him to do likewise. She released his arm to face him. "Please don't further seclude her. You've isolated her enough since the incident with Mr. Wickham."

Darcy took a half step back, stunned. "What do you know about the incident with Mr. Wickham?" Anger shot through him. "Earlier, you said another governess. Not a governess, but another. What did she tell you?"

"Given her frankness this morning, I suspect I know all there is to tell, which is more than you do."

He scowled. "Don't be absurd." Dread snaked through him. Had his sister been irreversibly compromised? Would she admit such a thing to Elizabeth when she hadn't told Richard or him? Had she told Richard and the two conspired to keep it from Darcy, so now he must learn it from a veritable stranger? "I know what happened," he added, but his voice lacked conviction.

Those delicate eyebrows rose again, but no amusement shone in Elizabeth's gaze. "Do you? You know, then, that your sister never intended to elope with Mr. Wickham? She only told you that so that you would remove her immediately."

Darcy shook his head. "It is impossible she would lie about such a thing."

"Even if I inform you that he'd plagued her for weeks, that she'd been deprived of food and rest, and that she was desperate to get away from there and feared you would launch an inquiry into the staff rather than remove her?"

Darcy rocked back on his heels. He had wished to do exactly that but had decided removing Georgiana from the temptation of Wickham was more paramount. "What did she tell you?" he asked.

Elizabeth gestured that they should resume walking. Darcy offered his arm. As they headed down the lane, Elizabeth gave him a concise, yet nuanced, description of what had befallen Georgiana in Ramsgate. By the end of her recounting, Darcy's relief held a sharp edge. If anything, Elizabeth's revelations made the incident less significant than before.

"She is very ashamed she lied to you," Elizabeth said after finishing her tale. "On the walk over, she told me that when your good opinion is lost, it is lost forever. I persuaded her that she should confess, but she said she couldn't face you. She asked me to tell you first, hoping, I think, to avoid your immediate anger. I hope you will forgive her, but even if you don't, it is best to get things out in the open. She feels very guilty about the lie and to compensate, she's been trying to act in the way they taught her to behave at school. Quiet. Speaking only when spoken to."

So, it was him and Richard, all along. Georgiana was not speaking when in their presence, specifically. No wonder she preferred the company of the Bennet sisters, where she could talk.

"Of course, I forgive her," Darcy said. "I don't understand why she thinks a lie is more significant than agreeing to elope with a fortune hunter. She would have been miserable if she'd married Mr. Wickham."

"Did you ever tell her not to lie?" Elizabeth glanced at him, amusement blooming to life in her eyes once more. "Did you, perchance, rail against lying?"

"Yes," he admitted.

"More than once?"

"Yes," he replied slowly. "Rather often."

"Did you ever tell her not to elope?"

"No. Nor did I tell her not to steal or commit murder. She should have known."

"She knew it was wrong," Elizabeth said. "She simply didn't think it was your priority. The eloping, I mean. She did mention that she felt admitting a plan to elope wouldn't upset you, whereas she realized actually eloping would, which is why she could never do such a thing."

"Even pretending she would wed Wickham is worse than a lie," Darcy declared, ignoring the contradiction inherent in that statement. He didn't look, but he could practically feel Elizabeth's supplication for patience. "She should simply have told me she wished to leave immediately."

"What would you have done if the possibility existed that Mrs. Younge was duped? How long would you have stayed and questioned Miss Darcy, Mrs. Younge and the other staff if the only thing that had happened was that Mr. Wickham had suggested an elopement?"

"I do not know," he admitted.

"Considering the stress Miss Darcy had been under for weeks, even half an hour was too much more to endure. Possibly, Mrs. Younge had no chance of retaining her job, but if her only error was to allow Mr. Wickham, a man who was brought up almost as your brother, to spend time with Miss Darcy, you would want to know. Had you given explicit instructions to keep Mr. Wickham away?"

"I had not," Darcy admitted. "It never occurred to me I needed to do so."

"It is easy to take things for granted," Elizabeth said.

She was right, he realized as they rounded a twist in the lane. "I took for granted that Georgiana would be able to get in touch with me if necessary. It never occurred to me that she wouldn't be free to write what she wished."

Elizabeth nodded. "How could it?" She glanced at him, expression worried.

His brows drew together. "Something is troubling you?" Beyond what they'd discussed?

"You should know, Miss Darcy repeated much of what I told you, the entirety of the incident in Ramsgate up until your arrival, to my mother and sisters. I could not stop her."

A pit opened in Darcy's gut. True, Georgiana had done nothing wrong, but there would still be rumors. They would be distorted. People would think the worst.

"It's years before she officially comes out," Elizabeth said, tone gentle. "This may be a good thing. The rumors will pass now, when they can do less harm."

He shook his head. What had Georgiana done? Wickham would hear. He would surely go about telling a false version. Between Darcy and Richard, they could do much to counter the ill will the story would bring, but they couldn't erase the tale from society. Exactly how much would Georgiana's prospects suffer?

Chapter Fourteen

Darcy mulled over his sister's prospects as Longbourn came into sight in the distance. Elizabeth, hand resting lightly on his arm, did not intrude on his silence. He continued to dwell on what Georgiana had done as he and Elizabeth finally turned up the drive toward the manor.

"In keeping with the standards of Miss Bingley, I invite you in," Elizabeth said as they walked up the drive, tone forcedly light. "She stipulated that a half hour is appropriate for walking a person home." Elizabeth cast him a quick glance. "Not that I shall attempt to persuade you to comply against your wishes."

Darcy forced a smile. Elizabeth had been nothing but convivial on their walk, and supportive. For once, she'd conversed with him normally, as he'd observed her do with Richard. Despite their uncomfortable topic, talking with her proved every bit as enjoyable as Darcy had anticipated.

He required a mind like hers to help him deal with Georgiana. His sister had become too complicated of late. She was no longer a young girl who skipped about Pemberley and played on the pianoforte all afternoon. Perhaps, if he encouraged Georgiana to spend more time with Elizabeth… But no, there were still her mother and younger sisters to think about.

Would their influence truly be so awful?

"I would not want to give Miss Bingley cause to think me derelict in my social duties," Darcy said as they neared the front door to Longbourn. If nothing else, a visit would remind him of why Elizabeth Bennet was not an acceptable companion for Georgiana…or for him.

As if to reinforce his thoughts, the youngest Bennet sister, Miss Lydia, came flying from the house. She ran toward them, then skidded to a stop before Elizabeth, halting their progress. The slightest blush touched Elizabeth's cheeks as she cast Darcy another sidelong look. It gratified him to realize she, too, didn't approve of Miss Lydia's behavior.

"Lizzy, you will never guess what has happened," Miss Lydia gasped out as she tried to catch her breath.

"Is Papa well?"

Darcy cast Elizabeth a sharp glance. Real concern filled her voice. Was Mr. Bennet ill?

"I don't know, but Mama visited him and decided he is dying and she said one of us has to marry Mr. Collins immediately so he won't throw us all out, but she told him he can't have Jane because she is for Mr. Bingley, and I said right away that I wouldn't marry him, because he's not an officer. Mama said he surely won't take Mary with her looks, so that leaves Kitty or you."

The blush in Elizabeth's cheeks deepened during Miss Lydia's babbled reply. Elizabeth held up a hand. "Lydia, slower, please, and keep in mind that we have a guest."

Miss Lydia glanced at Darcy. "Hello, Mr. Darcy," she said. He offered a nod, but she was already turning back to Elizabeth. "Mama suggested you because Kitty coughs, but before Mr. Collins could answer there was a knock at the door, and you'll never guess who showed up, but Mr. Wickham, who I still say is too handsome to be as awful as Miss Darcy says, meaning no offense, Mr. Darcy. Mr. Wickham was with Mr. Denny and Mr. Pratt, so we had to invite them all in."

Darcy didn't know which was worse, knowing Wickham had been at the Bennet's, his visit nearly overlapping with Georgiana's, or the idea of Elizabeth wedding this Mr. Collins fellow. Darcy hadn't met Collins, but he'd heard the man was the Bennets' cousin and a fool. Despite her undesirable connections and lack of a dowry, Elizabeth warranted better than a fool.

"I trust the subject of marriage was dropped," Elizabeth said, sounding hopeful.

"Yes, but Mr. Collins got all preachery."

Darcy didn't believe preachery to be a word, but he doubted Miss Lydia cared.

"What do you mean?" Elizabeth asked. A light breeze stirred the small curls about her face.

Miss Lydia grinned. "In a booming voice, like he was preaching in a large church, he denounced Mr. Wickham."

"Denounced Mr. Wickham?" Mr. Darcy repeated with a sinking feeling. Had Collins heard his sister's tale, too? A champion would only exacerbate the rumors. "For what?"

"For not showing proper respect for his patron," Miss Lydia said. "That's your father, Mr. Darcy. Mr. Collins went on and on, practically yelling. He said Mr. Wickham had shown a terrible disrespect to old Mr. Darcy by betraying the trust of Miss Darcy and you, Mr. Darcy, and that mistreating one's patron is a terrible crime against propriety."

Darcy grimaced.

Elizabeth shot him a look brimming with sympathy. "Did Mr. Collins elaborate?" she asked, tone somewhat pleading.

With a glance up at the bright blue sky, Darcy prayed, silently, that Collins had not.

Miss Lydia nodded. "Mr. Collins said that Mr. Wickham shouldn't have tried to persuade Miss Darcy to elope with him. Mr. Collins said that to even ponder marriage to her was improper of Mr. Wickham, since she is so above him in class."

Darcy winced. Apparently, his prayers came too late.

Elizabeth let out a sigh. "I see."

"Then, Mr. Collins said Mr. Wickham shouldn't have lied about Mr. Darcy denying him that living," Miss Lydia continued.

"He said what?" Darcy cut in. "Wickham has been putting out that I denied him the living my father left him?" Fresh anger at Wickham warred with Darcy's concern for his sister's future. "I paid him for that living, which was his idea."

Miss Lydia nodded as a gust of wind swirled the ladies' hems. "Miss Darcy already told us that."

"Georgiana knew?" Darcy asked. How had his sister found out?

"She told us this morning," Elizabeth said in a quiet voice. "She said he confessed as much to her in Ramsgate, after she asked him why he didn't have the living." She turned back to her sister. "Tell me there isn't more?"

"Oh, but there is," Miss Lydia said gleefully. "When Mr. Collins berated Mr. Wickham about the three thousand pounds, Mr. Wickham started yelling back. He said the living was worth more than three times that, and that Mr. Darcy told him he should take the money, because the incumbent was younger than Mr. Wickham, but that after he signed away his rights, he found out the incumbent was in his fifties."

"Wickham knew the incumbent," Darcy protested, though he suspected his denial was useless. From sad experience, Darcy knew that people were more likely to believe Wickham than him.

"Well, that's your word against his," Miss Lydia said with a shrug.

"Miss Darcy's assertion that Mr. Wickham confessed about the living to her corroborates Mr. Darcy's version," Elizabeth put in quickly.

"That's true," Miss Lydia said reluctantly.

"You won't be forced to challenge him, will you?" Elizabeth asked, turning a worried look on Darcy.

Darcy frowned. Should he? Georgiana's tale was public now. Those who believed her would feel that Darcy should challenge Wickham. Those who did not would see her as even more guilty if he did.

"Mr. Darcy doesn't have to," Miss Lydia said, bouncing up on her toes and back down again on the dusty front drive. "This is the best part. Mr. Collins and Mr. Wickham were shouting back and forth, and Mr. Collins said that Mr. Wickham had tried to steal the virtue of the very woman who gratitude should have him protect. He went on and on, chest all puffed out, about how Mr. Wickham had wronged the whole Darcy family, whose interests he should have put above his own, and how low that made Mr. Wickham. Then Mr. Wickham challenged him to a duel. Isn't it exciting, Lizzy? Only, Mama was in tears by then and she was screaming, too, and she says I can't go watch."

"Oh dear," Elizabeth said. She turned to Darcy. "Challenging a clergyman?"

Darcy shook his head. "Wickham had no choice. With two fellow officers there, he had to admit to wrongdoing or issue a challenge." And Wickham somehow never believed he was guilty of anything, no matter how many wrongs he committed.

"Still, to challenge a clergyman, especially one as inept as Mr. Collins," Elizabeth repeated, expression worried.

"Mr. Wickham said if he was maligned by a clergyman, he could challenge that clergyman," Miss Lydia said, eyes bright. "Mr. Denny is going to be his second. Mr. Wickham wanted to settle it immediately, but Papa came downstairs."

"Papa?" Elizabeth broke in, expression brightening. She cast a glance toward the windows of the manor. "He was well enough to come down? That's wonderful news. You should have begun with that, Lydia."

Miss Lydia tossed her curls. "It's only Papa. He seemed well enough to me. He was as grouchy as ever, at least. He said there was enough noise to wake the dead. He also said he would be Mr. Collins second, since Mr. Collins doesn't have any friends in the neighborhood. Then Papa said that he would talk to Mr. Denny about the duel in a few days when he is feeling better and people have had a chance to calm down."

"That seems sensible," Darcy said, relieved. Perhaps both sides might be made to see reason and no duel would take place.

"Mr. Wickham, Mr. Denny, and Mr. Pratt wanted to stay and talk about it more, but Papa made them leave." Sunlight bounced off Miss Lydia's bright curls as she let out a huff of annoyance. "After they left, Mr. Collins started shaking," she said with a tone of relish. "He said he is going to die, since he doesn't know anything about swords. Papa suggested he withdraw his accusation, but Mr. Collins got mulish and said right was right, even if he had to die for it."

"Really?" Elizabeth said, sounding impressed.

Miss Lydia gave a solemn nod. "Really."

Darcy felt a stab of worry for this Mr. Collins, and a pang of annoyance. Darcy hadn't even met the man, and Georgiana had spoken to him once, in company, so far as Darcy was able to determine. Now, Collins' name would be tied to Georgiana's, for better or for worse, and better seemed unlikely. Although their brief association would suggest to everyone that Collins' challenge sprang from knowledge, not amour, most wouldn't know the short length of their acquaintance. Rumor would abound.

Elizabeth turned to face him, expression grave. "I am so sorry about this." She glanced toward the manor. "I should have remained here. Perhaps I could have prevented their heated exchange."

"It stands in your favor that you escorted Georgiana home." Darcy forced the words out, for in truth he now wished that Elizabeth had remained in Longbourn. "You couldn't have known what would transpire."

Miss Lydia popped up on her toes again. "Anyhow, they've all seen you, so you have to come in, but Papa said I could come tell you."

"Papa?" Elizabeth repeated. "What of Mama?"

"She's still crying. Papa sent her to her room."

Elizabeth turned a worried look on Darcy. "Do you wish to come in, sir?"

"I believe it for the best."

She nodded and, taking her sister by the arm, led the way. They entered to no greeting but turned immediately into a parlor. Inside sat Miss Kitty, a poorly proportioned man Darcy could only assume was Collins, and Mr. Bennet. He was shaved and dressed, meaning he had not risen from his bed to come downstairs, but he'd lost at least a stone of weight since Darcy had last seen him, and the loss didn't suit him. His clothes were very loose. Miss Lydia hurried from Elizabeth's side to take a seat beside Miss Kitty.

Mr. Bennet started to rise, but Darcy stuck his hand out as if to push him back into the chair and said, "Don't get up."

Mr. Bennet settled back into his chair. He offered a nod of greeting. "Mr. Darcy. I believe you know my daughters. May I present Mr. Collins."

Darcy turned to the sallow-faced man, who stood and offered a bow. "Mr. Collins, forgive me for being forthright, but Miss Lydia informed us of what transpired. I cannot like a duel being fought over my sister."

Mr. Collins wrung his hands together. "The duel isn't about your sister. It is about Mr. Wickham's bad character. He should never have tried to persuade the daughter of his patron to elope. She said she was fifteen at the time. That's disgraceful."

"Perhaps you can make that clear to everyone," Elizabeth said. "I would hate to have Miss Darcy's name come into this at all."

Mr. Collins continued to twist his hands together, joints white. "I'm not certain what I can do. I don't know what to say or what to do." He held out his hands, which trembled, and issued an equally quavering laugh. "I'm shaking. I'm actually shaking in fear." He twisted his hands together again. "Mr. Wickham asked me to choose my weapon."

"And you chose swords," Miss Kitty said in a breathy voice.

Elbow propped on a chair arm, Mr. Bennet rubbed at his temples.

"Swords?" Darcy repeated. Collins didn't look like a swordsman. On the other hand, he was taller than Wickham and his longer reach would help.

Mr. Collins nodded. "I am inept with both sword and pistol, but if called to stand and face a man with a pistol, I would run away. I know that. With a sword, I will at least have the illusion that I might be able to defend myself, even if my mind knows I cannot."

Miss Lydia whispered something to Miss Kitty, who appeared not to notice. She had wide, bright eyes turned on Mr. Collins. "I'm certain you can win. You are in the right, Mr. Collins." She swiveled toward Darcy. "You could give him lessons, couldn't you, Mr. Darcy?"

Darcy stared at her, trying to formulate a reply. One look at Collins told Darcy that the man was physically inept. It would take years of lessons to make a difference.

"Please, Mr. Darcy?" Mr. Collins asked. "Perhaps, with a lesson or two, I wouldn't feel so doomed."

Darcy sought the right words. He held no desire to give the man false hope. He felt eyes upon him and turned to Elizabeth, still by his side.

She gave him a look he couldn't read and turned to Mr. Collins. "If Mr. Darcy gave you lessons, would you make a point of clarifying the nature of Mr. Wickham's offense?"

"Yes, I would. Of course, I would." Mr. Collins regarded Darcy with a painful amount of hope. "I'm really a coward, you know. I don't react well to pain. I will panic if I get the slightest scratch during a duel."

"Then why not apologize and withdraw your insult?" Mr. Bennet asked.

Mr. Collins drew himself up. "Because coward or not, right is right," he said, the statement losing some drama with the tremble in his voice.

"You are a hero," Miss Kitty breathed. "You are willing to face death for what is right."

Mr. Collins turned to Miss Kitty, his mouth gaping open in surprise.

"You will give him lessons?" Elizabeth asked Darcy, voice low.

Darcy suppressed a sigh. "I will."

"Thank you," Elizabeth murmured, fingers briefly touching his sleeve.

Mr. Collins cast a grateful look Darcy's way, then sagged, sinking back down into the chair he'd occupied when they entered. Miss Kitty clapped, expression joyous.

"Will you begin now?" Miss Lydia asked eagerly. "Can we watch?"

Darcy shrugged, looking to Mr. Bennet.

"I have a pair of masks and swords," Mr. Bennet said, tone one of resignation.

"Well then," Elizabeth said brightly. "Let us get started."

Chapter Fifteen

Darcy rolled down his shirtsleeves, then crossed the trampled grass to reclaim his coat from where he'd folded it over the back of one of the benches on the Bennets' lawn. He nodded to Mr. Bennet, who sat on the other bench, in the sun. Appearing even more pale out of doors, Mr. Bennet nodded back but didn't rise.

He'd been watching their progress. For a time, Miss Lydia had as well. Miss Mary had come out, shaken her head, and returned indoors. Darcy hadn't seen Miss Bennet, but he'd overheard Miss Lydia say she sat with Mrs. Bennet, trying to keep her calm. Miss Lydia had also remarked that watching him and Collins practice was much less fun than she'd hoped.

Sighting movement to his left, Darcy turned as he donned his coat. Elizabeth crossed to his side. Though she wore a bonnet, her cheeks were stained pink.

"You have been outdoors too long?" Darcy asked, worried she'd taken too much sun while he and Collins fenced.

The color in her cheeks deepened. She shook her head. "I am perfectly well, thank you. I came to ask if you would like me to show you the shortcut Miss Darcy and I took earlier?" Her eyes entreated.

"I would be most grateful," he said, though, from where he stood, he suspected he could pick out the path from his rides.

Mr. Collins walked over to them, Miss Kitty trailing him, gaze fixed on him. She wore an unsettlingly besotted expression.

Collins bowed. "Thank you, sir."

"My pleasure," Darcy said and was surprised to realize he didn't need to lie. Collins had no skill, but he seemed eager to learn and fencing outdoors in the crisp autumn air proved a pleasure. Darcy forbade his gaze to slip toward Elizabeth, even as he conceded that he'd also enjoyed the audience. "You will likely require more lessons."

Collins released his breath. "I hoped you would offer, Mr. Darcy. May I prevail upon you for further instruction tomorrow?"

Darcy searched his mind for previous obligations. "I intend to ride with Mr. Fitzwilliam tomorrow morning. Perhaps later in the day?"

"Mr. Fitzwilliam sometimes calls at the Lucases on his rides," Elizabeth said.

Darcy turned to her in mild surprise. He hadn't realized Richard called on Sir William often enough for others to note the frequency. Then, in truth, he didn't know where Richard rode to most days. Darcy assumed his cousin varied routes.

"What I suggest is that Mr. Collins visit the Lucases with us tomorrow," Elizabeth continued. "We do not, after all, wish to impose on you unduly, Mr. Darcy. Mr. Collins can practice with Mr. Lucas and his brothers, and if you and Mr. Fitzwilliam happen by, why, all the better." She turned to Mr. Collins. "While there, you can be sure to reiterate your reason for renouncing Mr. Wickham."

Darcy frowned. By taking Collins to the Lucases, did Elizabeth seek to see less of Darcy? Or, worse, was her goal to socialize more with Richard?

"That is, if you find no flaw in that plan?" Elizabeth said.

Darcy shook his head. "None." He turned back to Collins. "You did well today."

Mr. Collins stood a bit taller. "Thank you."

Darcy offered a nod and proffered his arm to Elizabeth. As they turned, he was peripherally aware that Mr. Collins offered Miss Kitty his arm. Collins led Miss Kitty toward Longbourn. Darcy and Elizabeth walked in the opposite direction.

"I assume you wish to speak with me?" he said.

Elizabeth cast him an amused smile. "You are astute."

"On what do you wish to converse?"

"I simply wished to thank you."

"For?" he asked, frowning.

"You were very patient with Mr. Collins today. Anyone can see he's terribly inept, and you were forced to repeat yourself often, but you never once seemed angry, even though he created this trouble for himself and..." She shot him a quick, worried look. "And his action may well harm Miss Darcy's reputation."

Darcy nodded. "They may, but that harm is already done. There is no point in Collins dying or being seriously injured, if it's possible to save him."

"You do not think Mr. Wickham would kill him?" she asked, tone startled.

"You have not met Mr. Wickham?" Darcy believed she'd said as much but wished to be sure.

"I have not, though all the rest of my family at Longbourn has, and my Aunt and Uncle Phillips."

"I know him well." Darcy searched for words as they walked. "He is charming. Most people like him very much. He has an easy way of making friends." He shook his head. "Keeping them, that is different. Once you come to know him, you become exposed to the baser side of his nature. He is almost childlike in his selfishness and greed." Darcy raised his gaze to study a cloud drifting slowly across the vast blue of the sky. "I like to think he would not kill Collins, but Wickham has disappointed me at every turn. Now, I cannot say for sure what he will do."

Elizabeth met Darcy's words with silence. A glance showed her brow creased in thought. "Mayhap he will find some honor," she finally said. "Or maybe, with your guidance, Mr. Collins will at least manage to defend himself. A duel is only to first blood, after all."

"That depends on how your father and Mr. Denny negotiate, but I assume your father will push for first blood."

"My father will push for no duel at all," Elizabeth said, her tone holding a bit of her usual wryness. "I'm certain he rightly believes the idea ludicrous."

They reached the taller grass, and the path his sister and Elizabeth took earlier that day. Elizabeth withdrew her hand from his arm. He turned to her, to study her face. The faintest dusting of freckles speckled across her cheeks and nose, somehow at odds with the drollness of her gaze. Then, her lips turned up at the corners and warmth pressed any hint of a sardonic edge from her expression.

"Regardless," she said. "I do thank you sir. You walked into a troubling situation. You could have made things worse for everyone. Instead, you made everyone involved feel better. Hopefully, yourself included."

Darcy's neck heated a bit with her praise and the knowledge that she was correct. He'd been a hairsbreadth away from taking the opposite track, demanding Mr. Collins rescind his insult, even if it was to Wickham. Darcy realized it was only by dint of Elizabeth's apology to him, delivered with all sincerity even though his sister's reputation wasn't

Elizabeth's responsibility, that he'd been reasonable. Her ill-placed guilt over the events had diverted Darcy from his usual quickness to find fault.

Darcy nodded, unsure how else to respond to her praise. He bowed over her hand, as if they parted at a formal event, then turned and set out across the field. He felt Elizabeth's eyes on him every step of the way, until he crested a hill and headed down the other side.

The walk, although shorter across the fields, still allowed plenty of time for introspection. Darcy strode toward Netherfield, attempting to organize what must be said to Georgiana. Despite Elizabeth's teasing, Georgiana must be made to know that disappearing without informing anyone of her whereabouts, or at least taking a maid, was unacceptable. Should he also speak to her about her lie, and Wickham's presence in Hertfordshire?

Elizabeth's wry smile filled his vision, followed by the memory not of hers, but Richard's words. Georgiana was not a child. Not yet a woman grown, but not a child. Darcy should speak to her, but not in the tone he intended. To find the right tone, it would be best to speak with Richard first.

That decided, Darcy lengthened his stride. Soon, he cut across the lawn toward Netherfield. He debated the kitchen entrance but went around to the front. Somehow, it didn't surprise him that Miss Bingley happened to be crossing the entrance hall when he entered.

"Mr. Darcy," she said in poorly feigned surprise. "Have you been out all this time? I trust nothing went awry?"

"I made the acquaintance of Mr. Collins, who is to someday take Mr. Bennet's place as master of Longbourn," Darcy said. "I spent some time offering him…guidance."

Miss Bingley's demeanor relaxed. She assayed a slight smile, the expression foreign to her lips. "Well, he must be a person worth knowing, then. I'm pleased to hear that is what kept you. I'd feared some ill had befallen Miss Elizabeth."

Darcy suspected that was more likely what she'd hoped. "I must speak to Mr. Fitzwilliam. Do you know his whereabouts?"

Miss Bingley nodded. "He retired to his room after luncheon, to compose a letter." Her frown reappeared. "Did the Bennets offer you luncheon?"

"The nature of my instructions to Mr. Collins precluded such an offer." In truth, he's forgotten about food. Now that Miss Bingley mentioned luncheon, hunger assailed him.

Miss Bingley sniffed. "A house full of women and not one a competent hostess. Of course, how could they be with Mrs. Bennet as their example."

Darcy made no comment, waiting to see if Miss Bingley would offer to have a tray prepared for him.

"Well, as you and Mr. Fitzwilliam will be occupied, I suppose there shall be no cards," she said after a moment. "I shall read in the green parlor. Miss Darcy is practicing there." Miss Bingley aimed one of her near-smiles at him. "I do so love listening to Miss Darcy play. I could listen to her for the rest of my days."

Darcy had no reply to that, either.

"Good afternoon, Mr. Darcy," Miss Bingley offered after a lengthy pause.

"Good afternoon, Miss Bingley." He turned and headed up the steps. Darcy sought his own quarters first, and his valet. He ordered a tray be brought, then headed to his cousin's room. "I hope I am not imposing," he said as Disher showed him in.

"Not at all." Richard turned from the desk, writing materials arrayed before him. "I'm only writing to Walter. He thanks you for your advice, by the way."

"He is most welcome."

"You missed luncheon," Richard observed as he stood. He crossed to join Darcy in the sitting area. "Miss Bingley mentioned that you were with Miss Elizabeth." Richard met Darcy's daze squarely. "Is there aught I should know?"

Darcy met his cousin's teasing with a frown. "There is, but not in the way you think," he said, and went on to inform Richard of the morning's revelations about Georgiana, and then the details of Miss Lydia's report and the subsequent lesson for Mr. Collins. The tray arrived as Darcy spoke, but he didn't avail himself of food until he'd finished his tale.

Richard sat back in his chair, expression thoughtful. "I don't remember fencing with Wickham. What kind of swordsman is he?"

Darcy speared a slice of cold beef. "Better than anyone could be after a week or two of training."

"If Mr. Bennet is sensible, he will delay the duel for months."

Darcy shook his head. "Wickham is pushing for a duel soon."

"Mr. Collins has every right to delay. Half the purpose of a formal duel is to give men time to have second thoughts."

"Wickham can't back down." Darcy slathered on mustard. "He would lose the respect of his fellow officers."

Richard offered a knowing grin. "And no one would take his word or his IOU's."

Darcy nodded, for that was likely Wickham's primary concern. Wickham always had trouble paying his debts and generally extended a significant number of IOUs. Not legally enforceable, debts of honor were only as valid as Wickham's façade. While Darcy doubted Wickham cared about his personal honor, having little, he surely cared about his ability to extend IOUs to his fellow officers. No, they weren't likely to dissuade Wickham from this duel.

***

Elizabeth woke the following morning feeling decidedly unsettled. Her night had been filled with dreams of Mr. Darcy. Over and over, she saw him in his waistcoat and shirt, sleeves rolled up, sword in hand. For a gentleman who generally appeared reserved to the point of being stiff, he moved with surprising grace when he fenced. Fluid, precise, elegant of form. Descriptions she'd never thought to apply to Mr. Darcy.

More than that, he'd been patient. He'd repeated words and movements over and over for Mr. Collins, who appeared even more awkward than usual by comparison to Mr. Darcy's polish. Elizabeth had heard the instructions enough times to try her serenity, but Mr. Darcy showed not a flicker of frustration.

To her continued annoyance, visions of Mr. Darcy in his shirtsleeves remained with her as she readied for the day, as she helped Jane with her hair, and even into breakfast. Elizabeth couldn't concentrate on Jane's attempts to converse, and repeatedly found herself shredding her food rather than eating it. Keen relief filled her when Mr. Bennet appeared, for Elizabeth required a more forceful distraction than Jane, who'd fallen silent after Elizabeth's second murmured apology for her lack of attention.

Mr. Bennet greeted them and sat. Though he usually filled his own plate, he gestured over a footman and requested food. Elizabeth observed her father carefully and decided he looked a bit improved. Mr. Bennet still ate less than usual, but at least he ate. She attempted to follow suit as more of her relations filed into the room.

Soon, the table was full. Elizabeth's mother and younger sisters saturated the room with chatter, but Mr. Collins appeared pale and spoke not a word. He, too, toyed with the food on his plate, but Elizabeth suspected he didn't suffer from dreams of Mr. Darcy, unless they were of Mr. Darcy commanding him to repeat a lunge over and over.

"Mr. Collins," Mr. Bennet said. "You were learning very quickly for someone who has never fenced."

Mr. Collins looked startled. "I felt very awkward. I doubt I have a chance against Mr. Wickham." He swiped a shaking hand across his face. "I am afraid he will kill me."

Mrs. Bennet looked over, expression pleased. "That would break the..."

"Our hearts," Kitty interrupted.

Everyone at the table, with the possible exception of Mr. Collins, knew Mrs. Bennet was going to mention the entail. Elizabeth doubted her mother was correct. Weren't there more male relatives lurking about, ready to swoop in when the time came? She glanced at her father and hoped that time was quite far off.

Mr. Collins aimed a surprised look at Kitty. "Your hearts?"

Kitty nodded. "Even though we've only known you a short time, we wouldn't want you to die."

"I think it would be exciting," Lydia said, earning a glare from more than Kitty.

Mr. Collins' expression clouded.

Kitty turned back to him, mien earnest. "She doesn't mean that, Mr. Collins. None of us want you to die. I pray you receive not even a scratch. The thought alone nearly breaks my heart."

"And there are other living heirs if Mr. Collins were to die," Mr. Bennet said, aiming his words at Mrs. Bennet. "Ones possibly less amiable. Mr. Collins came to us in good faith, after all."

Mr. Collins stared at Kitty, apparently oblivious to Mr. Bennet's words. "Would you really be heartbroken if I died, Miss Kitty?"

"Yes." She gave a vigorous nod. "You are so very brave."

Mr. Collins sat back in his chair, blinking rapidly, expression confused. "Brave? I'm shaking. Still. I am afraid of swords and more afraid of pistols." He swiped a trembling hand across his face again. "Even if I survived a duel with pistols, the thought of a ball being dug out of me gives me a cold sweat. I barely slept last night. Mr. Darcy fenced with me for less than an hour, and my muscles are sore. There is no way I can learn enough in time to beat Mr. Wickham."

"But you aren't backing down," Kitty said, adoration shimmering in her eyes. "You're doing what you think is right even though it frightens you. That's bravery."

"The very definition of it," Mr. Bennet added.

Mr. Collins spared him a glance before turning back to Kitty. "Miss Kitty, do you really admire me? I spent the night wondering what my life is worth. I have no one. No one cares for me. Yet, your family took me in. Your father got up from a serious illness and offered to be my second. I came here to find a wife because I need one, and not only to find someone who can run my household. I can't bear the thought of empty evenings with no conversation. Miss Kitty, if you truly do admire me, will you marry me?"

Several gasps sounded, Kitty's among them. Elizabeth pressed a hand to her cheek, shocked. A glance showed her father serene, her mother gaping, and revealed Lydia's frown. Mary and Jane, to their credit, both appeared happy.

Kitty's eyes glowed. "Yes. I will marry you, Mr. Collins."

"That is most generous of you, Kitty, if I may call you that? Know that you have made me the happiest of men."

Lydia's frown curled into a look of disgust, but Mrs. Bennet snapped her mouth closed and turned her lips up in a smile. Elizabeth smiled as well, for her mother didn't appear ready to engage in a fit, and Kitty truly did look happy.

Mr. Collins turned to Elizabeth's father. "Mr. Bennet, I would like permission to marry your daughter, Miss Kitty."

He studied Mr. Collins for long enough to make the man squirm, and cause Kitty to turn toward him in worry. "You have it."

"Oh, but this is marvelous," Mrs. Bennet cried. She stood and came around the table to wrap Kitty, chair back and all, in a hug. "This way, if Mr. Collins di—"

"Mama," Elizabeth cut her off. She leveled a hard look on her mother and stood to go about the table to hug Kitty. At that signal, Jane and Mary stood as well. They all took turns embracing and congratulating Kitty, except for Lydia, who watched with her lips pressed into a pout.

"When will you wed?" Jane asked, looking between Mr. Collins and their father.

"Oh, we must marry before Mr. Collins' duel," Kitty cried, expression aghast. "And then you must still wait longer, for they cannot expect me to let you risk yourself too soon after our wedding. That would be cruel."

Mr. Collins tugged at his cravat, shakiness returned. "Yes, I hope to delay the duel until after our marriage. The banns need to be read."

"It is my hope that I can delay it for months," Mr. Bennet said firmly. "Mr. Wickham pressing for an early duel is inappropriate. You must have longer to prepare. It may make no difference, for we have no idea of how good Mr. Wickham is, but you may stay at Longbourn and practice until you are married. Then you can take Kitty to your parish and I will delay the duel for as long as possible."

"I believe some of Sir William's sons fence," Elizabeth put in. "We were going to visit them this morning and see if they will assist Mr. Collins."

"So I overheard yesterday in the garden." Mr. Bennet turned to Mr. Collins. "I'm sure additional instruction will do you good. Already, your progress was impressive."

Elizabeth wondered if that were true or if her father simply attempted to bolster Mr. Collins' confidence.

"Thank you, sir." Mr. Collins expression grew a bit pained and he looked about the room. "There is one small thing."

Mr. Bennet raised his brows.

Mr. Collins cleared his throat. "Uh, that is, I have only my living and an income from a thousand pounds. Miss Kitty will not be living in the style to which she is accustomed."

Mr. Bennet took a sip of coffee. "After my death, she will live very much in the style she is accustomed to," he said dryly. "You will inherit an annual income of two thousand pounds. You could pay a curate and still have much more than fifty pounds left over from your living."

"But it is my hope you will live a great number of years more, sir," Mr. Collins said with evident sincerity.

Mr. Bennet nodded. "You make a fair point." He took another sip of coffee. "I would be happy to pay you fifty pounds a year in my lifetime, but after my death, the money will be needed for the remainder of my family."

Mr. Collins opened his mouth. Kitty turned a love-infused look on him. He shut his mouth, cleared his throat, and looked about the room. Jane still smiled. Mary's face was as blank as Elizabeth endeavored to make her own. Mrs. Bennet and Lydia both scowled.

Mr. Collins swallowed and tugged on his cravat again. "You are a very wise man, Mr. Bennet. It shall be as you say."

Chapter Sixteen

After breakfast, Elizabeth and Kitty took Mr. Collins on a visit to the Lucases. Jane remained to keep their father company, while Mary cited the many duties she liked to take on around Longbourn, as well as her studies, for declining to accompany them. Lydia simply refused, offering Kitty a glare for posing the question.

Elizabeth didn't mind. Charlotte was easier to converse with when Elizabeth's sisters weren't there. Aside from Jane, Charlotte Lucas was Elizabeth's dearest friend and much better company than Mary, Kitty or Lydia. Although, distanced from Lydia, engaged and pondering the prospect of having her new husband taken from her nearly as quickly as she gained him, Kitty behaved in a more thoughtful and subdued manner than normal, making her a better companion.

As Elizabeth suspected, the three older Lucas brothers were enthusiastic about helping Mr. Collins learn to duel. They quickly collected gear and went outside to mark off a practice area, which one of the Lucas boys insisted should be called a piste. Elizabeth, Kitty and Charlotte watched as each one, in turn, fenced with him, while he did his best both to learn and to fulfill his obligation to spread the real reason behind the duel. Much as they'd all feared, rumor already had Mr. Collins connected to Miss Darcy in various ways, most of which made Kitty scowl.

While the men moved about the practice field with varying degrees of grace and Mr. Collins' monologue filled the air, the Lucas brothers provided him with advice. Some of it may have been useful. A surprising amount proved contradictory. At each instance of opposing advice, Elizabeth and Charlotte exchanged amused looks. Kitty seemed too focused on the rumors flying about concerning her intended and Miss Darcy to notice what else the Lucas brothers said.

"Mr. Fitzwilliam," the Lucas' butler announced, standing inside the kitchen doorway.

Mr. Fitzwilliam thanked the butler by name and strode into the yard. Askance, Elizabeth didn't miss the way Charlotte's expression brightened. She turned to scrutinize her friend more fully as Mr. Fitzwilliam came over to bow to them. To Elizabeth's amazement, Charlotte's cheeks tinged pink.

Mr. Fitzwilliam bowed, greeted Charlotte, Elizabeth and Kitty in turn and finished by saying, "I am triply rewarded for calling today."

"Fitzwilliam," John Lucas, the eldest Lucas brother, called with easy familiarity. "Come, let me test your mettle. We're teaching Mr. Collins to duel. He could use an example of the real thing."

A frown played across Mr. Fitzwilliam's face. "Yes, Darcy told me of the challenge," he said in a low voice, aimed at Charlotte. Mr. Fitzwilliam shook his head, expression one of regret, but mustered his usual easy look before turning toward John Lucas. "I'd be delighted to put you in your place, Mr. Lucas."

All the Lucas brothers chuckled, as did Mr. Fitzwilliam. Mr. Collins attempted to smile, appearing unsure of the joke.

Elizabeth regarded Charlotte with raised eyebrows. She'd heard Mr. Fitzwilliam called on the Lucases frequently but... "Mr. Fitzwilliam seems to know your family well, and it's a bit early for general social calls."

"You are here," Charlotte said, but pink still tinged her cheeks.

"Yes, because I know you well enough to call early," Elizabeth said. Charlotte's blush deepened.

"How often does Mr. Fitzwilliam visit?" Elizabeth asked.

Charlotte turned redder still. "Shh. I'm trying to watch the duel."

Elizabeth left off teasing. Hope suffused her that Mr. Fitzwilliam, a very worthy seeming gentleman, returned her friends obvious affection. The way he'd addressed Charlotte, giving voice to his worry instead of putting on a good face, bespoke of a certain amount of intimacy, but was it simple familiarity or admiration?

The other two Lucas brothers hustled Mr. Collins off to the side and they all turned to watch as John Lucas and Mr. Fitzwilliam saluted. The bout began with several quick feints on Mr. Fitzwilliam's part, which Elizabeth judged were to test his opponent's skill, before he launched a full-fledged assault. In short order, it became obvious that Mr. Fitzwilliam held far greater skill than John Lucas. He made John Lucas look like he'd never before held a blade.

The bout ended with both men bowing. John Lucas laughed and wiped his brow. "I know when I'm outmatched, sir. I'd say you're the one who should be instructing Mr. Collins."

"And me," one of the younger Lucas brothers called.

The other nodded his agreement. Soon, Mr. Fitzwilliam became wrapped up in instructing all four other men. At one point, he cast an apologetic look Charlotte's way. She offered a shrug and a smile.

Mr. Fitzwilliam's gruffer style more fully revealed how inept Mr. Collins was than had Mr. Darcy's patient repetition of techniques or the Lucas brothers' fumbling attempts to instruct. Kitty bit her nails as she watched and resisted all attempts to draw her into conversation. Elizabeth gave up trying to ease her sister's mind and turned back to Charlotte.

"Mr. Fitzwilliam instructs like a general," Elizabeth observed.

"He was a colonel, until he inherited property from his aunt. An estate somewhere in Kent, I believe."

"Yes, Miss Darcy mentioned that." Elizabeth considered more teasing but decided to respect the privacy Charlotte obviously wanted. She changed the subject. "It looks like fun."

"It could be fun." Charlotte issued a droll smile. "And, if we ever actually got in a hit, it would be a great blow to our opponent's ego."

"Too bad we can't learn to fence and then challenge Mr. Darcy," Elizabeth said. "His ego needs a great blow." Though he'd behaved well the afternoon before.

"You tried to offer one," Charlotte said, in obvious reference to Elizabeth's actions at the assembly.

"Yes, but we have no idea if I succeeded." Could her set down be the reason for his improved behavior? "Have we?"

Charlotte offered a secretive smile with a shake of her head. "We don't know."

Charlotte's answer could mean that neither of them had the information or that they didn't both have the information, and Elizabeth suspected the latter. Having already resolved not to pry, she returned to watching the gentlemen. To her eye, Mr. Collins truly was improving at a steady pace, though he still appeared quite clumsy and slow, especially compared to Mr. Fitzwilliam. She wondered, unable to judge through watching each of them square off against Mr. Collins, who was the better fencer, Mr. Fitzwilliam or Mr. Darcy.

***

The next morning when they all met for breakfast, Mr. Collins walked with visible stiffness. He pulled out a chair for Kitty, then eased into his own with a grimace. He lifted his arm to reach for the pot of coffee before Mr. Bennet, but let it fall back to his side, coffee unclaimed. Kitty retrieved the pot and poured some for Mr. Collins. He offered a grateful smile that made Elizabeth's sister beam.

"Perhaps you should take a day off from fencing," Jane said sympathetically.

"Lady Lucas said Mr. Collins should take all the practice he can," Mrs. Bennet said.

Mr. Bennet, in better color this morning, reclaimed the coffee pot. "Recuperation is part of learning."

"I will take tomorrow off," Mr. Collins said.

Kitty smiled at him, as if his agreeing to take off the following day, Sunday, was the most intelligent decision a man ever made. Elizabeth stood and went to the sideboard to hide her amusement. She'd never thought to see either of her two youngest sisters more than superficially smitten, and certainly not by the likes of Mr. Collins.

"The banns will be read tomorrow." Kitty directed another besotted look at Mr. Collins.

"You should wear your green dress," Mrs. Bennet said. "You look sallow in any color but green."

"May I borrow your hat, Lydia?" Kitty asked. "The one with the green and cream ribbons?"

Lydia sniffed. "You may not."

Kitty regarded her with a hurt expression.

"I have extra green ribbon," Mary offered Kitty.

"And I have a hat I haven't had time to trim," Elizabeth said, returning to the table.

"Lydia already has a hat that goes with my green dress." Kitty glared at their youngest sister. "Why can't I wear it?"

"Loan Kitty your hat, Lydia," Mrs. Bennet said. "She is to marry, and she will be mistress of Longbourn someday, so you shall have to be kind to her."

Lydia crossed her arms over her chest, expression obstinate as she regarded Kitty. "She may borrow my hat when the officers stop avoiding us."

"What do you mean?" Jane asked, looking to Lydia in surprise.

148

"Aunt Phillips invited some officers for dinner last night and they declined. It's all because of Mr. Collins and his stupid duel." Lydia shifted her glare from Kitty to Mr. Collins.

"Mr. Collins didn't challenge Mr. Wickham," Mary said.

"But he insulted him. It's Mr. Collins' fault," Lydia complained.

This degraded into an argument that ended with Mr. Bennet retreating to his room. Mary gave up and went to the parlor to practice, hammering out loud, discordant notes that didn't overcome Kitty, Lydia and Miss Bennet's screeching. Mr. Collins fled to the yard to go through the practice forms Mr. Darcy and Mr. Fitzwilliam had given him. Elizabeth elected to take a walk.

She walked toward Netherfield, unaware of where her feet took her until she crested a hill to look down on the manor. She considered calling on Miss Darcy, but the hour was still quite early. Yes, Miss Darcy had taken that liberty, but Elizabeth wouldn't be so presumptuous. As she watched, a lone rider left the stable. The gentleman, taller than Mr. Bingley and not so rigidly upright as Mr. Darcy, angled his mount across country, toward Lucas Lodge. Though she felt a pang of sorrow, suspecting that she could soon lose not only Jane and a recently more-bearable Kitty, but Charlotte as well, Elizabeth smiled. She was desperately happy for her dear friend. With a sigh, she turned and headed back to Longbourn.

At church the following morning, sidelong glances and cold shoulders mingled with effusive greetings and smiles. Evidently, people had elected to take sides in the coming conflict. Elizabeth didn't mind, finding no surprises as to who remained friendly to her family.

As Mr. Collins made his way through the church, movements noticeably awkward and stiff, the cacophony of murmurs rose. Kitty, at his side, held her nose in the air and aimed a scowl at anyone she saw eyeing him unfavorably. Elizabeth hoped her sister couldn't sort out individual words from the general din of the congregation, for most were whispered predictions that Mr. Collins would lose the coming confrontation.

Still, no one protested when the banns were read, and Kitty received many congratulations. If some of their neighbors were notably absent from the well-wishers, and others offered their felicitations in tones tinged with sorrow, Kitty either didn't notice or didn't mind. With Mr. Collins by her side, her smile held a joy that made her beautiful, and her eyes sparkled. After the service, the first their father had attended in several weeks, Mr. Bennet confided in Elizabeth that, overall, the morning had gone more smoothly than he'd expected.

The following day practice at Lucas Lodge resumed, with several new additions in the form of Mr. Long and the two Goulding brothers. To Elizabeth's amusement, Lydia also joined them. She frowned as she watched, but Elizabeth could tell she enjoyed seeing the men in shirtsleeves and waistcoats, dancing about the practice areas they'd marked off.

"What are they all doing here?" Kitty asked, as two more young men arrived, asking to participate.

"I suspect they've felt a bit neglected by the women of Hertfordshire since the arrival of so many officers and other eligible gentlemen," Charlotte said.

"And they're here to support your Mr. Collins," Elizabeth added, mostly to induce Kitty's worried look to transform into a smile.

"They are not here to support Mr. Collins," Lydia muttered before raising her voice to call, "Mr. Long, are you here to support Mr. Collins?"

Mr. Long turned toward the benches where Elizabeth, her sisters and Charlotte sat. "I am. It was cowardly for an officer to challenge a clergyman, and everyone knows as much."

This evoked a round of *hear! hear!* from the other young men, though Mr. Fitzwilliam simply watched with mild amusement.

Lydia tossed her head. "A clergyman can't hide behind his profession."

"I'm sorry you feel that way, Miss Lydia," Mr. Long said and turned back to his opponent, one of the younger Lucas brothers.

Lydia's expression folded into a pout, but she didn't elect to defend Mr. Wickham again. Elizabeth was again called on to hide her amusement. Obviously, as she'd been deprived of officers, Lydia needed someone with whom to flirt. As uninterested in flirting as Elizabeth was, even she knew it was easier to flirt with a man when you weren't arguing with him.

Chapter Seventeen

After several days of trying, and finding Richard gone each morning, Darcy set an appointment to take a walk with his sister and cousin. They stepped outdoors to chilly, blustery weather, but that couldn't be helped. Not when Richard had been unavailable the past few mornings and Georgiana was becoming increasingly displeased with Darcy's constant hovering. He'd no desire for her to hear rumor of the duel until he and Richard could speak to her, so he hadn't permitted her from his sight during waking hours.

As they descended the steps of Netherfield, Darcy cast an appraising eye on the inky clouds. A little rain wouldn't deter him. In truth, it may be a boon. The inclement weather would keep Miss Bingley from one of her so-called accidental meetings with them. Bingley's sister would never risk appearing before Darcy and Richard bedraggled by rain.

With a glance about to ensure no one else trod the garden paths, Darcy set a quick pace. He led Georgiana and Richard to the shelter of a grove of ancient oaks and halted, praying the clouds wouldn't open in a deluge before he could conclude the upcoming discussion.

"Well?" Richard said as he and Georgiana turned to face Darcy. "You've obviously brought us out here for a reason, Darcy."

"So no one will overhear us," Georgiana said. She rubbed her arms and tugged her shawl tighter. "And they won't. No one sane would come out in this weather."

Darcy nodded. "Georgiana, Miss Elizabeth described what happened in Ramsgate differently from what I understood, and I repeated her words to Richard, but I would like to hear the story from you. Please recount what occurred." He locked gazes with her. "What truly occurred."

Georgiana let out a sigh.

Richard held up a hand, staying speech. "You were aware Miss Elizabeth shared your confidences?" he asked Georgiana.

She nodded. "I told her to. I wished my brother to know, but I've been too great a coward to broach the subject." She offered Darcy an embarrassed grimace.

Richard nodded. "Continue."

Georgiana drew another deep breath and launched into her tale. She gave details of her interactions with Mr. Wickham and Mrs. Younge, not in chronological order, but a clear picture emerged. Darcy attempted to keep his anger in check, aware that Richard studied his reactions as much as he watched Georgiana.

By the end of his sister's recounting, Darcy felt relief on two counts. He'd long worried that paying Mrs. Younge full wages and giving her money for transportation of herself and her belongings back to London was inadequate if she had been duped, but Georgiana's information painted Mrs. Younge as an accomplice, not a victim. It also pleased Darcy that the long, disjointed description matched what Elizabeth had told him.

Georgiana ended by saying, "I am so very sorry. It was not that I wished to lie. I simply wished the whole incident to end as quickly as possible." She turned beseeching eyes on Darcy. "I wanted you to take me away from there."

Darcy nodded. "So Miss Elizabeth made me understand." He put a hand on his sister's shoulder. "I forgive you."

He dropped his arm and they both turned to Richard, who made a dismissive gesture.

"I forgive you as well, cousin." Richard eyed her shrewdly. "And that really is why you've been so quiet? Out of guilt for lying to us? You conceal nothing more?"

"Yes. At school we were taught that girls who aren't out should be quiet, obey orders from their elders, and not speak unless directly addressed, and then do so in a manner so as not to garner attention." She raised her hands, palms up. "I wanted to be perfect, to make up for what I'd done."

"A truly ridiculous recommendation for any young woman's behavior," Richard said.

Darcy raised an eyebrow. "An accepted recommendation."

Richard shrugged. "Either way, you can forget that, Georgiana. By letting you dance at the assembly, you are out."

"That was only practice." Darcy didn't wish his sister to be as meek as she'd been of late, but he did not want her behaving like Miss Lydia Bennet, either.

Richard shook his head. "Women who are not out do not dance at assemblies. Impromptu dances at private parties are acceptable, and are good learning experiences, but an assembly is altogether different."

"We aren't even in London," Darcy protested.

Georgiana appeared thoughtful. "Once someone is out, they can't go in."

"I think the opposite of 'out' is 'not out,'" Richard said. "Georgiana is definitely out."

Darcy aimed a frown at his cousin, Georgiana's co-guardian. "If you felt the act would constitute a come out, you could have protested and told me I was wrong to promise she could dance at the assembly."

"But you had promised it. I am not saying that Georgiana should have a full season in London this winter but attending a few events as an adult would probably be good. If you remember, that is what my sister did."

Darcy frowned. He didn't recall well, being some five years younger than Richard's sister. "She couldn't have been as young then as Georgiana is."

"She was sixteen, as Georgiana will be soon enough," Richard stated. "The real question is who will chaperone her. You, as of yet, are unwed."

"What do you mean by a few events?" Georgiana asked, her eyes sparkling with anticipation.

Richard chuckled. "More than your brother would like, but considerably fewer than you would."

Excitement unwavering, Georgiana looked back the way they'd come, toward the manor. "We can start here. Miss Bingley can accept invitations and invite people here. There are lots of opportunities for impromptu dances at private parties. Maybe Mr. Bingley can even throw a ball."

"Georgiana," Darcy protested. He glanced at Richard. Although Wickham had nothing to do with his original protest, Darcy grasped at the idea of him to support his case. "You know George Wickham joined the local militia."

She tipped her chin up. "So I learned at the Bennets, and I do not care. George Wickham means nothing to me."

She obviously didn't understand how much trouble Wickham could make for her if he'd a mind to. Ignoring that, Darcy said, "Be that as it may, what you do not know is that the Bennets' cousin, Mr. Collins, is going to duel Mr. Wickham over Wickham's treatment of you."

Georgiana's eyes went round.

"Point of fact," Richard inserted. "Mr. Collins is dueling Mr. Wickham because he abused your father's trust, not because he abused yours, Georgiana."

Darcy shrugged. "The exact reason is not my point." He hoped his declaration would subdue Georgiana's desire to socialize.

"But it is important." Richard's gaze held sternness. "And, even scared as he is, Mr. Collins has been making a concerted effort to be quite clear on the subject. He is not dueling over Georgiana. I am sure you appreciate the distinction, Darcy."

Darcy most decidedly did, but he frowned. "Regardless, putting Georgiana in the same company as Wickham can only harm her reputation. We should go to Pemberley."

"No," Georgiana said firmly. "That is cowardly. I can face Mr. Wickham with a clear conscience. Perhaps I didn't conduct myself as well as I should have, but I can do better now. Mr. Wickham is the man who courted me persistently and asked me to elope with him. I refused. I wrote you about it, even if the letter was never delivered. I told my governess about it. She continued to allow him access to me." Fisted, Georgiana's hands found her hips. "I will meet him in company on those terms. Why should I hide?" She looked back and forth between Darcy and Richard. "If anything, we should confront Mr. Wickham. We should make him back down from the duel. Let poor Mr. Collins stop being afraid."

Darcy stared at his sister, rueful. He'd wished for a return of her spirit. He'd received that wish, tenfold.

"She's right," Richard said. "If we leave now, we will be perceived as running away. The scandal will be worse. We shou—"

Richard whirled and held up a staying hand. A moment later, Darcy, too, heard footsteps. Light and quick, and accompanied by the swish of skirts. He suppressed a groan. He'd been wrong about the strength of the threat of rain.

Miss Bingley flittered into view between trunks, hurrying down the path. She sighted them and slowed, a smile touching her lips. "There you all are. I was wondering to where you disappeared. It's almost as if you have secrets."

Chagrin shot through Darcy. Georgiana frowned.

Richard gave a chuckle. "We do. Georgiana was telling us she wished you to accept more invitations."

Miss Bingley's expression lit with pleasure as she turned to Georgiana. "Why, certainly, dear. I shall be more than happy to, but let's get you inside before it rains. You'll catch your death, like that poor Miss Bennet. It's so unfortunate such a lovely girl is beset by ill health." She proffered her arm.

Georgiana favored Darcy with a grimace, but accepted Miss Bingley's arm. As Miss Bingley led her away, her voice drifted back to them. "The whole family, really. The lot of them are sickly. Mr. Bennet, Mrs. Bennet, Miss Kitty. I'm sure we shall discover Miss Elizabeth is, too. Such a shame."

Richard cast Darcy an amused look and headed after the women, leaving Darcy alone and disgruntled under the ever-darkening sky, glimpsed through the lingering leaves of the oaks.

***

Miss Bingley took the opportunity to make calls with Georgiana quite seriously, undoubtedly hoping that if she could show Darcy and Richard how good a companion she could be, one of them would marry her to secure a chaperone for Georgiana. Suddenly, they were about the community day and night. It didn't deter Miss Bingley in the slightest that Darcy and Richard insisted on accompanying them on their calls, as did Bingley, in the hope of seeing Miss Bennet. Mrs. Hurst and Mr. Hurst sometimes joined them, but more often remained at Netherfield.

A few evenings after their meeting in the oak grove found all six of them on their way to Lucas Lodge. Darcy hoped the Bennets would be present at the Lucases, since that would permit him to ask after Collins' progress. That, surely, was the only reason he wished to see any member of the Bennet family…to assuage his guilt for neglecting Mr. Collins' training after their initial session, which he had. Though, in his defense, Darcy had heard that Richard had things well in hand on that front, and Darcy had needed to keep a close watch on Georgiana.

When they arrived, well-played strands of music spilled forth from the parlor, and Richard suggested to Sir William's butler that they not be announced so they wouldn't interrupt. As they traversed the entrance hall, a lovely contralto joined the playing, the notes tugging at Darcy's heart. Beside him, Miss Bingley appeared quite put out, but she said nothing as their party entered quietly and stood at the back of the room, only noticed by a couple of people.

Despite certainty that he was only interested in Mr. Collins, Darcy's gaze swept over him, searching the room. To his delight, Elizabeth sat at the pianoforte playing that delicate, sorrowful tune that had washed over them in the entrance hall. Her voice, lovely and sincere, filled the space. From the corner of his eye, Darcy noted two women dab at their eyes. Finally, Darcy could listen to Elizabeth play and sing, and he wasn't disappointed. Calmness settled over him as she performed. Worry and fears melted away.

When her song ended, the room filled with applause. She stood to the sound of protests, but shook her head, declining to play again. As she moved to stand with her mother and Miss Bennet, Miss Mary scrambled forward to take her place.

"Oh dear," Miss Bingley said. "Now we shall be subjected to hours of Miss Mary's squawking. The Bennet sisters are surprisingly devoid of talent."

"Miss Elizabeth sang prettily." Richard's expression was bland.

"She has a skill for melodrama and the ability to tap out very simple tunes, but she shall never be as accomplished as Miss Darcy," Miss Bingley said. "There are much more sophisticated pieces, more lovely than a simple country ballad, that a young woman ought to learn to play."

"Such as?" Richard asked.

"Show him how a truly accomplished lady plays, Caroline," Mrs. Hurst commanded.

"I certainly will."

Miss Bingley angled her nose a notch higher into the air and stalked across the room as Miss Mary began to play. Dragging Mr. Hurst along, Mrs. Hurst followed after. Bingley, Darcy noted, already wended his way toward where Miss Bennet and Elizabeth stood. If only Collins were with them, Darcy would have a reason to join him.

"You're mean," Georgiana whispered to Richard, who stood on the other side of her from Darcy.

"I was saving us," Richard replied in an equally low tone.

"Miss Mary plays perfectly well," Georgiana said.

"I wasn't saving us from Miss Mary."

Georgiana giggled.

Miss Mary did play adequately. By Darcy's thinking, it wasn't the quality of her skill so much as how laborious she made that skill appear. She frowned, eyes riveted on the sheets before her. No emotion, let alone passion, sparked in her voice, so different from Miss Elizabeth's poignant contralto. Finally, Miss Mary's piece ended, and Miss Bingley stepped forward.

"Play something for dancing," Miss Lydia called.

Miss Bingley shot her an annoyed look, though at the heckling or because she wished to try her hand at making the women of the room teary-eyed, Darcy couldn't say.

"No," John Lucas said. "We can dance anytime. Let's fence. Mr. Fitzwilliam and Mr. Darcy are both here. They should give us a match."

Miss Bingley leveled a venomous look on John Lucas, but everyone else turned about, seeking Darcy and Richard. A wave of affirmation went through the room. Sir William Lucas pressed his way through the gathering. Darcy caught Mr. Bennet's amused look, where the other man sat far across the room. Darcy was pleased to see Elizabeth's father appeared healthier, though still thinner than when first they'd met.

"Mr. Darcy, Mr. Fitzwilliam." Sir William stopped before them. "What say you, lads? We've yet to see you square off. We've only Mr. Collins' recounting of your skill, Mr. Darcy."

"Darcy would probably like to keep it that way," Richard said, grin touched with taunting.

Darcy felt an unexpected surge of humor, which he tamped down as inappropriate. "There is no need for a bout. Mr. Fitzwilliam is the better fencer."

About the room, some of the enthusiasm died down at his refusal.

"They want to see for themselves," Georgiana said. "It's not so much to ask."

"Five shillings on Mr. Darcy," someone called from the back of the room, the voice suspiciously like Mr. Bennet's.

"Ten on Mr. Fitzwilliam," Mr. Hurst countered, evoking a scowl from Mrs. Hurst, beside him.

This set up a bit of a ruckus, under the cover of which Georgiana elbowed Darcy and whispered, "Fence with Richard. Everyone will enjoy it."

Darcy nodded, seeing no harm. According to Richard, fencing had, in the days since Mr. Wickham's challenge to Mr. Collins, become something of a local pastime. "I would be pleased to test myself against Mr. Fitzwilliam."

Good natured cheers answered that. Everyone headed outside. Chairs were brought for the ladies, along with tables, punch and cakes. Several practice fields were already marked off, the trampled earth showing the daily dedication of the Lucas sons and their companions. Darcy stripped off his coat, which he handed to Georgiana, then accepted fencing gear.

He had no delusions of his skill compared to Richard's and so was quite pleased to end the match with four of the ten hits. As an added boon, the young men at the event, including Mr. Collins, all mobbed Richard after the bout. Darcy counted his loss as a victory, for he was free to step off to the side and not fight again.

"Are you sulking?" a familiar, amused voice said as Darcy shrugged back into his jacket.

He turned to find Elizabeth beside his sister. Georgiana offered a mischievous look and disappeared before Darcy could halt her. He frowned, then turned to Elizabeth. Had she sought him for the purpose of teasing? If she had, he found he didn't mind.

"Actually, I am pleased," he said, adjusting his cuffs. "Most days, Mr. Fitzwilliam can beat me eight or nine times out of ten." Seeing her raised eyebrows, Darcy added, "He was a soldier for most of his adult life. He's had plenty of practice."

"Yes, Charlotte mentioned that," Elizabeth replied.

"He is also a better shot."

Her eyes sparkled. "I suggest you don't get into a duel with him."

"There is no danger of that."

"He is truly so skilled as to cow the formidable Mr. Darcy?" She turned to study Richard where he instructed Mr. Collins and a row of young men.

Darcy nodded. "More than that, he is unflappable. He spent more than a year in Spain, and often faced enemy fire."

"Well then, we are lucky he is here with us now," Elizabeth said. "He came back because he inherited? Charlotte said something about an estate in Kent."

Darcy hid his surprise. Where had Miss Lucas learned that? Richard had instructed them not to bandy about his wealth. Mr. Hurst, Bingley and Darcy were all men of their word, and Darcy couldn't imagine Miss Bingley or Mrs. Hurst letting that information out. Not when Miss

Bingley had designs on Richard. He looked to where his sister had disappeared. That left only Georgiana.

"That would be logical, but no. He was wounded and returned to England. After he recovered, his father ensured he had plenty of duties here. He may be a third son, but that did not mean the earl was above using his influence to ensure Richard spent no more time on the frontline."

Elizabeth's eyebrows shot up again. "He's also the son of an earl?"

Her pleased smile sent an odd stab of emotion through Darcy. He cleared his throat. "He is." Did she fancy pursuing his cousin? Visions of the two chatting amiably filled his head.

"Did Mr. Fitzwilliam resent his father's interference or was he grateful for it?"

Darcy gave his head a shake to dispel the images. "Both, I believe. He was not eager to go back, but thought it was his duty."

"Speaking of duty, I'm surprised no one has taken on the duty of reporting that a duel is contemplated."

"I am not."

Elizabeth turned a slight frown on him. "Dueling is illegal."

"Yes, but it serves a purpose," he replied, surprised she disapproved. Didn't young ladies romanticize dueling?

Her frown deepened. "What purpose? Getting someone killed?"

"Upholding a code of conduct that is an important cornerstone of society."

"Being the better shot or more accomplished swordsman does not mean a man is more right than another," she said angrily. "Such skill is certainly not a qualification to judge and execute people."

Darcy turned to face her fully, undeterred by her ire. "In the first place, few duels end with a death. In the second, if a man insults someone, he should be willing to risk his life to defend that insult."

She narrowed her eyes. "Suppose a great wrong is done, but the only people who know about it are poor fighters. They may conceal that wrong in fear of their lives. What justice is there in that?"

"True. Dueling is not perfect, but the possibility of a duel has a containing effect on society." Darcy held up a hand when she made to speak. "Even if you don't agree with the overt premise, consider this: Imagine Mr. Wickham killed Mr. Collins, but not in a duel. Your father might feel the need to retaliate. If he proved successful in killing Mr. Wickham, Wickham's fellow officers might kill your father. Scotland is full of such feuds, some lasting for generations. People accept duels and are less likely to retaliate, because dueling is seen as fair."

"But it isn't fair. Right does not belong to the best swordsman." Her gaze left him to take in Mr. Collins, then shifted to her sister.

"Perhaps not, but a formal challenge also allows a cooling off period. Sometimes it allows people to settle their differences without a duel. As your father realizes, duels are often delayed long enough for people to calm down and think better of it." Darcy understood her dismay. Mr. Collins stood in the right, yet Mr. Wickham might kill him, and deprive Miss Kitty of a husband.

"I would still prefer the code of law to the code duello." She turned back to Darcy, eyes keen. "I am surprised at you, Mr. Darcy. I would have thought you would frown on any infraction in the law."

He shook his head. "There is the rule of law, and yes, I abide by it, but there is also an agreed-on code of conduct between men. A social construct. Maintaining that is just as important to the function of society, to staving off chaos and preserving our way of life."

"I will have to tell Charlotte that Mr. Fitzwilliam is the son of an earl," Elizabeth said.

Darcy blinked, taken off guard by the change in subject. "Why?"

She gave him a secretive smile. "We women have a code of conduct as well." Leaving Darcy flummoxed, she turned and headed around the practice area.

Startled as he was, Darcy simply watched her walk away.

Chapter Eighteen

The following morning, encountering Richard heading out for his ride, Darcy dutifully repeated his conversation with Elizabeth. He didn't wish to, but felt it his duty, as he did not wish to gossip behind his cousin's back. When he admitted to his inadvertent mention of Richard's father, his cousin grimaced, but didn't interrupt.

When Darcy fell silent, Richard let out a sigh. "She was bound to find out eventually."

Darcy frowned. "You care so greatly if Miss Elizabeth knows your father is an earl?"

Richard's startled look quickly morphed into amusement. "Do you?"

Darcy didn't know how to reply to that. Chuckling, Richard offered a nod and walked away.

That afternoon, as they had done for the past several days, they all piled into carriages to visit neighbors. Trying to sort out both his disquiet and Richard's amusement, Darcy avoided Elizabeth, instead standing off to the side. He repeated his withdrawal at their next stop, and the following, and into the evening.

Thus removed, he watched her interact with Richard, but saw nothing more than their usual easy conversation. Was easy conversation enough on which to base a relationship? Certainly, she smiled more often than when she spoke with Darcy, who usually ended up arguing with her.

From his self-imposed distance and without conversation with Elizabeth to distract him, Darcy had greater leisure to study those of his party. He noted, at each stop, how Georgiana entered, frame stiff with tension, but readily relaxed after surveying those present. Darcy suspected his sister feared meeting officers and felt relief each time they weren't in evidence. In addition to officers, they also didn't meet with several of the local families with whom they'd grown familiar. Darcy soon realized guest lists were being carefully selected along the divide the duel had created in the community.

Who they did meet, often, were the Lucases, Longs, Gouldings and, of course, the Bennets. Georgiana showed a growing preference for the company of Miss Lydia, which disturbed Darcy. He had little idea what to do about that, since avoiding Miss Lydia meant avoiding nearly all company available to them…and Elizabeth. He spent many anxious hours watching his sister and Miss Lydia laugh together and pondering whether to remove Georgiana to Pemberley.

In addition to watching Georgiana, Darcy took in the direct line Bingley made toward Miss Bennet whenever they attended the same gathering, and how his friend always spoke with her at great length. He watched Richard converse with seemingly every woman at each event, though always with Elizabeth and Miss Lucas twice. Darcy couldn't ascertain if this was deliberate, as the two were often side by side and Richard might count each interaction as half of their share of his time, as he spoke to both together.

Fencing marked many of their forays into the society of Hertfordshire. The community apparently couldn't get enough of watching Richard best their local men, who readily and good naturedly turned to him for additional instruction after each bout. Richard, true to form, fell into the role of commanding and instructing others with ease. But then, Richard did everything with ease.

Miss Bingley made a show of watching Richard in the makeshift pistes, though her sister disdained the bouts. While Mrs. Hurst wore an expression of perpetual aggravation during their outings, Mr. Hurst approached them with increasing livelihood. He started taking bets on who would win each match, and by how much, and soon was flocked by eager gamblers everywhere they went.

Mr. Hurst's gambling only increased his wife's general prickliness. Miss Bingley, to her credit, seemed unperturbed. She wasn't above a wager or two, especially if there were no card games to be played. She also added to their outings by entertaining on the pianoforte but declined to dance if Darcy and Richard weren't dancing. Darcy couldn't help but contrast her behavior with Elizabeth's, for she danced readily with other gentleman, then studiously avoided him when there was any opportunity to dance.

Did she believe he would belittle her again? How he wished he had not. His declaration that Elizabeth Bennet held no allure for him rang hollow in his memory. His own words taunted him. She held every allure, especially as she worked so hard to avoid him. If he asked her to dance, would she refuse and ruin her evening? Perhaps fear of that outcome made her avoid him.

If so, she was right to. He had every intention of asking her to partner him, if she ever allowed the opportunity, and, undoubtedly, she would refuse. She would see his attempt to dance as a repetition of the events at the assembly. And why shouldn't she? He'd never sought to make amends. As harm went, his unkind words at the assembly had been minor, but much as he would apologize if he accidentally bumped into someone, he should apologize for insulting her and for spoiling the assembly for her.

As he watched her each evening, usually across a room that resounded with chatter and mirth, he tried to plan the proper steps for such an apology. Should it be public or private? What could he say, other than that he was sorry?

At Lucas Lodge once more, over a sea of heads, some light, some dark, some with curled locks, others with straight, Darcy watched Elizabeth where she stood beside Miss Lucas. The two chatted with obvious amiability. Richard approached, bowed, and was readily welcomed. Darcy couldn't hear what they said, but he observed all three laugh. A wistful smile crossed his face, though he was glad they were enjoying themselves. Richard turned to Miss Lucas and said something more. She shook her head, still laughing, and made a shooing gesture as if to send him away. Richard placed his hands over his heart in mock hurt.

The way Miss Lucas' face glowed, her expression suffused with intelligence, made her almost acceptable to the eye. Miss Elizabeth added a look of feigned severity to the exchange. Richard regarded both with fondness. Darcy jerked back a half step.

If his offense of calling Elizabeth not beautiful enough to dance with should be apologized for, his offense against Miss Lucas necessitated an even greater apology. That he'd insulted her, he had no doubt, for she'd guessed the gist of it. Dancing with her had been the trial for losing the bet.

But if it was difficult to apologize to Elizabeth, an apology to Miss Lucas would not only be a strain on him, but on her as well. How could Darcy possibly apologize without compounding the injury. How could he admit to her that he'd thought she was the ugliest woman in the room? Even if, from what he overheard, she'd already guessed as much.

A sour feeling swelled in Darcy's gut. He glanced about at the cheerful, smiling assemblage. He had been the ugliest person in the room, even if it didn't show on his face.

***

Elizabeth and her family arrived at the Gouldings' lawn party to be informed the fencing was already underway. Jane, unmoved by the news, set out to find Mr. Bingley. Mary went inside to the parlor where the Gouldings kept their pianoforte, to ascertain if anyone lingered there in want of entertainment. Lydia and Mrs. Bennet set out in search of food. Both were bored with watching men who didn't wear red coats fence, but Mr. Bennet headed toward the fencing. He often assessed Mr. Collins' progress, and liked to keep tabs on Mr. Hurst's wagers as well.

Kitty took her intended over to Mr. Fitzwilliam, beseeching the former colonel for a practice duel with Mr. Collins. Elizabeth started to follow but caught sight of Mr. Darcy where he stood off to the side, watching. She angled toward him, happy to have some lively conversation. After all, at a garden party she was at little risk of his asking her to dance and ruining her day.

She moved to stand beside him, keeping her expression bland and her face angled toward the practice area. Mr. Fitzwilliam and Mr. Collins faced off. Across from where Elizabeth and Mr. Darcy stood, Kitty watched the two men fence with wide eyes and clasped hands. She cheered when Mr. Collins scored a hit.

Mr. Darcy frowned. "Mr. Collins looks leaner, but his clothes aren't loose."

"He is leaner. Kitty altered that shirt." Kitty was cheerfully doing for Mr. Collins what she resisted doing for anyone else.

As Mr. Darcy made no reply to that, Elizabeth returned to watching her cousin and Mr. Fitzwilliam fence. She was no expert, but it seemed that Mr. Collins' skill at dueling had increased tremendously. In no time at all, he'd won two out of four bouts.

When the fifth bout began, Elizabeth turned to Mr. Darcy. "He's made considerable improvement. I never thought I would see Mr. Collins score even one hit against Mr. Fitzwilliam, let alone reach a tie breaking fifth bout."

164

"He's not quite as good as he appears," Mr. Darcy said. "Mr. Collins is a tall man and long arms help, allowing him to win more often against a shorter man."

"Still, you cannot deny his hard work begins to pay off."

Mr. Darcy nodded. "He has improved more than I would expect anyone to improve."

"He asked my father for advice," Elizabeth said, feeling a touch of pride in both men. "My father isn't up to fencing, but he gave Mr. Collins some exercises to do, which he performs diligently."

"Exercises help," said a voice behind them.

Elizabeth turned, Mr. Darcy alongside her, to find Mr. Pratt, a lieutenant in the militia, who was not in uniform. She frowned at him. Out of the corner of her eye, she saw Mr. Darcy mimic the expression.

"You are wondering what I am doing here," Mr. Pratt said.

"Spying?" Elizabeth suggested. She hoped he hadn't overheard Mr. Darcy's statement that Mr. Collins was not as good as he seemed.

Mr. Pratt shook his head. "The Gouldings invited me, so I came. I'm not trying to take sides."

"So, you will report nothing that you've seen here to Mr. Wickham?" Elizabeth didn't hide disbelief from her tone.

Mr. Pratt shrugged. "That's not why I'm here, but I suspect Wickham will ask me, and I won't keep secret what I've seen."

"That makes you a spy," Mr. Darcy said.

Elizabeth cast him a quick look. Must he always sound so sure? "Not if he's open about it."

Mr. Darcy turned his frown on her.

Mr. Pratt gestured to the dueling men. "Mainly, I'm here because this is a very unusual form of entertainment."

Mr. Darcy still frowned, but Elizabeth knew that Lydia talked to members of the militia. The two opposing camps already shared information. Mr. Pratt reporting that Mr. Collins had scored a few hits on Mr. Fitzwilliam couldn't hurt Mr. Collins cause.

"You do not care for the other entertainments Hertfordshire has to offer, Mr. Pratt?" she asked, endeavoring to be civil.

"Fencing is an entertaining change from listening to music." Mr. Pratt offered an apologetic grimace. "I'm tone deaf." He gestured toward the practice area. "Mr. Fitzwilliam won."

Elizabeth turned to see Mr. Fitzwilliam, Kitty and Mr. Collins headed their way. Kitty scowled at Mr. Pratt, but both men wore neutral expressions.

"Pratt," Mr. Fitzwilliam greeted. "Come to evaluate our champion?"

Mr. Pratt looked Mr. Collins up and down. "Not specifically. I've come in hope of a bout."

"Mr. Collins is escorting me to get punch," Kitty said firmly. With another glare at Pratt, she clasped Mr. Collins' arm.

Elizabeth hid a smile.

Mr. Collins didn't protest Kitty's treatment of him, instead offering a stumbling bow as Kitty dragged him away and muttering, "Excuse us."

"I'll square off against you, Pratt," Mr. Goulding called.

Pratt nodded, offered them a bow of his own, and headed away just as Charlotte appeared. Elizabeth didn't miss that Charlotte had reached the practice area just after Mr. Fitzwilliam's bout ended, or that she walked up to stand beside him where he stood to one side of Mr. Darcy, not beside Elizabeth on the other. As one, all four turned to watch Mr. Pratt fence with Mr. Goulding.

"I'm surprised Mr. Collins did so well against you," Mr. Darcy said in a low voice to Mr. Fitzwilliam.

"It speaks well of your skill as a teacher," Charlotte said.

Much as Mr. Darcy had, Mr. Fitzwilliam spoke softly. "His first bit of success was legitimate. Then I saw Pratt circling the field and let Mr. Collins win again. It doesn't hurt to have Wickham more worried and Mr. Collins more confident." He gave a shrug. "Although it may not help. Wickham thinks I'm Walter."

"Who's Walter?" Elizabeth asked, a touch chagrinned to find Mr. Darcy in the right. Mr. Collins was not, indeed, as good as he appeared.

"Mr. Fitzwilliam's twin brother," Charlotte said, eliciting a startled glance from Mr. Darcy.

Elizabeth looked at Mr. Fitzwilliam in surprise. "You have a twin?" Was Walter as amiable as Mr. Fitzwilliam?

He nodded. "I do, and Wickham believes me to be him. Wickham saw me riding through Meryton a few days past and called me Walter. I turned to look at him and he touched his hat. As I am not Walter, I declined to return the salutation."

There was an uproar alongside the practice field. Elizabeth turned to see a group of men congratulating Mr. Goulding.

Mr. Pratt, expression rueful, wandered toward them. "I said I liked to watch fencing. That doesn't mean I'm good at it."

"I guessed as much and bet against you," Mr. Hurst said, following Mr. Pratt over, Miss Bingley trailing behind. "I set some pretty steep odds, too."

"Who had such unjustifiable faith in me?" Mr. Pratt asked.

Mr. Hurst chortled and nodded over his shoulder. "Miss Bingley. I don't mind taking a bit of money from my wife's sister, especially as I lost to her at cards last night."

"I should not have bet, especially at such odds," Miss Bingley said, joining them. "But I thought a soldier would be better at fencing."

"Not all soldiers are good fencers," Mr. Fitzwilliam said.

"Apparently not," Miss Bingley said, sourly. "You seem to fence well enough, Mr. Fitzwilliam."

Mr. Fitzwilliam chuckled. "I'm more interested in the fencing on a farm, the sort I need to keep my livestock from running off, although this is entertaining enough."

"You own a property?" Mr. Pratt asked. "I'm surprised you aren't there at this time of year."

Elizabeth was impressed that rumor of Mr. Fitzwilliam's inheritance hadn't reached the officers yet. Then again, he'd told Charlotte, and she'd told Elizabeth, who knew how to keep a confidence, not Lydia or Mrs. Bennet.

"I have someone managing my property who knows more about farming than I do," Mr. Fitzwilliam said. He cast Charlotte a sidelong look. "My property brings in a good income, but circumstances have made it so I'm short on funds. I'm happy to maximize my profit by not interfering with those who know what they're doing."

"You are lucky," Mr. Pratt said. "My income is dependent on my father's whim." He flexed his hand, as if it hurt, and Elizabeth wondered what she'd missed by not attending to the bout. "If you'll excuse me?" Mr. Pratt bowed, and left.

"What do you wager he runs and tells Wickham everything he heard and saw?" Mr. Fitzwilliam said.

"Not much," Mr. Hurst replied. "Terrible odds that he won't do that."

Chapter Nineteen

Mood light, Darcy, flanked by Richard and Bingley, strode up the steps to Netherfield. The three of them had been for a ride. Not fencing. Not to a luncheon. Not dancing, to a garden party, or any other such activity. Simply an afternoon with two of Darcy's most esteemed companions, spent riding about countryside that in its own way was nearly as lovely as Derbyshire.

The moment they entered, Bingley's butler, Andrews, stepped forward and cleared his throat, the sound the antithesis of Darcy's cheerful mood. "Sirs, there is a gentleman to see you, all of you." The butler's gaze lingering on Richard. "He claims extreme urgency."

"Did he give a card?" Bingley asked.

Andrews shook his head. "He said you would know him, sir, and I had a reason not to doubt him."

Bingley frowned, but nodded.

Darcy stripped off his outerwear, mind going over possibilities. A disgruntled officer, upset they'd sided with Mr. Collins? Worse, a disgruntled father? From Elizabeth, Darcy knew that Mr. Bennet was well enough to go about by carriage, but not to ride, though he improved daily. Was he now feeling up to a confrontation over Bingley's unsubtle attention to his eldest daughter?

They all followed Andrews not to one of the small front parlors, but the larger back one where the ladies liked to pass their afternoons. Standing near the fireplace, flanked by Miss Bingley seated to one side and Georgiana to the other, Walter waited within. He strode forward to meet them, then bowed.

"Walter," Richard greeted warmly.

Bingley looked back and forth between them, expression surprised. Darcy came forward to clasp Walter's hand in greeting.

Richard turned to wave Bingley nearer. "You know I have a twin brother."

"I do, but we've never met." Bingley extended a hand. "The resemblance is uncanny."

"So, I've been told," Walter said. "Please excuse my presumption in arriving unannounced. I'm afraid it's a matter of urgent, private family business. I don't mean to be an imposition."

"Not at all," was Bingley's predictable reply. "Do you wish to stay? Caroline can have a room made up."

"I would appreciate that," Walter said.

"What sort of family business?" Georgiana asked.

"Nothing to concern you, Cousin." Walter's tone was firm.

Georgiana frowned.

"No?" Richard looked between his brother and Georgiana.

"No. Especially not after the stunt she pulled," Walter said. Darcy raised his eyebrows, but before he could speak, Walter added, "If we could adjourn?" His gaze rested on Miss Bingley for a moment, then moved to Bingley. Walter ignored Georgiana's pout. "Please excuse my ill manners, but I really must speak with Richard and Darcy. Alone."

"Of course." Miss Bingley offered a brighter than usual smile. "Hopefully your business will be rapidly concluded. I should very much enjoy testing which of the two of you is better at cards."

Walter returned her smile. "That would be me, Miss Bingley. As the older brother, I am better at everything."

Richard snorted. "Hardly." He looked to Bingley. "May we monopolize your library?"

Bingley nodded. "As much as you like. I'm off to change."

Walter and Richard both bowed to the ladies. Georgiana's pout didn't waver. Darcy gave his sister a hard look, bowed to Miss Bingley, and followed the twins out.

They traversed the halls of Netherfield in silence, but as soon as the library doors closed, Darcy asked, "What did Georgiana do?"

"Bingley's butler let me in, likely thinking I was Richard," Walter said, taking a seat on one of the sofas that dominated the small library, Richard going to the one opposite him. "Miss Bingley and Georgiana were coming down the stairs, and Miss Bingley suggested I join her in the parlor for cards. Before I could correct her, Georgiana recognized me but called me Richard. I corrected Georgiana. I don't approve of deliberately trying to fool people, even if I fooled the butler accidentally."

Darcy nodded, taking a nearby chair. Perhaps he shouldn't have forgiven his sister for her lie about elopement so readily. Her return of spirit, coupled with the influence of Miss Lydia Bennet, seemed to be rendering her overly saucy.

"What business brings you?" Richard asked his brother.

"It's about Wickham." Walter's expression darkened. "And George Blackmore."

"George Blackmore?" Richard repeated, surprised.

"The man Richard saved Anne from three years ago?" Darcy added, in case there was another George Blackmore with whom the brothers were familiar.

"Yes, the George Blackmore that Richard killed."

"Defended himself and Anne against," Darcy corrected. "Richard was cleared of any wrongdoing."

Walter nodded. "He was. With two witnesses saying he attacked Richard with a sword," he nodded at Richard, "while you were unarmed. The magistrate could hardly do otherwise." Walter pushed a hand through his hair, a nervous habit picked up from the earl, but which Richard had long since shed. "Blackmore had a sister. She inherited what little he had."

"I know," Richard said. "She wrote me asking for money. I refused. She wrote me a second time when I inherited Rosings. I threw her letter into the fire and resolved not to pay to receive another from her."

"She sent me a package," Walter said. "Her brother's account book. She directed me to a page dated a couple of weeks before Blackmore presented himself to our aunt as a relative. There is a payment to G. Wickham for thirty pounds. Blackmore's sister said I should pay her whatever I think the information is worth."

Darcy frowned, trying to call Blackmore's letter from Sir Lewis to mind. The salutation had been penned, familiarly, to George, but the address had been somewhat obscured. "Have you paid her anything?"

Walter shook his head. "Not yet. I will pay her something though, because her information explains how Blackmore knew about Rosings. It also explains Sir Lewis' letter."

"So, Blackmore was never a relation." Darcy scowled. He should have followed his first instinct and had the man thrown out, no matter what Lady Catherine said. "Wickham described the Rosings of our youth and gave Blackmore that letter." That Wickham would trade a letter from a man who'd shown him care for a quick thirty pounds added to Darcy's ire.

"I've always wondered about that," Richard said. "Mystery solved."

Walter pressed a hand through his hair again. "I don't understand what Blackmore meant to accomplish."

"Likely, a legal, approved, marriage." Darcy's voice was flat. "Fortunately, Anne rejected his advances."

Richard's eyes glinted with suppressed anger. "She told me that she thought Blackmore meant to abduct her. That she almost escaped, but he caught her sleeve." He glanced at Darcy. "I never troubled you with the details, but I later discovered a carriage had been waiting nearby. One of the tenants saw the driver question the maid you sent out, and then leave rather quickly."

"Was he planning to take Anne to Scotland?" Walter asked.

Richard shrugged. "We'll never know if that was the plan or he only wanted to hold her for ransom. I attempted to locate the driver of the carriage but wasn't successful."

With his money, Darcy might have been more successful. He turned his frown on Richard. "You should have—"

Richard held up a staying hand. "I had resources enough. The man went to ground. The one thing I did get was a general description of the driver, from the same tenant. Enough that I can assure you now that the driver was not George Wickham."

Silence filled the library as they reflected on that possibility. Darcy hadn't considered that. Apparently, Blackmore, quite sensibly, hadn't trusted Wickham enough to have him drive the carriage. Or, Darcy grudgingly postulated, Wickham hadn't been low enough to participate in Anne's abduction. Low enough not to warn them, but not so immoral as to assist.

"I've always wondered, what was Anne doing in her father's office?" Walter asked.

Seeing no reason to go into three-year-old details of Anne's fears, Darcy said, "If you remember, Sir Lewis had been dead for about a year then. Anne was very close to him. She sometimes came downstairs to his office and curled up in his chair. Especially, when she wasn't feeling well."

"You should have written me in more detail," Walter said to his brother.

"Thanks to our father, I was sent to Spain very quickly after that. There was enough of a scandal that he wanted me out of the country." Richard smiled wryly. "He changed his mind when I was wounded."

"Does that make Wickham responsible?" Darcy asked.

172

Richard and Walter exchanged a long look. Walter pulled out a guinea and put it on the table. "My estate is not pulling in as much money as I could wish. I would like to marry, getting both a housekeeper and an heiress. Please tell me about Miss Bingley."

Richard picked up the coin and pocketed it. "Miss Bingley has twenty thousand pounds, which come from trade. She was educated in an exclusive private seminary and has manners that will allow her to pass in the best circles. She can be pettily nasty toward people she dislikes, but she is sufficiently awed by rank as not to create problems within our family. She plays the pianoforte quite well and has a fair singing voice. You've seen her, so I don't need to give a physical description. Her relatives will not cause you grief. In specific, her brother is a good connection to have, since he's universally liked. The Hursts have decent connections but have barely enough money to support their lifestyle and so may slightly impose on you."

Walter turned to Darcy. "Did either of us do anything wrong?"

Bemused by their demonstration, he said, "I suppose not," then turned to Richard. "Are you going to keep the money?"

"Yes." Richard ginned, but then his expression sobered. "I think it was a bit different when Blackmore tried to pass as a relative. He wanted more than simple information, all of which is publicly available." Richard shook his head. "Wickham must have known or guessed what Blackmore intended, and he obviously provided the letter."

"Perhaps," Darcy said bitterly. "Wickham will claim he sold information because he thought Blackmore was after a proper courtship. If pressed, he will probably claim that Blackmore stole the letter. There's no one to refute that." He turned to Walter. "Are you really interested in Miss Bingley?"

"Are you?" Walter replied.

Darcy's eyebrows shot up. "Heavens, no."

"Good. Heiresses are hard to come by. Especially those who are young enough to have children and would be acceptable to my family." Walter looked to Richard. "This isn't the woman you've hinted at being interested in, is it?"

"No."

A pang of jealousy hit Darcy. He readily conjured the easy way Richard and Elizabeth laughed together, and the way Richard sought her company twice at every gathering.

"Is there a problem, Darcy?" Richard's voice and expression were bland.

Darcy tugged at his cravat, suddenly too warm. "I beg your pardon?"

Richard exchanged another look with Walter and grinned. "It's not Miss Elizabeth."

"I didn't say—" Darcy halted his words even as Richard raised a hand to cut him off.

"You don't need to say."

"Who is Miss Elizabeth?" Walter asked, expression eager.

Darcy clamped his mouth closed.

"A local gentleman's daughter." Richard took no notice of Darcy's glare. "She's lovely and intelligent but has no dowry, a smattering of ill-mannered relations, and some relations in trade. So, no connections to speak of."

"Darcy doesn't need any additional connections or funds," Walter said.

"And Bingley seems sure to propose to Miss Bennet, so Miss Elizabeth does have connections," Darcy added.

Richard regarded him shrewdly. "Ones you already possess."

Darcy knew Richard was testing him, prodding to discover the depth of his interest. He glowered and asked, "What makes you think I'm interested in her?"

"Aren't you?"

Darcy wouldn't lie, even to himself, but a mixture of feelings swirled inside him. Foremost shone Elizabeth's bright eyes. He easily conjured her elegant form and often-wry tone, but behind that Mrs. Bennet screeched and Miss Lydia giggled, drawing Georgiana into worse and worse behavior. Instead of answering, Darcy stated, "I haven't seen you interested in anyone."

"Miss Lucas," Richard said.

"But she..." Darcy didn't want to voice that she was usually the least attractive woman in the room. He didn't need to. He suspected Richard knew what he was considering saying.

"Let's face it Darcy, my face is no prize."

"Hey," Walter protested with a chuckle. "We aren't that bad looking."

Richard spared him a half smile before turning back to Darcy. "I am of average looks. I know that. I also know that Miss Lucas isn't ugly.

174

She's simply plain, meaning ordinary. Bingley may go after beauty. You may go after liveliness and wit. Miss Lucas is sensible. Pleasant. Competent. And I love her."

"What's stopping you?" Walter asked.

"The very sensibleness that I esteem."

Darcy nodded with understanding. He'd faced the same quandary his whole adult life. "She would accept you even if she did not love or respect you."

Expression dour, Richard nodded. "I think she is in love with me, but I can't be sure. I wouldn't mind so much, except I want her to at least like me."

Walter sat forward on his sofa. "I would like to meet these women, and to get to know Miss Bingley better."

"You would marry her for her dowry?" Darcy asked.

"Probably. If she's acceptable, as Richard said." Walter frowned. "Oakhall Manor isn't grand. It isn't Pemberley or Rosings. It's not even Netherfield Park. I grew up in a grander place, but Arthur has two sons, so I'm not going to inherit. I don't mind. Oakhall Manor is my home." He grimaced. "But I've had some very bad luck the past few seasons. A hailstorm destroyed most of my wheat and that of my tenants. My stable was struck by lightning and it burned down, killing nearly all the animals in it. One of my most valuable tenants got sick and died. As a result, half of his spring planting didn't get done. His widow left with the children. I don't blame her, because she had relatives to take her in, but the timing was bad. I couldn't charge the new tenants very much because of the missed planting."

"You didn't write about all of that," Darcy said, taken aback. He may have offered different advice in his letters to Walter if he'd known the extent of the difficulties.

"I didn't want you to realize how badly I've bungled things," Walter said with a grimace.

"You couldn't have prevented all that," Darcy assured him.

"I hadn't realized how bad it's become," Richard said. "I'm sure I could find money to help you. When did the stable burn down?"

"Last week, and thank you, but no, little brother. Arthur already offered me a loan. I didn't take it. I don't like borrowing money. I'm not that desperate." Walter stood, prompting Darcy and Richard to do likewise. "But if I could add half the income Miss Bingley's dowry offers,

I believe I can recover. I would prefer not to sell or even to mortgage any land."

Richard shrugged. "Well then, let's go play cards with Miss Bingley." He turned and led the way from the library.

As they traversed the halls of Netherfield in search of an heiress and a card game, Darcy couldn't help but wonder if Miss Lucas harbored any affection for Richard, for he agreed with his cousin's assessment. The lady would accept almost any offer of marriage at this point, let alone one from a former officer who was the third son of an earl and master of an estate like Rosings. Few were the women in England who had enough in their own right to refuse a man like that.

Unbidden, Elizabeth's visage rose in Darcy's mind. Would Elizabeth refuse where her heart was not engaged? She hadn't deigned to dance with Darcy after his insult, but a dance was far from the offer of a lifetime of comfort and security. Still, mad as it might seem, Darcy had the unsettling suspicion that Miss Elizabeth Bennet was one to refuse any man she didn't hold in high esteem, no matter his standing or wealth.

And that idea terrified him.

Chapter Twenty

Two days before Kitty's wedding found Elizabeth heartily sick of sewing. They'd all come together to help Kitty with her trousseau, but they still weren't done. In general, the five of them, along with their mother, father and Mr. Collins, had spent many convivial afternoons together in the parlor, but with the wedding nearly upon them and a fair amount of work left to do, tempers were shortening.

"Ow." Mary stuck a pricked finger in her mouth.

"Did you bloody the fabric?" Jane asked, leaning over to look from where she sat on the other side of the same sofa, sewing the other end of the seam.

"I don't think so," Mary said around her finger. "Not this time." She offered Kitty a grimace. "I'm sorry. I know I keep stabbing myself."

"If Kitty had worked on this as she should have, we wouldn't have to do it," Lydia complained before Kitty could reply.

Kitty turned an overly sweet smile on Lydia. "Is your trousseau finished?"

"No." Lydia tossed her curls. "But I'm the youngest and it is logical that I get married last." She let out a huff of air. "I should have liked to get married first, but with us not being able to attend parties with the officers, I'm not meeting anyone." She leveled a glare at Kitty.

Elizabeth rolled her shoulders to loosen them. There was no use complaining either about the sewing or the lack of officers.

"If you are bored, Lydia, I'm certain Mr. Collins can be prevailed upon to read to us," Kitty said.

Mr. Collins looked up from the bible he studied, expression enthusiastic. "Yes, certainly. I should be more than pleased."

Lydia let out a groan.

Mr. Bennet lowered his paper. "Perhaps you can accompany me on a walk to Meryton, Lydia. I've indulged myself long enough. I'm still annoyingly weak, but I believe I can ride, and you can walk."

"All right." Lydia's tone held an undisguised sullen note.

Elizabeth exchanged an amused look with Jane. A trip to Meryton with their father wouldn't offer Lydia the chance to flirt with officers anywhere nearly as much as she wished.

"You never invite me on outings to Meryton," Mrs. Bennet groused. Unlike her daughters, Mrs. Bennet did not work on Kitty's trousseau. Having declared, 'the strain Kitty marrying a man who lives so far away is much too great,' Mrs. Bennet spent most of her time reclined on a sofa with a handkerchief over her eyes, napping.

Mr. Bennet folded his paper and eyed his wife. "Would anyone else care to join us? Mrs. Bennet? Mary? Kitty?" He turned to Elizabeth, expression slightly beseeching. "Lizzy?"

"I should be pleased to, Papa," Elizabeth said, aware her father didn't fancy an entire outing with only Lydia's chatter in his ears.

"And while you are gone, Mr. Bennet, since I will not be disturbing your reading of the paper, I can read psalms to the remaining ladies."

"Actually, Mr. Collins," Kitty said with a pleasant smile, "I believe it would do you good to stretch your legs. You've improved so with your practicing, and I realize you've done your routine for the day, but you haven't had a walk in some time. Walks are paramount for good form. Don't you agree, Papa?"

Mr. Bennet shrugged. Lydia scowled at Kitty.

Elizabeth set aside her sewing and stood saying, "Lydia, shall I fetch your bonnet?"

Soon all was in readiness and they made their way outside. Mr. Bennet had to use the mounting block, which he never had before. Elizabeth supposed it wasn't surprising, since he'd spent weeks in bed, but she didn't care for the stark reminder that he wasn't yet completely recovered.

The journey went more amiably than she expected. Mr. Collins and Mr. Bennet engaged in a debate about history. Lydia decided not to speak to any of them, presumably as some form of censure, which allowed Elizabeth to listen to the two men and insert occasional comments, to which both men attended and replied.

As they entered Meryton, Elizabeth's attention caught on four riders. She easily picked out Mr. Darcy, and she suspected two of the others were Mr. Bingley and Mr. Fitzwilliam, but, from afar, she didn't recognize the fourth gentleman.

The men adjusted their course to meet Elizabeth and her family. As they neared, Elizabeth's guesses proved correct and the visage of the fourth rider consolidated into a copy of Mr. Fitzwilliam's. Elizabeth looked back and forth between the Fitzwilliam twins and realized she would have difficulty telling them apart, especially if she met one without the other. The only clear sign she could pick out was that they wore their hair slightly different, but not enough to make it obvious who was who without both before her to compare.

The riders all dismounted, including Mr. Bennet. He did so slower than he used to, causing Elizabeth to look about for the nearest mounting block. Circumspectly, she moved to stand beside him, between him and Mr. Collins, whom she couldn't count on to notice if her father required a shoulder on which to lean. Her nervousness only increased when her father didn't immediately release his hold on his saddle, but he straightened and offered her a reassuring smile. The gentlemen from Netherfield each sketched a bow.

"Gentlemen," Mr. Bennet said. "A pleasant happenstance, meeting you all. Except, I feel I have not quite met you all."

Mr. Richard Fitzwilliam took a half step forward and introduced everyone to his brother, Mr. Walter Fitzwilliam. During the introductions, Elizabeth darted a glance past Mr. Bingley to Mr. Darcy, to see if he approved of her father's humor. His gaze, as was often the case, rested on her. He wore a slight frown, but she'd come to realize the expression was more thoughtful than censorious. At least, some of the time. She issued a quick smile to test his mood. His return smile sent a flutter of thrill through her. It was an oddly pleasant feeling, the realization that she could so easily evoke a smile from Mr. Darcy.

When the introductions were over, Lydia stepped forward and turned to Mr. Darcy. "Georgiana isn't with you?" Not waiting for him to reply, she focused on Mr. Walter Fitzwilliam. "Are you an officer?"

Mr. Walter Fitzwilliam shook his head. "Not me. That was Richard's ilk."

"Will Miss Bennet be joining you?" Mr. Bingley asked, looking past them, up the roadway.

"She will not," Mr. Bennet said.

Mr. Bingley appeared crestfallen, so Elizabeth said, "She is helping Kitty with her trousseaus." She couldn't resist adding, "I'm afraid Jane is very marriage minded of late."

Far from evidencing any alarm, Mr. Bingley's expression grew quite pleased.

"We could walk with you," Mr. Darcy said.

"Certainly," Mr. Bennet agreed.

"Let's stable the horses." Richard Fitzwilliam led the way to the stable, the others from Netherfield following.

Lydia watched with contemplative eyes. "At least he used to be an officer. That's something. I was too angry with him for helping Mr. Collins with fencing to consider him before."

Elizabeth shook her head. If Lydia paid any attention to other people at all, she would realize Charlotte already owned Richard Fitzwilliam's heart, and he hers. Elizabeth expected daily to hear the announcement of it.

"On your previous point, Mr. Bennet," Mr. Collins said. He turned to Elizabeth's father and resumed the discussion they'd been having.

Elizabeth turned to their father too, while Lydia's gaze searched the street for anything of interest. Mr. Bennet held his mount's reins loosely, no longer leaning on the animal for support, but his presence with them instead of the other men clearly meant he didn't feel up to walking the animal all the way to the stable, and then returning. Should she take the gelding? Or suggest that Mr. Collins do so? She waited for a break in Mr. Collins' monologue so she might do so.

The gentlemen from Netherfield returned before Mr. Collins ceased speaking and Richard Fitzwilliam went immediately to Elizabeth's father. "Mr. Bennet, allow me to take your horse."

"That would be appreciated." Mr. Bennet's tone held amusement, but no annoyance. With his insistence on risking his life for principle and his dedication to his daily training, they'd all grown in fondness for Mr. Collins and his idiosyncrasies, though Elizabeth strongly suspected only the latter point impressed her father.

As Richard Fitzwilliam led the animal away, Mr. Collins turned red. "I apologize, sir. I didn't think...that is, I wasn't aware...I mean, you rode here so I assumed..." He looked about as if for help.

"There is no need for concern, Mr. Collins," Mr. Bennet said. "I would ha—"

"Mr. Wickham," Lydia exclaimed happily, pointing.

Elizabeth turned to find not only Mr. Wickham, but also Mr. Denny, Mr. Pratt and Colonel Forster striding toward them, expressions a bit startled. Elizabeth realized they must have rounded the corner of the side street behind them and only just identified who they approached. To one side of her father, Mr. Collins's forehead instantly shone with sweat.

The soldiers could not turn around without appearing cowardly. Elizabeth's group wasn't moving at all. To walk away now would be a clear slight. Elizabeth turned slightly away from them, as did Mr. Darcy. Maybe the soldiers would ignore their group and move on.

"Mr. Wickham," Lydia repeated as they drew near.

Mr. Wickham was far from the only one to grimace. He pivoted toward her and halted a few feet away, the other officers doing likewise. "Miss Lydia."

Lydia's face split in a grin. "And Mr. Denny and Mr. Pratt and Colonel Forster."

Colonel Forster offered a nod but wore a deep frown. He stepped forward, toward Mr. Walter Fitzwilliam. "Mr. Fitzwilliam? Mr. Walter Fitzwilliam?" he asked, tone cold.

"Yes?" Mr. Walter Fitzwilliam's expression mirrored the confusion Elizabeth felt.

Colonel Forster's glower deepened. He squared his shoulders. "I understand you have been deceiving the good people of this district. You have been, subtly I admit, putting it out that you possess a large, wealthy estate. However, Mr. Wickham has informed me that your estate, Oakhall Manor, isn't very large or very rich. Indeed, it suffers what many similar estates do, a loss of tenants to factories. I think you owe the community an apology for allowing them to believe you are wealthy."

Mr. Wickham turned a false smile on Mr. Bingley. "This concerns you too, Bingley. I spoke to a servant from Netherfield Park who reported that Walter has been most attentive to Miss Bingley. I don't know how he managed to fool you, or why Darcy is permitting it, but I recommend you challenge both to a duel."

Mr. Bingley turned a look of confusion on Mr. Wickham. Mr. Darcy met Elizabeth's gaze, expression grimly amused. She returned his wry smile, quickly able to guess what transpired. Peripherally, Elizabeth also noted her father's amusement and Mr. Collins' confusion. Lydia appeared frustrated, likely due to being so near officers and not able to converse freely with them. Mr. Bingley opened his mouth to speak, but Colonel Forster took another step toward Mr. Walter Fitzwilliam. Mr. Denny and Mr. Pratt made a menacing wall behind him, but Mr. Wickham stood to one side, grinning.

"Although I owe nothing to the Bingleys," the colonel said, "I don't believe any woman deserves to be deceived by a scoundrel. Do you admit Oakhall Manor isn't as profitable as has been represented?"

Mr. Walter Fitzwilliam cast Mr. Darcy a questioning, disgruntled look. "I had no idea my wealth or lack of it was the common knowledge of the community, but I will readily admit that Oakhall Manor no longer has the income it used to. In view of a recent occurrence, Oakhall is probably worth even less than you now believe."

Colonel Forster gave a sharp nod. "And your comments about the absence of ready funds being available were misleading at best. You have no expectation of ever making up the deficit."

Mr. Walter Fitzwilliam shook his head, confused. "I have made no such comments."

"Come now, there were numerous witnesses who reported them," Wickham said with satisfaction.

"I think your witnesses were speaking of me." Everyone whirled to find Richard Fitzwilliam approaching. "My brother, Walter, arrived yesterday."

Colonel Forster looked back and forth between the two, expression shocked. "What is this now? Explain, Mr. Wickham."

"They are twins," Mr. Wickham said. "Richard and Walter Fitzwilliam, but I am sure it is Walter Fitzwilliam who we want. He's the one with an estate. Richard Fitzwilliam is an officer and has no land."

"That's where you are wrong," Richard Fitzwilliam said in his usual easy manner, joining the loose semicircle of men. "I now possess an estate. One with which I believe you are *very familiar* from your youth, Mr. Wickham."

Mr. Wickham narrowed his gaze, then jutted out his chin. "How would you have an estate? You can't have Oakhall if Walter is alive. And if not to deceive, why would you go by mister and not colonel?"

"Because I sold out when I inherited Rosings."

"Rosings," Mr. Wickham gasped, jaw hinging open like a gaping trout, causing Elizabeth to stifle a laugh.

Colonel Forster looked from one twin to the other, then back at Mr. Wickham. "Is Rosings valuable?"

"About nine thousand pounds a year from tenants," Mr. Wickham stammered. "And the estate owns some prime farmland."

Colonel Forster's eyes went nearly as wide as Mr. Wickham's. "And you have a funds flow problem?" Colonel Forster asked Richard Fitzwilliam.

He shrugged. "There were many bequests in my aunt's will. They took all the available funds."

Mr. Wickham jabbed a finger toward Richard Fitzwilliam. "But I called you Walter. You turned around."

"And ignored you as you were not addressing me," Richard Fitzwilliam said. "I've always responded to Walter, since so many people confuse us."

Mr. Wickham took a step back, face paling. He shot Mr. Collins a quick look. "Then it wasn't Walter who Pratt saw duel with Mr. Collins the other day."

"No. It was me," Richard Fitzwilliam replied in a hard voice.

Mr. Wickham whirled to face Mr. Pratt. "You said Mr. Collins won two out of five?"

"That's what I saw," Mr. Pratt replied.

Mr. Walter Fitzwilliam appeared perplexed, but behind Richard Fitzwilliam's hard façade, amusement lurked. Though not twins, Mr. Bingley and Mr. Darcy mirrored that mixture, with Mr. Bingley obviously confused and Mr. Darcy not bothering to hide a grim smile. Elizabeth glanced at her party to see Lydia was paying impatient attention, Mr. Collins collar was soaked with sweat, and her father looked wan but entertained. She took a step nearer him in case he needed her.

"I don't see what any of this has to do with my sister," Mr. Bingley complained.

"Two out of five?" Mr. Wickham repeated, voice a bit weak. "Against Colonel Fitzwilliam?" He swallowed, eying Mr. Collins as if he'd never seen him before.

Colonel Forster gave Wickham a look of disgust, but Mr. Denny stepped forward. "Mr. Bennet is clearly well enough to act as second and Collins is rumored to be marrying soon and then leaving. The duel should be fought."

"This is not the first time I've left Longbourn since I became ill," Mr. Bennet said, "but it is the first time I haven't required a carriage. I am by no means well."

Elizabeth moved nearer still, worried by her father's words. Maybe he simply wanted to delay the duel, but she would not take any chances. If he faltered for being made to stand so long in the street, with such high emotions playing about him, she would be there for him to lean on.

"You are here in town, sir," Mr. Denny said. "You are well enough." He turned to Mr. Collins. "Do you have any excuses, Collins? Rumor has it you've been making ready to depart. Running like a coward, are you?"

Elizabeth frowned at Mr. Denny's derisive tone, but Mr. Collins squared his shoulders. "I am marrying in two days' time and departing for my parish, not running."

"I suppose you'll use your wedding as another excuse to delay the duel?"

Mr. Collins shook his head. "There is no need to delay. Everything is in order. Mr. Phillips, soon to be a relation of mine, was kind enough not to charge me for helping me write my will. I've left all I have to my intended bride."

"Then why the preparations to leave, if you aren't running?" Mr. Pratt asked.

"If the outcome of the duel turns out to be felicitous, I will want to leave the area quickly, possibly never to return."

Elizabeth raised an eyebrow. Didn't Mr. Collins expect to return to Longbourn when her father died?

"Of course, someday, I may be required to return, or in a position to return," Mr. Collins continued. "Certainly, I will need to return to Longbourn when I inherit, but I hope that will not be for quite some time. If I survive the duel, especially if I kill Mr. Wickham, I hope Mr. Bennet will live long enough that any repercussions from the duel no longer affect me. Not that the repercussions of killing Mr. Wickham are the only reason I wish Mr. Bennet well. Of course not. Certainly not. I don't wish to imply any such thing." He turned to Elizabeth's father. "I am sorry if I did. Mr. Bennet, Miss Elizabeth, please forgive me. I was carried away in planning what I should do after I kill Mr. Wickham. Not, that is to say, that I will try to kill Mr. Wickham, but in the act of self-defense, these things might happen, after all, for which I also apologize."

Elizabeth touched Mr. Collins' sleeve, as she'd often seen Kitty do, to calm him.

Mr. Collins drew in a deep breath. "Tomorrow is Sunday, but if proper arrangements can be made, I am willing to fight the following morning, early, before my wedding. I certainly wouldn't wish to interfere with that."

Mr. Denny gave a sharp nod. "Well then, Mr. Bennet and I shall arrange for that."

Elizabeth's father let out a sigh. "If we must."

Mr. Denny and Mr. Pratt appeared pleased, but Colonel Forster frowned. Mr. Denny gestured Mr. Bennet off to the side and frowned when Elizabeth followed her father over. Mr. Denny didn't protest, however, or comment on the way Mr. Collins hovered behind them. The arrangements were made quickly, with no hitch until Mr. Denny insisted his principle had demanded well-bloodied rather than first blood.

"That's not reasonable," Elizabeth's father protested.

"Mr. Wickham insists," Mr. Denny replied, looking obstinate.

"Perhaps this hasn't been enough time for tempers to be restored," Mr. Bennet said.

"Is Mr. Collins so great a coward?"

Elizabeth glared at him, but Mr. Denny ignored her glare as he did her presence.

"I actually do not believe I am a coward," Mr. Collins, who probably shouldn't have been listening according to code duello, said. "I will accept well bloodied," he added with surprising firmness.

"Then we're agreed" Mr. Denny said. He proffered his hand.

Mr. Bennet let out a sigh and shook, expression resigned.

Mr. Denny turned back to the other officers. He raised his voice, saying, "It's settled."

"Let's go," Mr. Wickham snapped, expression worried, and turned away.

As the officers left, Mr. Bennet murmured, almost to himself, "I'll take the carriage."

Elizabeth clasped his arm as the officers strut off, worried for his health. Lydia hurried back toward the group, but not quickly enough that the officers couldn't reasonably ignore her as she called after them. Mr. Darcy took Mr. Walter Fitzwilliam aside, and what Elizabeth caught of their quick exchange revealed that Mr. Darcy had not, indeed, made any of the other man's circumstances public knowledge. Both gentlemen concluded that what Mr. Wickham did know, he'd heard by rumor of another source or conjectured. Meanwhile, Richard Fitzwilliam explained the confusion to Mr. Bingley and assured him that Mr. Walter Fitzwilliam had only honorable intentions toward Miss Bingley.

Mr. Bennet, leaning on Elizabeth, watched the exchanges wearily. "Mr. Collins, if you would fetch my horse?"

"Yes, of course. Certainly." Mr. Collins bobbed a bow. "Right away. I won't be long." His words trailed off as he headed toward the stable.

"If you will excuse us," Richard Fitzwilliam said to Elizabeth and her father. "We shall collect our mounts as well."

Mr. Bennet nodded.

"We're leaving already?" Lydia complained. "All we did was walk here and then everyone argued. None of the officers would even talk to me." She leveled a hard look in the direction Mr. Collins had gone.

"Yes, we are leaving already," Mr. Bennet said in a tone that brooked no argument.

They waited in silence for the gentlemen to return. When they did, Mr. Collins immediately offered to assist Mr. Bennet to mount, tone apologetic. Obviously, he keenly felt his neglect in not offering to take Mr. Bennet's gelding to the stable earlier.

"It was...entertaining to see you all," Richard Fitzwilliam said, bowing.

"And a pleasure to meet you," his brother added.

Mr. Bingley bowed. "I must attend to the errand that brought me to town, a purchase for Caroline, but please tell Miss Bennet I hope to call on her soon."

"We shall," Elizabeth replied.

"You return to Longbourn?" Mr. Darcy asked.

"We do," Elizabeth's father said from where he now sat on his horse.

Mr. Darcy met Elizabeth's gaze. "May I walk with you?"

She looked to her father, who offered a slight nod. Elizabeth turned back to Mr. Darcy. "That would be pleasant," she said, and meant it.

"But I don't want to go back," Lydia said.

Ignoring Lydia, they all exchanged a few last farewells, then parted ways. Mr. Darcy turned his horse over to Mr. Collins, who started to lead it, until Mr. Darcy suggested he ride. Mr. Darcy then fell in step with Elizabeth. Riding beside Elizabeth's father, Mr. Collins immediately resumed their earlier discussion, while Lydia trailed behind. A glance back showed her expression quite sullen.

Elizabeth turned her gaze forward as they strode down the lane, contemplating their outing to Meryton. If they hadn't met Mr. Wickham and his fellow officers that day, the duel might have been put off for weeks longer. The more she thought on it, the more she wished they'd never ventured into Meryton that morning. Soon, her mood became at least as dour as Lydia's.

Chapter Twenty-One

As they walked, Darcy became aware of a growing frown turning down Elizabeth's lips. Darcy had thought her happy to accept his company. He added a frown of his own, wondering if she now wished him well away, and why.

"Exactly what does 'well-bloodied' mean?" she asked, voice edged with anger.

Darcy shrugged, keenly aware how near his shoulder was to her slender form. "I don't believe it is clearly defined, but sometimes the offense is not considered sufficiently punished by first blood, which could be a scratch."

Elizabeth pondered this, gaze going to Mr. Collins' back where he walked with her father. "Do they take a measure? A teaspoon or less is a scratch? Maybe we'll be generous and make it a tablespoon." Her words were clipped. "Or does it have to be a cup to be 'well-bloodied?'"

"I think a cup of blood would clearly qualify and a teaspoon would not. It would be impractical to measure the amount." Aware arguing would only amplify her mood, he gentled his tone and observed, "You are upset."

After a time, she let out a long sigh. "I am."

"May I know why?"

Silence drew out between them. Darcy didn't press her.

Finally, she glanced at him, lips set in a firm line. "Because people can be killed in duels, and it will not accomplish anything."

"You mean, Mr. Collins could be killed," he said, addressing the problem head on.

Elizabeth nodded. "I realize he's not a very sensible man, and he can be longwinded, but soon he will be my brother and I find I don't mind. Kitty is marrying him because he's brave and standing up for what he believes is right. His diligence in training and daily exercise has improved him and shown good character. He has noble qualities."

"What he believes is right?" Darcy reiterated.

Elizabeth offered a wry smile. "I beg your pardon. I meant, what is right. I believe you and Miss Darcy, not what Mr. Wickham has said."

Darcy felt something unclench within him. He hadn't realized how much her qualification hurt until she removed it. "Thank you."

"It wasn't Mr. Collins' place to denounce Mr. Wickham, yet now it is everyone's business." She shook her head. "Maybe it should be. It could be argued that Mr. Collins acted in the best interests of the community. By exposing Mr. Wickham's actions, he's protected other young women." She cast Darcy a quick glance, touching concern on her face. "I only hope Miss Darcy doesn't suffer repercussions for this."

It was his turn to sigh, but he suppressed the urge. "I wanted to take her away from the scandal, but the community has been surprisingly supportive. Everyone is very kind to her. I misjudged the people here."

Elizabeth offered a quick smile. "Mr. Wickham made a mistake. He described her as very proud. Mr. Bingley's sisters might be considered to deserve that description, but Miss Darcy doesn't. At the assembly, she danced with those who asked her and was more talkative with partners she'd just met than with those of her party."

He could almost hear the accusation at the end of that statement, her silent, 'unlike you,' but didn't broach the subject. It pleased him too much to speak amiably with Elizabeth to further sour her mood. "Then why haven't people stopped supporting Mr. Wickham?"

She turned her gaze up the roadway, expression thoughtful. "I'm not sure. Maybe because those who support him have not encountered Miss Darcy? Or maybe due to malicious gossip, for some are always willing to believe the worst." She grimaced. "Our community has become divided."

"I am sorry our presence has divided your community." He shook his head, still surprised at the treatment Georgiana enjoyed in Hertfordshire, especially after his own blundered introduction to their society. "It is unexpected. I had assumed most all would rail against my sister and me."

***

Elizabeth studied Mr. Darcy askance. She could find no hint of sarcasm in his tone. Still, angry he should think the people of Meryton so readily fooled, she couldn't contain the derision coating her words as she said, "Of course, it would be preferable that we unite around Mr. Wickham's lie."

"It has happened before." Mr. Darcy's tone bespoke of bitterness. "When we were both at Cambridge… No, there is no point to reliving that."

She studied him again, this confusing man who strode beside her. Handsome, to be sure. Wealthy. Possessed of good friends and caring relations. Yet, not happy. How much of that unhappiness was perpetuated by Mr. Wickham and the acute difference between the two? Admittedly, she knew Mr. Wickham mostly through reports from her family, but where Wickham exuded easy charm, Mr. Darcy proved stiff and withdrawn. Where Wickham offered compliments he did not mean, Mr. Darcy offered insults that he did.

"I'm sorry." She reined in her aggrieved tone and tried again. "I'm sorry he has blighted your life. You must hope he will lose the duel."

"I do. But if he does, he will somehow twist things so he gets everyone's sympathy."

Sympathy and annoyance warred within her. A man of Mr. Darcy's means and connections had no right to wallow in self-pity. "Again, I'm sorry. I'm sorry he's made you bitter."

"I thought I had moved past any care for George Wickham's machinations." Mr. Darcy shook his head slightly, as if disagreeing with his own words. "No. I thought he was out of my life and so I needed no longer think on them. Then he showed up. He showed up at Ramsgate and nearly ruined my sister's life. He showed up here and may ruin your sister's life."

"Or did he improve Kitty's life?" Elizabeth wondered.

Mr. Darcy cast her a startled look, much more becoming than his inwardly aimed recrimination. "I beg your pardon?"

"I don't think Kitty would have been attracted to Mr. Collins if Mr. Wickham hadn't shown up," Elizabeth said thoughtfully. "Lydia has always been the leader, and she persuaded Kitty that the militia contains wonderful men. Then Mr. Collins stood up to the man Lydia likes best. There must be a little bit of competitiveness in Kitty, for that to stir her interest in Mr. Collins. Basically, Kitty found someone who is better than Lydia's favorite and who is eager to have her, while Lydia's choice shows no such inclination toward matrimony."

Mr. Darcy's expression became thoughtful. A wave of pleasure stole through Elizabeth. She'd made a point so good, Mr. Darcy considered her words, rather than instantly arguing. She savored the feeling as they continued down the road, some distance now behind her father and Mr. Collins.

"I don't want anyone killed in the duel," Mr. Darcy said.

"What outcome would please you?" she asked, though she felt she knew.

"It may be petty of me, but I would be very pleased if Mr. Wickham knew humiliation, especially at Mr. Collins' hands."

It was a pleasure to speak with Mr. Darcy both amiably and honestly, instead of having to choose one or the other. Recovered from her fit of temper, Elizabeth sought to further lighten the mood. "How about if he gets a scar? On his face. Not a romantic one that would make him more interesting, but an ugly scar."

Mr. Darcy walked in silence for a while. Elizabeth wondered if she had offended him. She'd only meant to tease.

"Thank you," he finally said.

"For what?"

"For making me realize the pettiness of my anger toward him."

"My intention was not to reprimand you."

"Yet a reprimand was deserved." He glanced at her, gaze oddly intent, before turning his attention back up the roadway. "Mr. Wickham and I were friends as children. I should not forget that. I cannot wish him well, but I do not wish him dead. You can jest about a scar, and yes, I said I would like to see him chastened, but mainly, I would like people to know that I am an honorable man."

Elizabeth thought that over. Mr. Darcy, she'd found, was ever complicated. "Will a duel accomplish that?"

His lips quirked upward. "No. Most people will continue to believe whatever they wish to believe." He shook his head. "As they will not think as I wish, perhaps I should try to place less value on what others think."

His words were reasonable and spoken without rancor or condescension. She frowned, unable to reconcile this Mr. Darcy with his behavior when he arrived in Hertfordshire. She didn't wish a return to their usual animosity, but couldn't refrain from asking, "If you care what people think, why did you behave the way you did at the assembly?" With his aloofness and unwillingness to dance with a single woman outside his party, save Charlotte as part of a bet, Mr. Darcy had offended more than Elizabeth that day.

"My behavior in general?" he asked, tone tentative.

"There is that." Did he also consider his insult to her?

He clasped his hands behind his back, expression thoughtful. "I was a fool. I thought myself above my company which, in truth, brought me below it. Yet, even after my behavior, many here are still polite to me, even friendly, and many more are good to Georgiana. The kindness and understanding offered to Georgiana, when I know how London society would treat her in similar circumstances, humbles me."

"You mean, we've offered more compassion than you would have, under similar circumstances?"

He grimaced, showing her barb hit. "I would not have been impolite to a younger sister of an acquaintance who was similarly affected, but I would have ensured no further contact with her. Or with him, if he pressed the issue."

"And now?" Elizabeth pressed.

"Now, I would seek to find the truth, not let rumor define my view. I should also endeavor to judge the characters of those involved, not shun them due to general opinion."

Elizabeth allowed a smile. "You truly have learned." Dare she bring up his insult? Were they going to be amiable, his words must no longer linger between them. He'd stung her pride. As much as she wished to, Elizabeth could not forgive him. She was not so magnanimous as Charlotte. Still, if she must coax an apology from him, would he mean his words?

"There is also my behavior in specific," Mr. Darcy said into the silence.

"Oh?" Her heart took up a disconcerting, strong beat.

"Let me take this opportunity to apologize to you." His voice held an odd tension. "I am sorry that I said you are not beautiful enough to dance with. If I did not wish to dance, I should have sat down and conversed with some of the local populace. There was no reason for me to insult you. Richard and Georgiana rightfully reproached me for my behavior."

Her heart resumed a more normal beat. It wasn't the apology she'd hoped for, but she suspected the words were difficult for him, which meant she should be gracious. "Your apology is accepted."

He halted his stride. Elizabeth stopped and turned back to face him, expression questioning.

"Thank you."

She tried to smile, but a tremor swept through her at the intensity of his gaze. "You do not need to thank me for accepting an apology, sir."

"I believe I do. I also believe my apology is not complete." He held out a hand.

Unable to suppress her trembling, or even pinpoint the source, she placed her hand in his. Instantly, she became acutely aware of the layers of gloves between them. Looking up, she searched his face. Was he likewise affected? Did he feel how her fingers shook?

"Now I may offer the second portion of my apology." He pressed her fingers gently. "You are very beautiful. To say what I said, I must have been blind. I—"

A call behind them caused them both to whirl. Elizabeth's hand fell to her side. Lydia, the source of the call and far behind them on the roadway, waved to a group of riders.

Elizabeth glanced toward Mr. Darcy to take in his frown. Unaccountably, for they'd done nothing wrong, her face heated. She willed the warmth away before he could turn back.

"I believe that to be the two Mr. Fitzwilliams and Bingley," Mr. Darcy said, voice chagrined. "Miss Bingley's purchase must have been easily achieved."

"Apparently so." Elizabeth felt pleasure that her voice sounded normal, for her heart beat fiercely once more. What words had Mr. Darcy been about to speak?

The gentlemen came abreast of Lydia, their greetings indistinct, then passed her to head toward Elizabeth and Mr. Darcy. When Elizabeth glanced back up the road, she found her father and Mr. Collins had halted. They must have observed the approaching riders, for Mr. Collins turned his mount and headed back toward Elizabeth and Darcy. Collins reached them moments before Mr. Bingley and the Fitzwilliam brothers.

"Darcy," Mr. Bingley said as they drew abreast. "The delivery has not yet arrived with Caroline's order."

"So I suggested we catch up to you." As he spoke, Richard Fitzwilliam's gaze moved from Mr. Darcy to Elizabeth, and back again. "Perhaps I erred."

Mr. Darcy's customary frown turned down his mouth. Elizabeth wished she could smooth the expression away. "No. How could that be an error?" he asked.

The Fitzwilliam twins exchanged an amused look. "I suppose it couldn't be."

"Perhaps now we may all call on Longbourn?" Mr. Bingley exuded hope.

Elizabeth forced a smile and nodded, though she wished nothing more than a continuation of Mr. Darcy's words. "Certainly. My mother will be very pleased to see you all." Her smile grew in sincerity. "As will Jane."

"I am pleased, too," Lydia said, reaching them. "It means no more sewing."

The gentlemen dismounted to walk with them, Mr. Darcy taking the reins of his horse from Mr. Collins, who hurried to rejoin Mr. Bennet. Elizabeth fell in step with Mr. Darcy once more, Mr. Bingley on her other side. She supposed she should be pleased to be in the company of two amiable men, instead of wishing for only one.

Behind them on the roadway, Lydia walked between the Fitzwilliam twins. "Do you think you'll ever retake your commission?"

"I do not believe so," Richard Fitzwilliam said.

Elizabeth shook her head. Her youngest sister possessed a very single mind.

"Do you intend to serve, Mr. Walter?" Lydia asked.

"I do not, Miss Lydia," Mr. Walter Fitzwilliam said.

Even from her position up the roadway, between a now silent Mr. Darcy and an eager-faced Mr. Bingley, Elizabeth could hear Lydia's despondent sigh.

Chapter Twenty-Two

Darcy wondered when they would get word of the duel or, alternately, confirmation of Mr. Collins and Miss Kitty Bennet wedding, which would somewhat tell the morning's tale. Of course, there was no reason for anyone to send word of either event to Netherfield Park, but nearly everyone there eagerly awaited news. Even Miss Bingley feigned an interest, for she'd latched onto Walter's advances quite willingly, and proceeded to evidence care for anything he did.

In view of her shift in devotion, Darcy had briefly wondered if she knew about Walter's financial situation. Based on their interactions, he'd concluded she did, but valued another advantage Walter offered more than she did a fortune. As a close neighbor to his older brother, and on excellent terms with him, Walter gave Miss Bingley something neither Darcy nor Richard could; direct and frequent access to Sir Arthur, Earl of Matlock and his association with other members of the peerage.

As the morning wore on, Darcy became increasingly agitated. He wondered if he should send out for news. He wanted to be available to console Elizabeth if she required consoling. Mr. Collins' death would plunge the family into weeks of mourning, perhaps even months if they decided to honor him as if the wedding planned for after the duel actually took place. After one visit of condolence, Elizabeth would be absent from those events at which Darcy customarily met her, possibly for some time.

Darcy scanned the room and took in a general disquiet. He felt certain that Bingley held thoughts regarding Miss Bennet that were similar to his regarding Elizabeth. Richard's and Walter's interests were more marital, but Mr. Hurst required the outcome for his gambling venture. Georgiana, appearing particularly nervous, likely felt the outcome would affect her reputation, which it would, even though logically it should not. Only Mrs. Hurst seemed unconcerned.

When Netherfield's butler showed Colonel Forster into the parlor, all movement paused. Miss Bingley broke off mid-sentence. Richard's hand halted with a card halfway to the tabletop. Even Mrs. Hurst paused mid-stitch to look up. Darcy and the other gentlemen stood to greet the colonel.

"Refreshments, sir?" Miss Bingley asked as they were all seated.

From the chair across from Darcy, Colonel Forster shook his head. "No thank you. I shall be brief."

"Don't leave us in suspense, Colonel," Bingley said when the man didn't continue. "What happened?"

"No deaths, no serious injuries." Colonel Forster did not sound pleased, though Darcy counted the news as good. "If you remember, it was finally agreed that the duel was going to be fought until they were well-bloodied." About the room, eager faces nodded. "Mr. Collins was injured first. A scratch on his cheek. Collins became enraged." Forster shook his head. "Rarely have I seen the like. Collins' onslaught forced Wickham out of the area marked off for the bout."

Mr. Hurst let out an exclamation of delight. "Wickham lost."

Colonel Forster nodded. "And more than lost. He kept retreating. Many cried to Collins that he'd won, but he would not halt his pursuit. Wickham tripped and fell. Collins stood over him and roared that he should admit he'd lied. Wickham did so. Even though the only blood drawn was Mr. Collins', he was declared the winner."

Satisfaction eased tension from Darcy's frame. Elizabeth's sister would have her husband, Georgiana's reputation would be somewhat restored, and Wickham had shown his true nature.

Colonel Forster's hard look didn't waver. "I was so upset by Wickham's cowardice, that I confronted him to demand clarification. One by one, Wickham's lies were exposed." Forster turned to face Darcy directly, expression morphing into a look of apology. "He knew who held the living. He did conspire with Miss Darcy's governess to persuade your sister to elope. Miss Darcy did tell him repeatedly that she would not. He also admitted that you and others have paid his debts."

Darcy's sister wore a look of satisfaction. Walter let out a low whistle and he and Richard exchanged a glance. Bingley appeared startled, and Miss Bingley and Mrs. Hurst wore matching expressions of condemnation. Mr. Hurst didn't seem to have heard anything beyond the declaration of Wickham's loss. He'd pulled out a small ledger and eagerly consulted the pages.

Darcy offered Colonel Forster a nod, surprised how pleasant vindication felt.

"There is more." Colonel Forster sat forward in his chair. "You should know that Mr. Wickham admitted to providing information to a one Mr. Blackmore." Forster turned to Richard. "The man you slew in Kent, sir."

Richard's countenance went flinty. "Did Wickham know Blackmore intended to kidnap Miss de Bourgh?"

"He confessed only to providing information so the man might court your cousin." Colonel Forster shrugged. "As some of his other transgressions involve theft, for which Mr. Darcy could press to have him hung, I feel he told the truth."

"Thefts?" Georgiana repeated, startled.

"Darcy would never have Wickham hung for theft and he knows as much," Richard stated. He offered Darcy a look that clearly bespoke of his lack of faith in Wickham's protestations. "Regardless, I am willing to consider the matter involving Blackmore closed. Darcy?"

"You are Anne's champion and master of Rosings. If you see the matter as closed, it is closed."

Richard gave a sharp nod. "Please continue, Colonel. What thefts did Mr. Wickham report?"

Colonel Forster sat back in his chair again and began to list various other misdeeds to which Wickham had admitted. The colonel ended with, "Wickham's cowardice exonerates you, Mr. Darcy. I am sorry I doubted your honor."

***

Elizabeth leaned against the doorframe to the room Kitty once shared with Lydia. Lydia's possessions occupied the full of the space now, strewn about haphazardly. Ignoring the mess, Elizabeth smiled. Kitty had set off for her new home with Mr. Collins. She hadn't coughed once since he won the duel, dutifully described and re-described by Mr. Bennet, and directly followed by Kitty and Mr. Collins' nuptials. Elizabeth had never seen Kitty so happy.

A commotion sounded in the entrance hall. Elizabeth eased the door closed, for Lydia wouldn't appreciate the intrusion, and went to ascertain the source of the ruckus. As she drew near the staircase, she clearly heard Mr. Bingley greet her mother. Mr. Darcy's voice followed, and Elizabeth hurried her stride.

She came down the steps to find Mr. Darcy looking up, seeking her. When their gazes met, a smile formed on his lips. Elizabeth didn't hide her own. The world seemed a lighter place now that Mr. Darcy had apologized to her, Miss Darcy's reputation was upheld, and Mr. Collins had emerged all but unscathed from the duel.

"…in and have tea," Mrs. Bennet was saying, directing her words at Miss Darcy, who stood between Mr. Bingley and her brother.

"We hoped to invite Miss Bennet and Miss Elizabeth to walk with us," Mr. Bingley replied. "I believe Miss Darcy may care for tea."

"That would be lovely," Miss Darcy agreed. "I should enjoy visiting with you and Miss Lydia."

"May we, Mama?" Jane asked, just out of sight behind their mother.

"Walk? Yes. Of course. I will gladly keep Miss Darcy and Lydia company. You walk."

"I'll fetch Lizzy and my bonnet."

Not until Jane appeared around the corner and started up the steps did Elizabeth realize she had stilled the moment her gaze met Mr. Darcy's, and hadn't yet continued down.

Jane smiled up at her. "Lizzy, there you are. Fetch your bonnet. We're to walk with the gentlemen."

Elizabeth dutifully turned around and headed back up the steps. When a few weeks ago it would have displeased her not to have her wishes sought, to simply be thrown together with Mr. Darcy so that Jane might have time with Mr. Bingley, now, Elizabeth knew pleasure. She looked forward to a walk with Mr. Darcy by her side.

In short order, they were reassembled in the entrance hall. Mrs. Bennet had withdrawn into the parlor, where she, Lydia and Miss Darcy could be heard. From deeper in the room, Mary's pianoforte practice sounded. A footman opened the door and Mr. Darcy offered Elizabeth his arm.

The day proved sun-filled, though Elizabeth would have walked with Mr. Darcy in wind or rain. As they both preferred a quicker pace, they soon outdistanced Jane and Mr. Bingley. A light breeze ruffled Elizabeth's curls. Mr. Darcy's arm was solid and warm beneath her hand. They headed along a path that would skirt the meadow and take them to a high bluff, where the view should be particularly fine. A feeling of contentment stole through her.

"Colonel Forster reported the duel to us," Mr. Darcy said as the path curved to skirt an ancient elm.

"Father reported it to us. Mr. Collins proved too agitated to convey his own story. Kitty took him aside to tend the cut on his cheek."

"Disfiguring, or a romantic scar?" Mr. Darcy's tone held amusement.

"I believe it shall be romantic, especially to Kitty."

"Then perhaps Mr. Collins deems the entire escapade worthwhile."

Elizabeth quirked an eyebrow. "I should hope so. From it, he proved his bravery and gained Kitty."

"And I am exonerated."

Elizabeth tried to school her expression. Mr. Darcy's actions were not on trial, or shouldn't be, but those in the community who'd sided with Wickham had also believed his lies about Mr. Darcy denying him the living, among other slights. They must now take Mr. Darcy at his word, which was good, except that she refused to see a test of arms as a fair trial. "It's all a bit…" She sought a word less offensive than 'idiotic.' "Nonsensical."

"I agree." He scanned the horizon, thoughtful. "This duel has been strange from the start. From what I understand, Mr. Collins declared Mr. Wickham's offense as not being properly respectful of my father."

Elizabeth nodded. "Ignoring whether Mr. Wickham was guilty of conspiring to persuade a fifteen-year-old girl to elope because she has a large dowry. That would be wrong regardless of the identity of the girl's father."

"And may I assume, given your view of dueling, that you object to the general agreement that Wickham's defeat proves his guilt?"

"I do." Although she was certain Mr. Wickham stood in the wrong, she wished Mr. Darcy to acknowledge the folly of employing a contest of arms to ascertain rightness. "He could fight well and be guilty or fight poorly and be innocent."

Beside her, Mr. Darcy stiffened. "He made a full confession. Didn't your father share with you all to which Mr. Wickham admitted?"

Elizabeth shook her head. "He mentioned that Colonel Forster and the other officers took Wickham aside and they spoke at length, but Father was occupied with Mr. Collins." They crested a hill. "But even a confession should be suspect. Mr. Wickham might have confessed to things he didn't do because he was frightened."

Mr. Darcy halted them at the top of the hill. "Do you doubt my good behavior in all this?"

Elizabeth cast him a surprised look. "You know I do not. I have said as much. I simply wish you to acknowledge a flawed system of reasoning. What if a woman with no male relations were wronged? She cannot stand against a gentleman. Is she, then, automatically guilty? What of a father who dare not risk death and the subsequent abandonment of his children? There are many reasons a contest of arms might end in a way that has nothing to do with right or wrong."

Mr. Darcy frowned. "I agree, dueling is not the best way to discover the truth, but in this case, in main part due to Wickham's cowardliness, the practice proved a success."

"And due to Mr. Collins' bravery, which he may not have found. He could easily have proved the coward." She smiled wryly. "I am saddened to admit, I assumed he would."

"You are correct, of course." Mr. Darcy studied her face. "Dueling is a flawed way to determine a man's honesty."

"Thank you." She tamped down her elation at his agreement, not wishing him to see her gloat, and turned them and started back toward the bluff, asking, "To what else did Mr. Wickham confess?"

"Quite a number of things, including some of which I was not aware."

"Oh dear." Perhaps there was some slight validity to dueling, if guilt had weighed so harsh on Mr. Wickham's conscience that he could not win. "He's committed even more transgressions than you realized?"

Mr. Darcy nodded. "I'd no idea about the pilfering. Twice, he took small but valuable items found in our home and hid them with the intention of selling them if they went unmissed."

"And did he sell them?"

"My mother noticed the absence of her earrings. I should have been more suspicious when Wickham managed to find them for her, under a sofa in the parlor. The second item was a gold picture frame with a miniature painting of my great grandmother. The picture wasn't missed so he sold it."

"It wasn't missed eventually?"

"It was, but not for months after his visit. We never connected him to the painting's absence. I also learned something I'd suspected, but of which I was never sure." A glance showed Mr. Darcy's visage had gone as grim as his voice. "Wickham helped someone plot to kidnap a cousin of mine. He claimed he believed the man was only going to court her."

"I assume your cousin was an heiress." Elizabeth narrowed her gaze against the brightness of the sky. They neared the highpoint of the hillock and the breeze strengthened.

"Very much so." Mr. Darcy's voice took on a wistful note. "When I was ten or eleven, my mother told me that I should consider marrying my cousin, who was a small child at the time, to keep our fortunes in the family. I was fond of my cousin, so I always assumed that, when the time came to marry, I would consider her, but Anne was too ill to marry anyone."

Tightness constricted Elizabeth's chest, but she forced a normal tone to ask, "Did you love her?"

Mr. Darcy shook his head. "Not in that way. I loved her more in the way I love Georgiana, though less so."

The tightness eased. "Did she love you?"

He gave another head shake. "No. If anyone, she loved Richard. He saved her, you know, from the man who tried to kidnap her. I believe that's why my aunt left the estate to him. Rosings, along with all that went with it, was meant for Anne."

Elizabeth couldn't think of a more worthy man to bequeath an estate, except perhaps Mr. Darcy. But he already had Pemberley, and any who heard him speak of his home must know he loved it beyond measure. "Maybe your aunt thought Mr. Fitzwilliam and your cousin would have wed, if your cousin had lived, and so passed the estate on to him."

"No. Anne died first, after which Lady Catherine rewrote her will. Since her only child was dead... Well, Richard was the right choice among her nephews."

They crested the hilltop in silence. Hertfordshire's verdant, rolling hills spread out before them against a backdrop of blue sky. Lazy, puffy white clouds drifted high above.

Elizabeth's lips curved in a smile. "It's lovely, don't you think?"

"Very." His single, quiet word brought her head around. He studied her once more, gaze intent.

Heat rose in her cheeks and she turned quickly back to the view. She gestured to their right. "You can't see from here, but Meryton is not far beyond that hill."

"The place of my newfound acceptance," he said in a normal, if slightly amused, voice.

"You mean because, in view of Mr. Wickham's lies, you now have Colonel Forster's approval?"

"As well as Mr. Pratt's and Mr. Denny's, as they are angry with Wickham for deceiving them. More than that, when Bingley and I rode through Meryton on our way to Longbourn, two people greeted me. Not only did I return their greetings, I stopped and exchanged a few words with each."

"You'd best be careful," she said lightly. "You might find yourself unable to pass through Meryton without squandering your time being friendly."

"That would be a terrible fate." His words had a lightness to them. "On future visits, I may have to employ the shortcut you showed me the day you walked Georgiana back."

She swiveled from the view to study him. "There will be future visits?"

"If you will permit it, I plan to visit many times."

Her breath caught. "How many times?"

The breeze ruffled his neat locks. "As many as it takes."

Elizabeth studied him. He could hardly be clearer in his meaning. Yet, weren't they near adversaries? At least, they had been, until his apology. Since then, she saw him in a kinder light. How did he see her? That day on the road, before his companions caught up to them, he'd called her pretty. Fresh warmth suffused her cheeks. She dropped her gaze to the grass and stone beneath her feet. After a long moment, he shifted back toward the view. Elizabeth looked up to find him studying the sky above.

"Perhaps I may seek your advice," Mr. Darcy said.

"Certainly." The word came out so breathy, she wished to call it back. She tried for a stronger tone and asked, "On what topic?"

"I apologized to you, and you were gracious enough to accept my apology, but there is the issue of Miss Lucas. I know she is aware of my transgression, but there is no way I can say anything without adding to my insult."

Elizabeth drew in a slow breath, reordering her thoughts. Amusement sparked. "You say she knows of your transgression. Is this because you overheard the two of us talking?"

He turned to her in surprise. "Yes. But how do you know I overheard you? I didn't tell anyone and neither of you looked my way."

She couldn't contain a laugh. "You heard our second conversation. We had the conversation, and at the end Charlotte said it was too bad you hadn't heard what we said about you. She claimed that if you had even an ounce of decency, you would be embarrassed." She cast him a smile. "I admit, I suggested you did not. She then proposed we repeat the conversation while in your hearing, as a test." Elizabeth shook her head, curls tumbling with the mixture of movement and wind. "It was very difficult to avoid looking at you. I wanted to see your reaction."

She looked at him now and watched the succession of emotions that stole across his features. The changes were subtle. When they met, she would have seen only one, his usual stoic lack of expression. Knowing him better, she observed surprise, annoyance, guilt and, finally, wry amusement.

"I was embarrassed. Chagrined. It never occurred to me that anyone would guess why I danced with Miss Lucas."

"So, it was on a wager?"

"It was. On top of that, you may have suggested I do not hold an ounce of decency, but I proclaimed not only would you stand up with a wealthy man minutes after he'd insulted you, but that if you did not, you wouldn't have the integrity to then refuse other gentlemen."

"My goodness but we had terrible opinions of one another, did we not?"

His expression filled with recrimination. "Yes, but my opinions of you were incorrect. I'm afraid you were more justified in your assessment of me."

"Not entirely. You do feel guilty, so I must conclude that you do have at least an ounce of decency, maybe even a quarter pound." His look of self-loathing didn't lessen, so Elizabeth added, "The real question is, how do we measure the true weight, for I suspect you hold more than an ounce of fine qualities. Do you suppose decency, honor and integrity fit in a teaspoon? Though, I imagine, we'll need a cup at least."

His severe expression eased. "It would be impractical to measure." As quickly as his mood had lightened, he became grim again. "How can I tell Miss Lucas that I danced with her because I lost a wager that…" He grimaced. "That is, we stipulated the incorrect party must dance with the ugliest woman in the room. The apology would be as bad as the original offense. Yet I owe her an apology. A profound apology."

Elizabeth tucked her hair back behind her ear. "I see your point. Charlotte has always been very realistic about her appearance, but I can't believe she wouldn't be hurt by being so characterized." Elizabeth met Mr. Darcy's gaze. "I cannot but think your words would carry a harsh weight for her. I have been told I'm pretty my whole life, and they still stung me."

As he had on the roadway, he caught one of her hands. Gaze wedded with hers, he brought her fingers to his lips. Elizabeth's heart took up a now familiar pounding. His thumb caressed the back of her hand as he lowered it, sending a thrill of delight through her.

"Again, I beg your forgiveness. I cannot comprehend what had me say those words. Yours is the loveliest countenance I have ever seen."

Elizabeth pressed her free hand to her chest, trying to slow her heart before she succumbed to dizziness. Would she learn what he'd meant to say on the roadway?

He started to bend a knee. "Elizabeth, I—"

A giggle brought Mr. Darcy up straight. They both swiveled toward the sound. Jane's and Mr. Bingley's heads appeared, followed by more of each as they crested the rise. Sharp regret and something akin to anger sped through Elizabeth. Reluctantly, she slipped her hand from Mr. Darcy's grasp. He frowned at her sister and Mr. Bingley. They looked up and sighted Elizabeth and Mr. Darcy.

Mr. Bingley cleared his throat. "We apologize for lagging quite so far behind. Miss Bennet and I were..." He turned to her.

Jane's cheeks bloomed with pink. "Unexpectedly detained."

"Oh?" Joy for her sister quickly chased Elizabeth's disappointment away. "Who or what detained you?"

Jane exchanged a positively doting look with Mr. Bingley. "Each other," she said softly.

Mr. Bingley's face split with a grin. "We're engaged. Or at least, we will be if I get Mr. Bennet's consent."

"Oh Jane." Elizabeth rushed to hug her sister.

"Congratulations," Mr. Darcy murmured.

Chapter Twenty-Three

The four of them made all haste back to Longbourn. Mr. Bennet's permission was sought and given. Mrs. Bennet collapsed but insisted on remaining in the parlor. Miss Lydia sat beside her and dabbed her forehead with a damp cloth, while Georgiana took a turn on the pianoforte to provide more soothing accompaniment than Miss Mary knew how to play. During the ensuing commotion, Darcy found no graceful means of separating Elizabeth from her family. So much so, he began to fear she deliberately avoided being alone with him.

When they'd stood on the hill, her smooth skin bathed in the morning sunlight that crept beneath her hat and her silken curls dancing about her cheeks, she must have guessed his intention. A proposal had all but left his lips. Was avoidance her way of declining him gently?

He sat off to one side of the Bennet's parlor while the womenfolk and Bingley laughed, conversed and assayed plans. Mr. Bennet had already retreated to his library, saying Mr. Phillips would draw up something for Bingley to sign. Bingley hadn't even asked for the specifics of the document. Looking at his friend's overjoyed expression, Darcy wasn't sure Bingley would bother to read before he signed.

"Oh, and the banns can be read this Sunday," Mrs. Bennet cried, not for the first time. "Three weeks. In three weeks, my Jane will be mistress of Netherfield Park. Netherfield Park!"

Unlike everyone else, Darcy watched Elizabeth as her mother spoke, and so saw Elizabeth grimace and cast a quick look his way. Not wishing to give insult, he kept his expression bland.

Insult…Perhaps that was the trouble. After his apology for maligning her, Elizabeth had warmed considerably. Miss Lucas was Elizabeth's dearest friend. Did Elizabeth require full amends for Miss Lucas before he offered for her hand? If so, Darcy's desire to apologize to Miss Lucas had more than doubled, but he would require Elizabeth's help.

Unfortunately, the moment a wedding was planned, Mrs. Bennet became shockingly conscientious about leaving Miss Bennet alone with Bingley. This, in turn, meant Darcy could find no time to speak with Elizabeth, as she became her sister's shadow. Apparently, Mrs. Bennet would have gladly seen her daughter compromised into a union, yet now feared too much time with Miss Bennet would satisfy Bingley's need for her and see him on his way.

Darcy would be insulted on behalf of his friend, if he weren't so frustrated by an inability to speak privately with Elizabeth. He attempted several singular rides and walks, but Bingley pounced on anyone leaving Netherfield in the hope they intended an outing that offered an excuse to see Miss Bennet for even a moment. Finally, Darcy claimed an errand in Meryton on behalf of Georgiana. That he had an insignificant stop to make there did little to ease his conscience as his real goal was Elizabeth. But, between Bingley and Mrs. Bennet, they all but forced Darcy into subterfuge.

As he entered the village, two officers stepped from a storefront into the street. Darcy didn't slow, accustomed to being ignored by anyone in a red coat, but one of the men raised a hand in greeting. He nudged his companion and they started across the street toward Darcy. Unable to claim he hadn't seen them, Darcy brought his mount to a halt.

"Mr. Darcy," the first greeted in cordial tones. "Sir, I should like to tender my apology. You were in the right, and Mr. Wickham in the wrong."

"Thank you," Darcy replied, surprised.

"That goes for me as well, sir," the second officer said. "The next man who questions your honor won't have us on his side, you can be sure."

"Thank you." Darcy refrained from saying he did not foresee a repetition of such slander. He didn't usually permit people such as George Wickham in his association. He'd learned enough to know voicing that would only alienate them, but realizing he should be more than minimally polite, he added, "It takes a good man to admit he has been wrong."

"Thank you, sir," one said. The other nodded.

The two men tipped their hats. Darcy did likewise and parted ways. A few doors down, he dismounted and went into a shop to pick up a length of ribbon Georgiana had ordered in preparation for Bingley and Miss Bennet's wedding. Darcy came back out to the sight of Mr. Watson, a man whose family had refused to fraternize with those who supported Mr. Collins, coming down the street.

Sighting Darcy, Mr. Watson bowed. "I heard the good news from Netherfield Park. That makes another Bennet daughter happily accounted for. I trust the first wedded couple are well on their way?"

Darcy realized that Mr. Watson, as part of the other camp, hadn't been part of the Collins' celebration. Therefore, he assumed Darcy had been, not aware that the Bennets, unsure if Collins would survive the duel, had kept the wedding breakfast small. In the same moment, Darcy also realized he'd never asked Elizabeth how her sister's wedding celebration had gone, or for any news of the newly made Mrs. Collins.

Seeking back for what little knowledge his sister had provided, garnered from Miss Lydia, Darcy offered, "They left from the church door."

"Then I can't be blamed for missing them. If you come across the opportunity, wish them well from the Watsons." Mr. Watson let out a lugubrious sigh. "Terrible thing, us being taken in by that Mr. Wickham."

"Yes."

Mr. Watson accepted Darcy's brevity with a pleasant nod and continued down the street. Darcy turned toward his horse, only to find four more officers headed his way. They professed to being suspicious of Wickham all along but said they hadn't spoken up because the general opinion of him was so positive. Darcy hid his skepticism and pretended to be impressed by their acuity.

After the officers came several more gentlemen and two ladies. Darcy behaved as genially as he could. He didn't wish to squander the good will of the community, or take their esteem for granted, as he had when he'd first arrived. It wasn't only a personal issue. Georgiana's good reputation, at least in Hertfordshire, was partially dependent on how people perceived Darcy.

Quite obviously, their good reputation also hinged on Mr. Wickham's bad one. It was like a seesaw. As Wickham went down, Darcy and Georgiana went up. Darcy wished it could be otherwise, that they could shed even so tenuous a connection to Wickham, but he did his best to converse in a friendly manner. It took him nearly half an hour to remount his horse and head toward Longbourn, and Elizabeth.

Frustration gnawing at his temperament, he urged his mount up the lane. A short distance outside the village, a carriage drew into view. Darcy didn't know if he should be elated or defeated as he recognized it as Mr. Bennet's.

When they met, the carriage drew to a halt. Darcy's heart leapt as Elizabeth alighted, a smile on her lips, and swung the door closed behind her. Darcy dismounted to greet her. From the carriage, Mrs. Bennet, Miss Mary and Miss Lydia all peeked out.

"We're on our way to Meryton to see what gifts we may contrive for Jane." Elizabeth gestured over her shoulder, toward the carriage, but didn't break from his gaze. "You seem to be headed in the opposite direction. Toward Longbourn?"

He nodded. "To see you."

"Lizzy, get back in so we can go," Miss Lydia called.

Elizabeth angled her head to look over her shoulder, showing off the long, graceful sweep of her neck. "I should like to walk with Mr. Darcy."

"But we're meaning to—" Miss Mary began.

"Shush," Mrs. Bennet hissed before turning her face back toward them to smile ingratiatingly. "Mr. Darcy, how kind of you to wish to walk with our Lizzy. I know she isn't as pretty as Jane or Kitty, but you've missed your chances there, haven't you? Best not to miss again, because Lydia is bound to win an officer now that this terrible ordeal with Mr. Wickham is over."

Elizabeth, facing him again, raised her gaze in silent supplication.

"Thank you for the advice, Mrs. Bennet." Darcy gestured to the carriage driver. "Do not let me detain you. I shall see her home."

The carriage started forward and Elizabeth stepped to his side. "You were on your way to see me?" Elizabeth prompted once the carriage dwindled behind them.

Darcy glanced about, finding them quite alone. He regretted the horse and the dusty lane, but perhaps they were for the best. The roadway was no place to propose, and he needed to put things right with Miss Lucas before declaring his intentions. Not only to clear any objections Elizabeth may have but, also, for the sake of his relationship with Richard. It had occurred to Darcy that his cousin might wed Miss Lucas, and he had no desire to be estranged from Richard.

"I am in need of guidance."

"And you seek mine?" Her voice rippled with interest.

He nodded. "I remain committed to rectifying my behavior toward Miss Lucas, yet my quandary is the same. How can I apologize? Yet, how can I not? I want to ask forgiveness of Miss Lucas without hurting her further."

Elizabeth issued a slight sigh. "I'm not sure that is possible."

"Then I must do something for her."

"Not offer her money," Elizabeth said quickly. "She is so practical that she would accept, but…" She shot him an assessing glance.

Darcy supplied, "It wouldn't be appropriate, and she would still resent me."

They continued down the roadway at a mildly quick pace. Darcy appreciated that Elizabeth didn't balk at stretching her legs. Georgiana had remarked on that as well. His sister enjoyed the ease of associating with Miss Lydia, but sometimes tired of her silliness. On top of that complaint, Georgiana said Miss Lydia did not care to walk without a goal and, if made to, dawdled so much as to render the activity unenjoyable, unlike Elizabeth. His sister's observations pleased him and eased his fear of Georgiana succumbing too much to Miss Lydia's influence.

"Charlotte is eminently practical and even tempered," Elizabeth said, interrupting Darcy's musing. "Perhaps we worry unduly and overcomplicate the matter. The best course is likely to speak with her in a direct manner."

"You truly believe so?"

"I do."

Darcy frowned. He preferred being direct. In his experience, most women did not. Still, he'd sought Elizabeth's advice. He ought to abide by it. "It will be difficult to speak with her alone. I should not wish to unfairly raise her, or her family's, expectations."

"There is no trouble there. We shall visit Lucas Lodge now, together. I will invite Charlotte to walk."

"She will not mind you being privy to our conversation?"

Elizabeth cast him an amused look. "We are dear friends. She would share each word with me after speaking with you. I may as well hear them as they are voiced."

Though Darcy hadn't intended an extended walk, they changed their course for Lucas Lodge. There, they were greeted cheerfully and give the news that they'd recently missed Richard's visit. Darcy expressed his regrets at that. He also asked for his horse be taken to Longbourn and stabled there until he could claim the animal after escorting Elizabeth home later. That agreed to, Elizabeth suggested Miss Lucas walk with them, to show Darcy a decorative pond in the far corner of the garden.

The Lucases' garden had nearly recovered from being so often used as a practice field for dueling, but Darcy had little eye for the beauty of the day. The moment they reached the pond, he turned to Miss Lucas. "I should like to speak with you on a matter of import, Miss Lucas. Miss Elizabeth assures me she may remain, but if you wish her to, I am certain she can be prevailed upon to observe us from out of earshot."

Miss Lucas offered a slight smile, the bright wit in her eyes increasing her appeal. "Lizzy may stay. On what do you wish to speak, Mr. Darcy?"

"First, I extend an apology for what I am about to say."

"Then I extend an offer to think carefully on my reaction to your words."

Darcy wished for a bit more assurance than that but knew he did not deserve it. He launched into an account of the events of his first assembly in Hertfordshire, in so much as they concerned Miss Lucas. He did not hide that he considered her the ugliest woman in the room.

When he finally fell silent, she remained beside him, gaze trained over the pond. Darcy rubbed his palms against his trouser legs, more nervous than he'd been in many years. A splash sounded. He looked across to see ripples spreading near the far bank. He angled his gaze past Miss Lucas to where Elizabeth stood. She offered an encouraging smile.

"Mr. Darcy, I have a mirror," Miss Lucas finally said. "I am not a fool. Even so, your behavior was objectionable, and yes, I was and still remain somewhat hurt by it. But due to your behavior, I had the most enjoyable time I've ever had at an assembly."

Darcy considered that. "Because of Mr. Fitzwilliam?"

"Yes."

He waited, but she offered nothing more. Was her stoicism part of the reason Richard couldn't discern the nature of her interest in him? Well, if Darcy had begun their relationship, maybe he could further it. He owed Miss Lucas, and Richard, at least that much. "I am violating a confidence to say this but—"

"Don't," Miss Lucas interrupted.

"Why?" Elizabeth asked. "What do you fear he will say?"

Miss Lucas kept her attention trained across the pond. "With his brutal honesty, I believe Mr. Darcy will inform me that Richard Fitzwilliam is not prepared to take me to wife." Only the slightest hitch in her voice betrayed the anguish he suspected lurked beneath her calm words. She lowered her lashes.

Darcy wondered if her lids pressed back tears. "And you would miss the opportunity for his fortune?"

On the other side of Miss Lucas, Elizabeth gasped. Darcy winced. He believed Miss Lucas in love with his cousin. His question sprang more from a doubt of his ability to comprehend the emotions of others than from doubt in her. Hopefully, Elizabeth would permit him to explain that.

"Because I will miss him," Miss Lucas whispered. Tears slid down her cheeks. She pulled free a handkerchief to wipe them away. "If you will excuse me?" She turned her back to Darcy.

"Charlotte." Elizabeth drew her friend into an embrace, casting Darcy an angry glare.

"I will not excuse you, for I will speak my mind." Obtuse as he often proved, even he could readily interpret the anger in Elizabeth's gaze. He had little time to set matters right. "I believe my words will lead to greater happiness for all involved. I hope you and Richard will forgive me, but the two of you seem to be making little progress finding a resolution on your own. Miss Lucas, Richard will not propose. He is too concerned that you would marry him even if you don't care for him, both for his wealth and to spare you from being a burden on your family."

Eying him over her friend's shoulder, Elizabeth's expression grew stony. "Charlotte would never do that."

Miss Lucas pulled free of Elizabeth's arms to look her in the eye. "Elizabeth, you are seven years younger than I am. You still believe you can wait for someone you love. For me, that is no longer true."

Elizabeth's eyes betrayed shock. "No, Charlotte, you—"

Miss Lucas shook her head. "It's true, Lizzy. I am sorry you must know it, but it is true. I will marry any man who asked, so long as he seems able to provide a decent home to me and any children I bear him."

Elizabeth shook her head. "Surely not any man."

Miss Lucas captured Elizabeth's hands. "Remember how much you disliked your cousin, Mr. Collins, when first you met him?"

Elizabeth nodded.

"I swear to you, Lizzy, I would have married Mr. Collins if he'd asked me. Not the reformed Mr. Collins who dueled Mr. Wickham, but Mr. Collins as he arrived on your doorstep."

"I can't believe that." Elizabeth's tone bespoke of desperation. "I won't believe that of you, Charlotte."

Miss Lucas gave Elizabeth's hands a squeeze and released them. "Well, we can't test that." She turned to Darcy and squared her shoulders. "You should know, Mr. Darcy, that I would marry Richard Fitzwilliam even if he was a lieutenant and we had to live on his pay."

Darcy narrowed his gaze, less sure of her devotion to Richard in the face of her words about Mr. Collins. "I would like to compensate you for insulting you. Suppose I offered you ten thousand pounds not to marry Richard?"

Elizabeth's hands came up to cover her mouth, her eyes wide once more.

"If you did, I would accept. Then I would go to Richard and offer half of it to him to help him with his monetary problems." Miss Lucas gave a smile which made Darcy wonder why he'd ever thought her ugly. "But you wouldn't make such an offer. And you either believe my honesty or you don't. It's not dishonest for a woman to accept the proposal of a man she doesn't love. All I can say is that I do love him. Do what you will with that information."

Darcy met her gaze for a long moment, but her calm didn't waver. She added no more tears to her plea. No histrionics. Any man would be lucky to take Charlotte Lucas to wife.

Darcy dipped his head, the gesture half in acknowledgement of her declaration, half a bow of respect. "I will convey your words to Richard, along with my assessment and advice. You should know, he loves you as well, regardless of circumstance."

"Oh, but Charlotte, this is wonderful," Elizabeth exclaimed, coming to stand shoulder to shoulder with her friend.

Miss Lucas cast Elizabeth a wry smile. "We shall see."

"I am certain it will all come right." Elizabeth angled a look Darcy's way that bespoke well enough who she would blame should it not.

Miss Lucas looked from Elizabeth to Darcy. "I believe we should head back now, so Mr. Darcy may walk you home." Meeting his gaze, she offered the barest smile.

She was very intelligent, Miss Lucas. Darcy had no doubt she knew every motive behind his apology, and what course he plotted next. Richard would do well with such a wife to guide him in managing Rosings, and Darcy liked to think his aunt would approve. Not of Miss Lucas' standing, for Lady Catherine would think her too low, but that a strong, intelligent woman would have a hand in managing her beloved estate. Though it was always clear Anne would never become the type of force Lady Catherine had been, that sort of leadership was what his aunt had wanted for Rosings.

"Certainly, we may return to Lucas Lodge if you wish," Elizabeth said, taking Miss Lucas' arm. "Unless you care to speak more of Mr. Fitzwilliam? I'm very happy for you, Charlotte."

"You must endeavor to tamp down your happiness, Lizzy. Nothing is set. Far from it."

"Oh, but it will be." She looked to Darcy. "Won't it?"

"I will endeavor to accurately convey Miss Lucas' feelings in this matter."

Elizabeth offered the same supplicative look evoked by her mother on the roadway, much to Darcy's chagrin.

"I'm sure Mr. Darcy will do his best, Lizzy. Let us return. The Lucases and Fitzwilliams have taken enough of Mr. Darcy's time for one morning."

Though Elizabeth appeared slightly mutinous, she permitted Miss Lucas to walk her back. Darcy trailed behind, jealous of the way Elizabeth hugged her friend's arm to her, of the ease with which they conversed as they traversed the path, and of Richard, who would soon have the hand of the woman he loved, if Darcy read the situation aright.

They made their goodbyes to the Lucases, the pleasantries more difficult for Darcy than usual. He yearned to get Elizabeth alone. He wouldn't be put off any longer. Not by the Lucases, Elizabeth's family, or pursuit of Richard's future happiness.

When they stepped free of Lucas Lodge, he said, "Is there a cut across the fields?"

"So eager to be away from me?" Elizabeth accompanied her light tone with a smile.

Darcy offered his arm. She placed a hand on his sleeve. He wished she would wrap her arm about his and walk close, as she had with Miss Lucas. He also wished to avoid any potential interruptions on the roadway.

"We have taken up a great deal of your day, between the lot of us," Elizabeth said before he could form a denial of her teasing words. "Come, if we cut through that hedge, and you can see where Charlotte and I often do, we have only meadows and a few trees between us and Longbourn."

They set off and, soon enough, traversed one of the promised meadows. The sky remained blue and the breeze light. Darcy set a slower than usual pace, needing time to compose his words.

"You were headed to Longbourn to seek my advice about Charlotte, then?" Elizabeth asked after a time. Although the trees were bare, their silhouettes graced the skyline.

"Yes." Should he tell her why he'd so vehemently wished to make amends? He could use his reasons for apologizing to broach the subject of wanting Elizabeth's regard.

"And when we spoke of the best way to make that apology, you said that you didn't wish to converse with Charlotte alone. You did not wish to raise her hopes."

"True. If I seemed to seek her company, it may have created false expectations." Darcy frowned. He didn't wish to speak of an imagined interest in Miss Lucas, but rather his very real interest in Elizabeth.

She halted them as they reached the intricate shadows traced by the bare branches of a maple. "You mean, you felt that if you spent time alone with her, she would expect you to propose?"

"That is the general assumption." He worked to keep irritation from his tone. He must direct the conversation away from Miss Lucas.

Elizabeth clasped her hands tightly before her, studying his face. "You spend time alone with me."

His heart stilled, then stuttered to life again. Was she providing him his chance? The nervousness he'd felt when apologizing to Miss Lucas became nothing compared to the tension that seized his every limb.

"Are you not worried you shall raise my expectations?"

He gazed into those lovely, intelligent eyes and found his voice. "I hope I have raised your expectations, and that I have atoned for the misdeeds of our first meeting. It is my wish for you to be happy when I propose."

"Not if." She unclasped her hands and held them out before her. "But when?"

He captured her hands and dropped to a knee. The face that turned to gaze down at him was pure perfection. He squeezed her hands to halt the tremble that threatened his. "I never understood kneeling to propose," he admitted. "It seemed demeaning. I always believed that I would bring so much more to a marriage than any woman could that she would be grateful to marry me." He shook his head at his foolishness. "Your value to me is so great that kneeling is a small price to pay. More than that, it is your due. You are worth more to me than I ever imagined anyone could be. It isn't simply your beauty. It is you. Your charm, your wit, your kindness and integrity. Everything. I never considered myself as a man who would be at loss for words, but words are inadequate to describe the wonder that is you. Miss Elizabeth Bennet, will you marry me?"

She parted her lips to speak and his heart stopped beating. "I will marry you, Mr. Darcy." A smile curved her perfect mouth. "My answer is yes."

Heart pounding once again, Darcy rose to his feet and gathered Elizabeth in his arms, where she was always meant to be.

Chapter Twenty-Four

They arrived back to Longbourn to find the manor empty of all but Mr. Bennet, which suited Darcy eminently. Hand in hand, they entered Mr. Bennet's sanctuary and sought his permission, which he readily granted. He then went on to list some terms for Mr. Phillips to draw up before permitting Darcy a half hour alone in the front parlor with Elizabeth. Darcy had never realized a parlor could feel like heaven.

The sky had never been so blue, nor the sun as bright, as they were along Darcy's ride back to Netherfield Park. Bemused, he realized he recalled nothing of what Mr. Bennet had said pertaining to the marriage contract. Darcy supposed it mattered little. He trusted Mr. Bennet and, in truth, couldn't bring himself to care. So long as Elizabeth became his wife, little else mattered.

The announcement of his engagement caused quite a stir at Netherfield. Darcy regained enough control over his emotions to note that, unexpectedly, Miss Bingley seemed genuinely happy for him, while Richard appeared glum. The first he could only give thanks for, but the second was enough out of character that Darcy took his cousin aside as soon as the commotion his news created died down enough to make their absence from the parlor acceptable.

Darcy followed Richard into Bingley's library and closed the door behind them. He gestured to the cluster of sofas and chairs. Expression still morose, Richard took a chair, Darcy sitting opposite him.

"You are displeased with my engagement?" Darcy asked, seeing no reason for preamble.

"What? No. I am happy for both of you. You professed an interest in her and now you have her. Felicitations."

Darcy narrowed his gaze. "Then you are unhappy because?"

Richard let out a sigh and slumped back in his chair. "You've been at Longbourn quite a bit, but you must have noticed that Walter and Miss Bingley regard one another with growing affection?"

"I have, but surely you do not find her that objectionable? True, she can be overbearing, but her connections are good, she possesses a large dowry, and she is a skilled hostess."

"I don't find her objectionable." Richard grimaced. "I find everyone wedding, with affection no less, objectionable." A never-before-seen look of entreaty transformed Richard's features. "What about me?"

Darcy tamped down his shock at seeing Richard Fitzwilliam bleat. "What about you? You love Miss Lucas. Do something about it."

"You know my quandary, Darcy. I'm at a stalemate."

"Perhaps I can break it for you," Darcy said and gave Richard a detailed account of his conversation with Miss Lucas. He concluded with, "So, you have a choice. She confirmed your judgment of her, but she also says she loves you."

"What choice is that?" Richard's tone held an edge of anger. "I stand where I have always stood."

Darcy raised his eyebrows. He'd expected Richard to rejoice at news of Miss Lucas' declaration. "Do you judge her to be a liar as well as a fortune hunter?"

"I don't know." Richard shook his head. "I'm in such agony, it's difficult to think. I'd almost rather be back at the front than endure this." He frowned, silent for a long moment. "If she were a liar, she would be a clever one."

Darcy could only agree with that, in view of Miss Lucas' keen intelligence. "She would not tell a lie that could ever be revealed as a lie." He shrugged. "We can't know if she is lying. We can only know the alternatives."

"And I do not relish the alternatives." Richard stood, clasped his hands behind his back, and began to pace the small library. "One, I marry her, and she never reveals what she truly thinks. Two, I eventually find out that she doesn't love me. Neither choice is good."

"You forget three. You marry and eventually find out that she does love you."

Richard didn't halt his pacing. "One out of three odds. Not good."

Darcy resisted the urge to order his cousin to sit. "Have you considered that there are also alternatives if you do not marry?"

Richard turned to face him. "You mean, that I will regret losing her for the remainder of my days?"

Darcy turned a bark of laughter into a cough. Richard smitten was a much more dramatic man that Darcy would have guessed. He tried another tact. "Ask yourself this question. Are you ever going to find a woman who isn't influenced by your wealth? You will not face this quandary with Miss Lucas alone, but with every woman you meet."

Richard shook his head in disagreement. "If I pick someone young and naïve enough, she might not be able to hide her true feelings. The trouble is, that is not the kind of woman I want to marry."

Darcy sought for another angle to break Richard's indecision. He obviously loved Miss Lucas. He would therefore wish her well, regardless of if they wed. With that inspiration, Darcy said, "Try looking at the alternatives for Miss Lucas. She might marry a widower who wants a good housekeeper. Or a brute of a man, desperate because no woman will accept him." Richard flinched, though Darcy considered that scenario unlikely. Miss Lucas was too sharp to make that error. Richard required prodding, though, for his own good. He should know the happiness Darcy had found. "She might never marry and be a burden on her family." He met Richard's gaze squarely. "You claim to love her, yet you would condemn her to one of those fates on the possibility that she might not love you? Your regard must not be so strong as all that, then."

Richard whirled toward the door.

"Where are you going?" Darcy asked.

"To propose."

***

Elizabeth couldn't suppress a grin as she, Jane and Charlotte alighted from Mr. Bennet's carriage and started up the steps to Netherfield Park. Jane, of course, was always meant to marry well, but Elizabeth had held little interest in gentlemen before meeting Mr. Darcy, and Charlotte had given up years before Richard Fitzwilliam asked her to dance twice at the assembly. The miracles that were their gentlemen aside, even Elizabeth's fondest dreams had never aspired to her and Jane wedding close friends, or Charlotte becoming Elizabeth's cousin by marriage. She could imagine no happier course.

They handed their outerwear to waiting servants and followed Andrews, Netherfield's butler, toward the large parlor. Elizabeth knew great familiarity with the room from her time nursing Jane at Netherfield, but the chamber no longer held the dread of sharp tongues and boredom. Now, eager steps carried her through the halls.

"Jane, Miss Elizabeth, Miss Lucas." Mr. Bingley's voice stayed them. He hurried down the hall toward them with a sunny smile, eyes only for

Jane, and offered a bow. When he straightened, he held out a hand to her, which she readily clasped. "I do not mean to break you up before you make your greetings, but there is something I wish to show Jane."

"Oh?" Elizabeth couldn't help asking.

Mr. Bingley darted a glance her way. "A, uh, painting she asked about. We located it in the attic and brought it down."

"I very much wish to see it," Jane declared, cheeks glowing pink.

Elizabeth did not doubt there was a painting, or that her sister would look on it. She also suspected that Jane and Mr. Bingley desired time alone. Elizabeth's mother had given strict orders against such a thing. Elizabeth smiled and gestured for Andrews to resume leading the way. As they set off down the corridor, Mr. Bingley led Jane the opposite direction.

They entered the parlor to find it empty of all but Georgiana, who sat at the pianoforte in the middle of a piece far too elaborate for Elizabeth to attempt. She looked over and smiled but did not break off her practice. Her expression of concentration revealed that, even for her, the music was difficult to play. Rather than take any insult at Georgiana's lack of greeting, Elizabeth was pleased. For the younger woman not to break off to greet them showed her ease in their company, and a proper adolescent disregard for what her brother would say.

"I shall inform the household that you have arrived." Andrews bowed his way from the room.

Elizabeth didn't know if they would see the Hursts, who'd spoken of spending time in London before returning for Jane and Mr. Bingley's wedding, and who didn't approve of her, Jane and Charlotte anyway. She would not mind conversing with Miss Bingley, transformed into a genial companion by the attention of Walter Fitzwilliam. Most of all, though, she simply wished Mr. Darcy would appear, the sight of him making the presence of all others melt away.

As she and Charlotte settled on a sofa, Elizabeth observed her joy mirrored her friend and asked, "Is it love or your upcoming marriage that makes you so happy?"

"It is my upcoming marriage to the man I love." Charlotte offered a contented smile. "Every year my prospects of marrying became dimmer. For the past several years, I've been resigned to accepting the proposal of anyone who could support me. Then Richard came along. He is everything I ever wanted in a husband. And he's wealthy as well. I can't believe my good fortune."

"Nor I mine. Not only am I going to marry someone I love, but he is also wealthy. We shall want for nothing and be able to give good lives to our children."

A teasing light lit Charlotte's eyes. "Mr. Darcy is very handsome as well."

"Yes, but I wasn't going to point that out."

Charlotte issued a happy sigh. "I don't hold any envy. To me, Richard's face is the most wonderful face in the world. I don't care if he isn't as well-favored as Mr. Darcy. I like Richard's face better."

"What about my face?" a teasing voice asked as Walter Fitzwilliam entered the room, Miss Bingley on his arm.

Charlotte shook her head. "I am sorry, Walter, but I prefer Richard's face."

"Well, I prefer Walter's." Miss Bingley, arm laced with Walter Fitzwilliam's, looked up at him through long lashes, aiming her words at him rather than Charlotte.

Georgiana gently closed the pianoforte. "I should hope so." She arose from the bench and headed toward Miss Bingley. "You seem even more cheerful than usual, Miss Bingley." She shifted her gaze to Walter Fitzwilliam. "Is there something we should know?"

Miss Bingley offered Walter Fitzwilliam a questioning look.

He patted her hand on his sleeve and turned to Georgiana. "Yes. I have asked Miss Bingley to be my wife. We're to be married, assuming Bingley holds no objection. We'd hoped to find him here, to seek his approval."

Georgiana turned back to Miss Bingley. "I am certain he will approve. Let me welcome you into the family. We will be cousins." Tugging Miss Bingley away from her intended, Georgiana embraced her.

Surprise raced across Miss Bingley's features, but she returned the hug. "Thank you."

When Georgiana stepped back, Walter Fitzwilliam reclaimed Miss Bingley's arm. "We don't mean to abandon you, but we're off to search out Bingley. I'm sure my brother and Darcy will be along shortly."

"Mr. Bingley took Jane to see a painting he found in the attic," Elizabeth advised, voice bland.

Walter Fitzwilliam offered her a quick grin and led Miss Bingley from the room. Georgiana came over to join Elizabeth and Charlotte, taking a chair to Elizabeth's right.

Elizabeth turned to her. "It was good of you to be so kind to Miss Bingley."

Georgiana shrugged. "I can be much more relaxed with her now that she isn't chasing after my brother or trying to persuade me to marry her brother."

"She did used to be rather single minded," Elizabeth agreed.

"Double minded," Georgiana giggled. "Two marriages."

Charlotte turned toward the door, expression expectant. A moment later, Elizabeth too heard the footfalls. Strong, even treads. She came to her feet with a smile.

Mr. Darcy entered the room and cross to take her hands. Dimly, Elizabeth knew Richard Fitzwilliam entered as well, and spoke to both Georgiana and Charlotte. All Elizabeth could see was Mr. Darcy's fine countenance, which no longer held any hint of arrogance to her.

"...in the garden," Richard Fitzwilliam was saying.

Georgiana laughed. "I know when I am not wanted."

Mr. Darcy's head snapped around. "Nonsense. You are always wanted, Georgiana."

"Almost always," she corrected. "Wanted or not, it is time for me to study French, which I believe I shall do in the library. Elizabeth, Charlotte." Georgiana offered them each a smile and headed from the room.

"Yes, well, I suppose Miss Lucas and I shall be forced to walk in the garden alone," Richard Fitzwilliam said, offering Charlotte his arm.

"I suppose so." Mr. Darcy didn't watch them leave, his gaze returning to Elizabeth.

Under his scrutiny, color rose in her cheeks. As if from far away, she heard the parlor door swing shut. "We're alone."

Mr. Darcy nodded. A gentle tug of her hands brought her a step closer, nearly into his arms.

She endeavored for a teasing tone, but her words came out a whisper as she said, "This is very scandalous, Mr. Darcy."

"Is it?" he murmured. "We're simply standing here. Only our hands even touch."

"People will think the worst."

"I would not wish us falsely accused." A final tug brought her up against him. His arms slid around her. His lips found hers.

Elizabeth knew no concept of time. She could have stayed thus forever, but Mr. Darcy raised his lips from hers to look down into her eyes. Quickened breath sounded about them and she realized they both inhaled and exhaled rapidly. She knew she should be scandalized. She reached up and tugged his head down for more.

Again, it was he who broke their kiss. This time, he took a step away from her, bracing his hands on her shoulders. She knew not if he wished to keep ahold of her or force her to remain at arms' length.

"Elizabeth, please, you tempt me too far. We are not wed yet."

A blush stained her cheeks, but she raised her chin and met his gaze. "I would that we were."

"As do I. Believe me."

She drew in several long, deep breaths and smoothed the front of her gown. He released her shoulders to take her hand. He led her to a chair and pressed her down to sit, then took the chair beside her.

"Wouldn't we be more comfortable on the sofa?" she asked, enamored with the obvious effect she had on him.

He shot her a startled look. "You, Miss Elizabeth Bennet, are a hoyden."

"I never pretended otherwise."

"I am sure the others of our acquaintance will soon appear, ready for tea. I do not mean for us to be in a disheveled state."

His tone was very serious, but Elizabeth saw the way his gaze raked over her as he spoke. For a moment, she wondered into how disheveled a state she could entice Mr. Darcy. She'd never felt so sure before as she did when he wrapped her in his arms. Still, she was not truly a hoyden and, as he'd said, they were not yet married. She must gather her resolve and behave in a more proper manner.

Conversation would help, so she turned to the first topic that came to mind and said, "I understood your need to apologize to Charlotte, but didn't you run the risk of hurting Richard?"

"Yes, there were risks," he said. "My apology to Miss Lucas was not a selfless act by any means. It made me feel less guilty about my behavior, and hopefully showed you that I am capable of admitting my faults and endeavoring to change. The apology didn't help Miss Lucas in any way."

"If I am a hoyden, you are a gambler, Mr. Darcy," Elizabeth teased.

"That was a single risk, which does not make me a gambler."

"As I recall it, you took two risks, sir. You also gambled on whether or not Charlotte truly loves your cousin."

Mr. Darcy nodded. "I admit, that was also a gamble. If I'd learned that Miss Lucas was only interested in Richard's wealth, then I still hurt her, and an honest apology hurt her more. But she is your dear friend and I believed that, to be such, she must share the sort of honesty and honor you have."

"Even if she was willing to marry without caring for her husband?" Elizabeth meant to continue their levity, but her mood soured slightly. She did not like to think of Charlotte as having so little integrity.

"Consider what the rest of her life would have been if she never found a husband," Mr. Darcy said gently.

"I have trouble putting myself in her position, even knowing that if you and I hadn't fallen in love, I could be." Elizabeth shook her head. "Whatever she claims she would have done, she didn't."

"Which is good, both for your sake and for hers."

"I would never have forsaken our friendship," Elizabeth protested.

"As with the truth of Miss Lucas' declaration, we fortunately need not find out." He reached to capture one of Elizabeth's hands, his warm grip dispelling some of her unease. "It is like the duel. The truth came out, but coincidentally, not because of who was the better duelist. Although, in Miss Lucas' case, honor and self-interest coincided, both for me and for her. There was no dilemma of believing in the process even if it led to a bad result."

Elizabeth thought about that for a moment. "Did you even weigh losing your cousin's affection in your decision to confront Charlotte?"

"I did, but I thought more of his happiness should she love him, and I thought of you and your loyalty to your friend."

"Then I appreciate the risk you took when you intervened. I know you are close with your cousin. It would have been unfortunate if you'd damaged your relationship with him." She tipped her head to the side, questioning. "You truly felt you must apologize to Charlotte to gain my affection and esteem?"

He turned more fully to capture her other hand, clasping both. "Elizabeth, I have come to realize that I want to be a good man for you. I always thought I would never have to change for anyone." He grimaced. "I had delusions I was perfect, but I have at least temporarily changed for Georgiana and now I realize I need to continue to become the best possible person for you. Marrying you is not enough. I don't want you to be dissatisfied with the man you married."

"How could I be? I love you."

He pulled her back to her feet and into his arms. This time, Elizabeth broke off their kiss, but only to murmur the words her heart felt. "You're perfect, Mr. Darcy."

"No, I'm not," he whispered back. "But to be worthy of you, I will try to be."

Epilogue

Forty years later

The journey to Rosings took longer than ever, although their actual travel time was less. Neither Darcy nor Elizabeth were comfortable traveling more than a day at a time, and they preferred to make those short days. Sometimes Darcy wondered if Elizabeth exaggerated her discomfort to give him an excuse to stop for, in his eyes, she'd hardly changed from the girl he'd met in Hertfordshire, nearly a lifetime ago.

Several switches occurred between carriages and trains, each train of a different gauge. The changes were eased by a stay at an inn or with someone for whom they cared. One such stay was with their younger son and his growing family. Another was with their only daughter, who lived in London with her husband and three children. Catching up with both friends and business kept them in London for weeks.

But eventually, they journeyed on. Darcy and Elizabeth both looked forward to their visit at Rosings, even if reaching there proved momentous. The burden fell on them, for Richard was seventy and found travel very difficult. The older he got, the more the wounds of his youth troubled him.

They arrived to find Richard now walked with a cane for even a few steps. Charlotte, as lovely as ever, greeted them with an ease of movement her husband no longer had. Like Elizabeth, she'd aged well. Now, no one could say if she was pretty or not, her face a collection of lines, but to Darcy she would always be beautiful. Beautiful as his friend, as an intelligent, diligent, shrewd steward of Rosings and, most of all, beautiful as the woman who'd shared with Richard a lifetime of steadfast happiness and love.

They retired to a small front parlor, one Lady Catherine had never deigned to use, but which filled with welcome sunlight. After initial inquiries about family were answered, Richard said, "You know, today is the fortieth anniversary of the duel."

"Is it?" Elizabeth asked. "I'd forgotten."

"I prefer to remember the anniversary of the assembly." Charlotte reached for her husband's hand. "Just think, if I had been beautiful, I would probably not have been lucky enough to marry you."

"I'm the lucky one," Richard said.

Mimicking Charlotte, Elizabeth reached for Darcy's hand, where he sat beside her on a sofa. "Darcy and I will both argue with you over which of the four of us is luckiest."

Darcy shook his head, always ready to disagree with his wife...on the little things. "No, I will not make that argument today. Instead, I will point out that if I hadn't been a tactless idiot, I might never have had my luck."

"Hadn't been?" Richard gestured at Darcy with his cane. "You speak as though you still aren't. I saw you eying this when you entered."

"Only because he's considering one for himself." Elizabeth offered Darcy a sweet, teasing smile.

"Be careful, Lizzy." Charlotte's tone held equal amusement. "Canes are all the fashion. Sometimes bad comes with good. Another woman might try to steal him away."

Richard snorted. "No woman's been able to catch Darcy's eyes since the moment his gaze settled on Elizabeth. In this instance, I do not believe we need to worry about bad coming from good."

"As this is the anniversary of Mr. Collins' duel, we should be more focused on good coming from bad," Elizabeth said.

Darcy squeezed Elizabeth's hand. "I think we can all affirm that sometimes good results from bad actions."

This met with general agreement. Darcy leaned back on the sofa to listen as Elizabeth and Charlotte began a comparison of grandchildren. Where he sat beside Charlotte, Richard dozed, head drooping against his chest but one hand still resting on the top of his cane. In his other, he held Charlotte's.

The conversation moved from the accomplishments of their and Richard and Charlotte's grandchildren to Georgiana's, then Walter and Caroline's. Nor did Elizabeth's sisters' grandchildren escape scrutiny. All the Bennet sisters had been blessed with the fortitude of their mother, but only Jane had surpassed Mrs. Bennet. She and Bingley had raised five daughters and two sons, and now knew the joy of over twenty grandchildren. With so many relations, Darcy knew the conversation would go well into that evening, and likely the following as well, and he didn't mind. Elizabeth and Charlotte had much to speak on, the result of happy, full lives.

~ The End ~

About the Authors

Renata McMann

Renata McMann is the pen name of Teresa McCullough, someone who likes to rewrite public domain works. She is fond of thinking, "What if?" To learn more about Renata's work and collaborations, visit **www.renatamcmann.com**.

Summer Hanford

Starting in 2014, Summer was offered the privilege of partnering with fan fiction author Renata McMann on her well-loved *Pride and Prejudice* variations. More information on these works is available at **www.renatamcmann.com**.

Summer is currently partnering with McMann as well as writing solo works in Regency Romance and Fantasy. She lives in New York with her husband and compulsory, deliberately spoiled, cats. The newest addition to their household is an energetic setter-shepherd mix...not yet appreciated by any of the three cats. For more about Summer, visit **www.summerhanford.com**.

Get Your Thank You Gift! Sign Up for Our Mailing List Today!

Visit: **www.renatamcmann.com/news/**

Printed in the USA
CPSIA information can be obtained
at www.ICGtesting.com
LVHW040330091023
760556LV00014B/208